Desire Burn

Desire Burn

WOMEN'S STORIES
FROM THE
DARK SIDE OF PASSION

*Edited by Janet Berliner, Uwe Luserke,
and Martin H. Greenberg*

Carroll & Graf Publishers, Inc.
New York

The editors wish to acknowledge Laurie Harper of Sebastian Agency for her support and assistance; Robert L. "Cowboy Bob" Fleck for his hard work and constant sense of humor; Jennifer Prior for being cheerful, efficient, and working miraculously quickly, and Kent Carroll, especially for a great title.

Additionally, Janet Berliner wishes to thank the authors, and her mother, Thea Cowan.

First edition 1995

Carroll & Graf Publishers, Inc.
260 Fifth Avenue
New York, NY 10001

Library of Congress Cataloging-in-Publication Data is available.

ISBN 0-7867-0259-1

Manufactured in the United States of America.

2   4   6   8   10   9   7   5   3   1

PERMISSIONS

CONTENTS

INTRODUCTION

A friend of mine, a psychiatrist who specializes—personally and professionally—in dealing with sexual problems, introduced me to the word "limmerance." He defined it as that early state of being in love, in lust, or both, when two people see each other as perfect.

The word stems from "limmer," which means a loose woman or, in the case of a man, a scoundrel.

Interesting, no?

Before the loving, even the dark side of desire and fulfillment is encompassed in a glorious state of limmerance; after the loving, when reality sets in, we are limmers.

Before the loving, satin sheets are erotic, and the end justifies the means; *after* the loving, satin sheets are a nuisance, and the end still justifies the means.

In each case, the "end" is the obsession.

I, for one, am fascinated by obsessive and compulsive behavior—in life and in print, in others and in myself. I am also an incurable romantic, which means that I consider a permanent state of limmerance to be ideal.

Romantic love and pure lust, combined forever in one partner. Who would not want that? It's even PC (Politically Correct), for heaven's sake.

Seeking limmerance, *being* in limmerance, dealing with the *loss* of limmerance—in the past that was surely the construct of literary paths leading to strange, dark places, and to unlikely liaisons. Isn't that what drove Thomas Hardy's protagonist in *Return of the Native,* Flaubert's in *Emma Bovary,* Brontë's in *Wuthering Heights?*

Yes, but that was then, you say. What of now, as we head toward the end of the nineties?

Now, would we not be likely to write of Emmanuelle (of the R-rated movies) posturing on the cliff at Wuthering Heights, while she fast-talks Brontë's Catherine into coming with her to England. Their mission, to rescue Hardy's Eustacia Vye from Egdon Heath and from the wimps who have prevented her from realizing her full romantic potential. The sequel might have the three of them seeking out Emma Bovary for an all-girl discussion about being true to yourself and the romantic ideal.

Being ever in search of stories that combine these elements, it made sense to me to put together a collection of contemporary noir stories above love, lust, and the search for romantic and physical fulfillment—and for revenge, with secret longings and imaginings, with descriptions of actions once hardly even contemplated behind closed shutters.

When I started looking for just the right stories, I knew full well that it would be a challenge, for even now these themes spawn thoughts mostly confined to journals and to the confessional, rather than to the pages of fiction. But I kept on looking because I knew they existed, those fictional explorations of the dark side of human longing.

Having found some in print which satisfied me, I decided to confine this collection to stories written by women, of women, and to see what specific writers might come up with if I solicited stories dealing with those themes. I asked for noir stories, tales dealing with the more sinister side of these all-too-human emotions, and with the actions that emanated from them.

What emerged was a stunning collection of stories that simultaneously challenged the intellect and attacked the viscera of the reader. I believe that women will identify with them, and men will learn secrets long withheld.

In "Wife of Fifty Years," for example, the protagonist is an old woman dying of cancer. Though repulsed by the very idea, she allows her senile husband to make love to her for what she knows will be the last time. She is not sure that he understands what is happening to her or that he really remembers what is driving his pitiful grasping at her body. Barely tolerant of his touch at first, she finds herself needing him, too.

Lisa Mason's "Felicitas" is about a young Mexican woman, an illegal immigrant, who works as a servant by day and prowls by night. Under cover of darkness, she is ravaged repeatedly by her rich employer. She can't stop him except to stop prowling herself or to kill him. The choice she makes is only less shocking than the denouement.

In P.D. Cacek's "Mime Games," a woman takes silent revenge on the mime who violated her in the park. The rape is conducted without physical contact, yet you won't doubt the act—or the revenge.

And then there are two stories by Martha Soukup, "Having Keith," and "The Arbitrary Placement of Walls." The former is a tightly executed obsession story; the latter is about a woman who, in living with the psychic remains of her former lovers, discovers that when they die, so does the pain. Since there was no way I could choose between them, I herewith present to you both of Soukup's stories.

There are twenty-two stories in all, twenty-one outside of my own. Their strength and diversity knock me sideways.

I trust they will do the same for you.

Desire Burn

Janet Berliner

❧ ❧

CASTOFF

Exercising editorial prerogative, I slid one of my own stories into the volume. It's one I particularly enjoyed writing: A Bayou woman knits a sweater for the lover who has abandoned her. Each "Knit one, purl one," reinforces the curse that she weaves into the gift.

❧ ❧

Knit one, purl one.

Cast off.

The sweater was finished.

Stretching, Bethany rubbed the small of her back and stared at the empty street outside her window, her ears tuned for the crunch of his footsteps in the snow that had been falling all night. "Come back to me, Nicholas," she whispered, swearing that if he had not returned by morning she would unravel the last row of the right sleeve and go on knitting, this time weaving one of her Cajun grandmother's curses into each tiny woolen loop. She would punish him for the broken dreams and the worthless promises. He had been strong once, in body and spirit. But that was before he had decided to come to New York; dragging her here from the Bayou; telling her that if she did not come she would lose him. Now the bottle had claimed his soul and she had lost him anyway. She had nothing left to cling to, nothing except the knitting and the waiting and the knowledge that her curses would reach out and touch him, no matter where he had gone.

Knit one, purl one.

Bethany watched the sleeve grow, counting one extra inch, then a second and a third, pushing the stitches across the needle like rosary beads sending prayers to the ears of God. Only Bethany's god was a different one; it was guided by her need for vengeance.

When her knitting was done, Bethany went out into the Bowery. From dawn until dusk and through the night, pausing neither for food nor rest, she haunted the alleys, searching for Nicholas in the unshaven faces of every broken-down bum she could find. She did not give up until that moment of greatest darkness, that instant shortly before the dawn when the night seemed to take a deep breath and briefly renew its losing battle against the encroachment of daylight.

Tired and hungry and cold, her eyes raw from the debris being whipped up by the wind and her jacket gaping open over Nick's bulky sweater, its right sleeve so long that it had to be doubled up into her armpit, she started for home.

But picturing the dingy room she had shared first with Nicholas then with her loneliness and her knitting, Bethany stood still. That wasn't home. She couldn't go back there, not now, not without even the knitting to sustain her. There was nothing in that room she could not live without and she had enough money in her pocket to take a bus to her real home. She was going back to the Bayou where she belonged. Now, before she had time to change her mind.

"I'm leaving, Nicholas."

She had not meant to say the words aloud, to yell them and let them echo against the buildings and flow into the sour-smelling doorways. She had meant only to weave the last of her curses into each syllable of his name.

Angrily she removed her jacket and drew Nick's sweater over her head. Holding it with the tips of her fingers as if it were a dead roach, she headed for the nearest garbage can. Almost without breaking her stride, she lifted the lid and dropped the sweater inside. She would leave it for one of the unwashed creatures hovering in the shadows, a vulture whose only raison d'être was the anticipation of disemboweling the Bowery's refuse. She and her gods had done their work; though she would never see what she had wrought, she was going home.

Half-listening for the rattle of aluminum behind her, Bethany walked on. The scavenger moved quickly; she had hardly taken a dozen steps before she heard the sounds of his rummaging in the trash. She hesitated; stopped; shivered in the damp chill.

Turning around, she watched the man who listed into the glare of a streetlight, his gait singular, lop-sided, pushed askew by the disproportionate length of his right arm. Balancing himself with difficulty, he pushed his arms through the sleeves of the sweater and pulled it over his head. When it was on he stroked it, as if he could not quite believe his new good fortune.

Suddenly, he felt her there. Knew it was she who had done this to him. He raised his head and she saw his eyes. They were filled with questions and pleading with terror.

Slowly, lurching, Nicholas moved toward her.

Smiling, she let him advance. Allowed him to hope. Watched the long fingers of his right hand brush the wine-spattered sidewalk. When he was close enough to touch her, he lifted his elongated right arm and held it out to her in a gesture of supplication.

"You really should have come back to me, Nicholas," she said, admiring the perfect fit of the sleeve and the stitches on the cuff that encircled his distended wrist. "You really should have come home."

Martha Soukup

❧ ❧

THE ARBITRARY PLACEMENT OF WALLS

There was no way that I could choose only one of the two **Martha Soukup** *stories offered to me for this volume—so I took them both. In this story, the writer's down-to-earth, literary style gives the hammer of the story an edge that stays with you, and makes you want to keep the lights on and the lovers away from your own bed.*

❧ ❧

The trip to the kitchen like this:

Stand up from the folding chair six feet to the left of the far corner of the living room. Wide circle around the red armchair. The television is on. It makes a lot of noise. Basketball. Laura doesn't know anything about basketball; the confusion of the game comforts her a little.

Crossing the living-room floor in four big steps. A wide semi-circle, to avoid the coffee table. She replaced the coffee table a year ago, but it didn't make any difference. She'd known it wouldn't.

Up the hall: left side, left side, right side, left side, right side, right side, right side, left side. A whispering at the fourth step. It can't be helped.

Dining room best ignored. Past the back bedroom, which is best ignored too: more whispers, many whispers; she tightens her inner ears to make a roar to drown them out. Finally into the kitchen. The thin blue line on the linoleum around the stove is one of the first she painted. There used also to be ribbons, ropes, strings around corners and chairs and places, different colors, color-coded. She's taken them down. Sometimes she can't keep intruders out of the apartment, and anyway she knows where all the ghosts are now. She steps around the line to the refrigerator. Takes a Pepsi and pops it open. She likes Coke. So did Eric.

She looks at the line around the stove and wonders how much acetone it would take to remove it. Maybe she could just paint lines around the refrigerator, the microwave stand, the kitchen table. Make it look like a Statement.

Thinking about Statements she missteps her way past the stove, stepping on the line. Blue ghosts. Donald memories. Donald frying bacon, naked, dancing away from the sizzles. She remembers yelling at him not to be an idiot, laughing at him. She has long since forgotten exactly what she said. Donald is always there to say what he said.

"It takes a real man to brave elemental fire for his woman," Donald says. Pauses, listening. Dusting of bright blond hair down his belly. "You think I'm afraid of a little bit of grease?"

"You should be, jerk," Laura says into the unresponsive air. "I only wish you'd cauterized your favorite parts." But she can't make herself sound as hostile as she wants.

"Yes I'm crazy and I love you too," Donald says. Suddenly— her memory times it perfectly—he yelps, clutches his buttock, leaps. "My god, I'm hit!" Pause. He laughs. Turns down the burner. "That's right. Kiss it and make it better—" He's collapsing in laughter. Kissing.

The Pepsi jerks in her hand, spraying Laura with sticky cold cola. She's squeezed a dented waistline around its middle. She breaks away form the blue Donald zone, wiping her hand jerkily on her jeans.

Back down the hall: right, left, left, left, right, left, right, right.

She sits two-thirds from the left side of the sofa and stares at the television screen, sipping too-sweet Pepsi. Michael Jordan leaps and spins. She tries to pay attention to the announcers, pick up the subtleties of the game. Donald taught her football, Frank taught her hockey, she taught Eric baseball. Basketball's new. Hers.

The doorbell rings. If it's a meter reader, he can wait for the Martins upstairs to answer. If it's not a meter reader, it's a Jehovah's Witness and child. She doesn't have visitors.

"Laura, I know you're in there. I saw you through the curtains."

Damn it. Life is complicated enough. She takes a wide arc to the front door, backtracking once as she nears Frank. She opens the apartment door to the lobby, crosses the narrow lobby space in two steps and peers through the front door peephole. If she squints down angled form the left she can barely see through it. Not Eric and three dozen roses. She sees her mother, two plastic grocery bags dragging down her arm.

What to do? Laura closes her eyes and opens the door.

"I'm not feeling very—" she begins, but her mother, a stout energetic woman in a perm Laura hasn't seen before, is already in the lobby. "You keep saying you'll come for dinner and you never do," her mother says. "So I have a nice chicken from the Jewel"—lifting one bag—"and a little something to drink with it"—lifting the other. "No arguing now. You let me in your kitchen and I'll have it in the oven in a flash. Then we can chat while it cooks."

Furious thought. "That's so much work, Mother. Let me take you out to a restaurant."

"Don't be ridiculous. I could do a chicken in my sleep, after forty years of it. What are you eating, that terrible microwave food? You could let your mother make you a real meal once a year besides Thanksgiving."

No way out. As she crosses the worn tiles of the lobby her mother's sturdy pink-sneakered foot squeals on the ceramic. In a flash Frank is solidly between them, jogging in place, his running shoes squeaking. "You look fine already, why jog so much?" she asked, four years ago.

Frank grins and gathers up a nonexistent love handle under his t-shirt. "When this body is perfect, your highness, then you'll really be in my power." He leans forward for a kiss, misses, stumbles, his new shoes squealing again. "See? Not irresistable yet. But soon—soon you'll be begging—and then I'll laugh—" and chortling, mock-sinister, he turns and runs out the door through her mother. Goodbye again, Frank.

"Laura?" She jumps. "I swear, you're always daydreaming, honey. Are we going in, or do we stand in the lobby all day?"

"I'm sorry, Mother. I've been feeling a little tired." A fumble with the key. Her stomach hollows as she sees her mother seeing the place, realizes what it looks like through orderly, domestic eyes. Christ. What a mess it is: old newspapers piled at apparent haphazard to block off bad places, traces of old chalk outlines lingering in worn carpet which hasn't been vacuumed in months, furniture in odd places —sofa in a corner, television on the mantelpiece, chairs angled erratically, the big red armchair near the center of the floor.

"Have you been sick? It looks like you haven't cleaned in ages. Is the whole place like this?"

A tally of bad places and the arbitrary placement of walls around them: living room, sunporch, big bedroom, little bedroom, study (the barest, least comfortable room, where she sleeps on a sprung mattress retrieved from someone's trash), the bathroom, and the lobby whose floor she hasn't mopped or even swept— "I'm afraid I've done better. We're busy at work. A lot of overtime." She grabs the red armchair and wrestles it to the nearest corner, its former corner, so mortified she barely

sees the kaleidoscope of ghosts she plows through in the process. Back in place, Eric snores softly once, curled in red velvet,
rubs his eyes, smiles sleepily up at her, murmurs: "Love you,
Lauracakes. . . ."

She whirls away. "Really it's not usually like this at all—"

"I hope not, honey. You'll make yourself sick living like this."
Her mother shoves her sleeves up her sturdy arms. "That's it,
then. We're going to give this place its spring cleaning. I've got
the whole evening free."

The whole evening? Dear God, Laura thinks. "I don't," she
lies. "I have to go out and run some errands."

"Then don't let me stop you." Her mother is already gathering
up newspapers. "You just leave me here and you'll see how
much better this place looks when you get back."

"No, you can't—"

"Don't argue with your mother. What would your grandparents have said, if they knew you'd let their home get like this?"
She is unstoppable. Laura can't leave her alone here.

So the whole evening it is, three solid hours caught helplessly in a domestic whirlwind, in the wake of a cheerful
blur of activity. Her mother digs up brooms, vacuum cleaner,
garbage bags, and Laura follows unable to defend her for-
tresses of boxes, paper and carefully positioned furniture from
being torn down and restructured into normal and deadly
order. Her mother knows where everything used to be. She
helped Laura move here from the dorm, years back, in the
first place.

A helpless accomplice in the destruction of her wards, if Laura
tries to move a chair back from a danger spot, she comes face
to face with Donald Frank Eric and must retreat to hold bags
for her mother's disposal of Pepsi cans, or to sweep furiously,
staring at the floor where she can see only feet. Air fills with
dust. Windows fling open. Nothing stops the juggernaut. It's a
sickening feeling, like being dragged carelessly, at great speed,
at the end of a tether across slick and dangerous ice. All she
can do is pray for it to stop.

Suddenly she is taken by the shoulder and plunked into the sofa, a sweaty cold bottle shoved into her hand. "All done! That wasn't too bad, was it?" Her mother produces another bottle of wine cooler—Laura hasn't had alcohol since Eric—twisting the top off. Her mother sits in the red armchair and, though Laura sits six feet away, she can faintly see Eric sleepily stir and smile, sitting up until his curling lips are inches out of synch with her mother's. A swing band, her mother's cleaning music from the stereo, drowns out his loving murmurs. Her mother pours herself some wine cooler. The smell of roasting chicken drifts from the kitchen.

Laura takes a long pull from her bottle, gets hold of herself. The thin bite of alcohol unfamiliar on her tongue.

"I hope you like this brand, dear." She sips. "Nothing tastes better than a cold drink after a good day's cleaning."

Nothing hurts like old happiness, trapping her.

"You should be more careful with the things people leave you. Your grandparents willed you this building because they loved you, honey. You should treat it better."

'It's so big for one person," Laura says. "There's so much to do. If the Martins upstairs didn't do the yardwork, I don't know how I'd keep up."

"Then sell it," her mother says. "It would break your grandparents' hearts—but I suppose they're not around to know it."

"I can't." There are so many reasons, worn around the edges: the repairs it would need before she could put it on the market, the time it would take up, the Martins who were old friends of her grandparents and would never get such a low rent rate from any new landlord. What kind of person would put the Martins out on the street?

And no money at all to make the sort of repairs the place would need, even to cover the building's age with a bright coat of paint. Donald's investments saw to that; eternally, back in the study, he explains the columns of figures that prove his cousin's novelty factory will triple her money, give them enough for a honeymoon in Switzerland. He believed it. Any time she cares to look in the study she can see the excitement in his eyes. She saw it, unwillingly, an hour ago. She is still paying back the debts.

"Whatever you think is best," her mother says. Covering her mouth, she yawns with Eric. "Excuse me! All this exercise." She deftly rebuttons her sleeves. "I haven't moved so much furniture in years. I used to do it all the time, you know, whenever I was really upset about something. When we couldn't pay the bills, or when your father and I fought, or when you went away to college and I missed you so much, dear. I'd just roll up my sleeves and move the furniture all around. It really gets rid of the ghosts."

Laura starts. "Ghosts?"

"Oh, you know, all those stupid old memories. It does help to keep busy. Anyway, now we can sit and catch up."

Her mother sits, pleasantly waiting for news. Laura can't think of anything to say.

"So, are you dating anybody?"

"No," she says.

"Oh, honey. Now I know I'm not supposed to push for grandchildren, and I'd never do that. But don't you think you're working too hard? It couldn't hurt you to get out now and then. Aren't there any nice young men where you work?"

"They're all married."

"Oh, that's too bad. You know, I thought it was such a shame when that Eric moved to Wisconsin. He was such a sweet boy. Do you know he phoned me the other day?"

Oh Christ. Eric sits up sleepily through her mother and rubs his eyes. Her mother always liked him. Everybody liked him. He was good at that. After Donald and Frank, she hadn't been able to trust anyone, not until nice sweet Eric, polite to mothers, wonderful listener, gentle in bed. The bastard. She looks away from his smiling murmurs.

"He didn't sound like himself. He's in the hospital up there, poor boy."

"The hospital? Why?"

"He wouldn't say. He said it wasn't anything important, but

you know he really didn't sound so good. Hasn't he called you? Maybe you should call him. I'll give you his number." She takes her little address book and a notepad from her purse and starts to copy a listing.

I'll never talk to him, Laura thinks. Then she thinks: AIDS, the bastard gave me AIDS and ran out, oh Jesus.

"Here you are, honey. I never did understand what happened between you two. If he's not very sick maybe this is a blessing, get you two together for a talk and who knows what could happen?"

The bastard would just lie to her again. "Mother—"

"Not that I'd ever pressure you, dear. You know I'd just like you kids to be friends."

"Mother—"

The oven timer sounds. Her mother stands.

"Mother." She jumps up and grabs her mother's arm. "Mother, I can't eat now." Her mother looks startled. "You understand. It's upsetting. Not knowing. I have to call the hospital, okay?"

"He said it wasn't anything important, honey."

He lied all the time. "Don't forget your purse. We'll do this again. Thank you for everything." She propels her mother to the apartment door, through the lobby, to the building door.

"Don't forget the hospital number—"

She grabs it and shoves it in her pocket. "Thank you. I'll call. Goodbye!" The door slams in her mother's concerned face. Laura retreats three steps and shoves the inner door shut, stepping around where the end table used to keep her from Donald. She miscalculates. His bags are packed and he glowers without looking at her. "Bastard!" she screams at him. She thrashes the empty air, makes herself stop.

She stands trembling in the wreckage of her protection, tidy rational apartment with nowhere to hide. Every chair and table, bit and piece has used her mother as its agent to find its way back to sinister order. Closing in on her.

She has survived everything else. She will survive.

She will leave the slip of paper wadded in her pocket.

The chicken slowly turns to carbon in the oven.

❧ ❦

Ghosts.

Frank lifts weights in the back room, in the corner once marked out with brown chalk. "You're a self-involved jerk," she shouts at him. "I don't know what I ever saw in you!" He clamps another weight on the bar and grins at her. "You don't think I can lift this? Ah, but you forget how you inspire me, oh beauteous one. Watch!"

"I don't care!" She throws her glass through him. It shatters against the wall. Frank doesn't stop grinning. The bar bends under the weights' mass as he lifts it over his head.

"What do I get for a reward?" he says, grunting the bar back down, reaching out—

On the floor against the coffee table, Donald hunches, knee-hugging, in rare tears, his only tears. His father's death. Weeping, bruise-eyed, he reaches up for comfort—

Eric is setting the dining-room table; it's roast goose, a sort of asparagus souffle, German wine. She can almost taste it. Smiling, pleased with himself, he reaches out to pull her in to him—

The shower is horrible: her mother threw out the hose she rigged to the other side of the tub, shaking her head, telling Laura she really should call a plumber if she can't deal with shower pipes. Laura can't bathe without Donald Frank Eric swirling around her with the water. She sponges her armpits, washes her hair in the bathroom sink, not looking up to see who is shaving in the mirror—

She tries sleeping in her bed where it's been moved back. (Her mother threw out the mildewy mattress in the back room.) Donald makes love beside her. His lean torso moves slowly, sensually; sweat gleams along his smooth jaw; his broad hand reaches to stroke her hair. He whispers things she could barely hear the first time, can barely hear now. Nonsense.

She turns her back, squeezes her eyes shut. Still the indecipherable murmuring. Gets up and takes two sleeping pills, jams the pillow down hard over her ears. Can't shut out the murmurs. Even the bed seems to rock, slowly, sensually—

Sobbing with anger she drags the massive bed across the floor. It takes five long minutes to move it, gouging four broad pale lines in the floor. Her shoulders ache. Shake.

The bed away from where Donald touched a girl who used to be Laura, she still can't sleep. The house murmurs with the hundred ghosts of three living men.

Slip of paper wadded in her pocket.

The workday seems infinite when she's in the office. She thinks she hears gossip behind her back. Nobody says more than hello except her supervisor, Bob, who lingers too long at her desk. His smug flirting brings bile to the back of her throat; she clenches her jaw until he moves on to the next woman. She routes forms, stacks and stacks of forms, trying to lose herself in the mindlessness of it. The routine is abysmal, the whispering unbearable, and the day goes on forever; and then she has to go home.

To each infinite, unbearable night.

⋅৵ ৡ⋅

Finally she calls the number on the lined paper.

Eric is putting a big box of Godiva chocolates on the end table next to the telephone, bidding for her attention with another present. The phone rings twice on the other end.

"Yes, could you tell me about your patient Eric Kennelly?"

"I can connect you."

Eric pulls away the chocolate box and points coyly to his lips.

"No, I don't want to talk to him. I just want to know how he's doing. Could you tell me what he's being treated for?" She knows it's not AIDS—Eric was too clever, too controlled to forget any precautions—but she tells herself she has to be sure. It's only sensible.

"I'm afraid that's not hospital policy, ma'am. I can connect you, if you like."

He unbuttons two buttons, pulls away the shirt from one shoulder and balances a chocolate on his pale skin.

"Ma'am?"

She hangs up.

An hour later she walks eight blocks to the car rental place and lays down her credit card.

He didn't even leave her for another woman. He'd just been killing time in Chicago until he could wangle an assistant professorship at UW. She was something to do in the meantime. Hindsight. "Do you know how many PhD's in history are working in personnel, or selling insurance, or sweeping high schools? And this isn't some podunk college, either. This is my big break!" But he never asked if she'd move north with him. And was packed and gone before she could ask him.

It's only a couple of hours drive to Madison, far too short. She has to stop at a gas station to find out where the hospital is. She circles it a couple times before she pulls in and parks near the Visitors sign.

"It's probably not visiting hours," she says to the woman at the desk. "I can leave if it's the wrong time."

"No, there's half an hour left." The woman smiles. "Who are you here to see?"

"That's okay, I have his room number." 258. She can almost feel the number, burning her hand from the wad of paper. Into the elevator, down the hall to the right nearly to the end; she faces the door. Hand on the knob. Opens it.

A wasted pale figure lies half-curled on a hospital bed. Tubes all over. It looks like nobody she's ever seen, barely like a human. The figure turns and opens Eric's gray-green eyes. "Laura. Well. What brings you by?"

The door gapes open behind her, air blowing through it, chilling her as if she's naked. She closes it carefully.

"I'll bet it's two weeks since I had a visitor." The voice is a rasping whisper, not Eric's soft tenor at all. He manages a lopsided sort of grin. "People get bored of watching a guy die. Can't blame them. Liver cancer's not a showbiz way to go."

She is silent.

"I knew you'd come eventually. You cut it close, though, hon."

She stares at him. She can't let herself feel sorry for the sweet and lying Eric who haunts her days and nights, so she mustn't make this miserable stick-figure look like any Eric at all.

Except the eyes. Hard not to look at the eyes.

"Laura? You going to say anything?" The stick-man swallows painfully. "I feel like I'm being visited by a ghost. You didn't go and beat me to the other side, did you?" He laughs briefly, coughs at greater length. "Sorry. Gallows humor. My psychiatrist tells me it's normal.'

Just a stick-man, she tells herself. Something too big moves, like broken wings, inside her. All right! she thinks. Eric! Sick. Pitifully sick. But don't let him fool you again, don't let him—

"Laura?"

"Why did you call my mother? What do you want?"

The stick-man blinks Eric's eyes. "I don't know. Nothing. Whatever. It's so damn boring, dying. To see if you were still as uptight as you ever were. Amazing—you're even more uptight."

If she moves even an inch she'll be lost, he'll have won; in grief and sympathy and love she will do anything for him. She struggles to stand still, firm. So he'd be using her. Is that bad? Was he really just using her before?

He grins again, a parody of the smile that used to be his best feature. "It's something to do." Why did you move in with me if you just expected to leave in four months? she had asked him, desperate, as his car backed down the driveway. It was something to do, he said, and drove away.

"You never needed much reason," Laura says. She wonders if anaesthetics linger in hospital air. Her heart beats slow and her body feels dull. Antiseptics must be stinging her eyes to tears. But she pushes down the crippled part inside her. Things die in hospitals.

The stick-man frowns. "Laura—"

"You knew how Donald and Frank hurt me, and you made it your little project to get me to trust you. Then you walked out." Something almost chokes her voice; she doesn't let it. "Kept things from being boring, I expect. I don't know. I've never been so bored I'd do that."

The stick-man coughs, starts to speak, coughs again. Lopsided grin. "Is that any way to talk to a dying man?"

"I don't give a shit what you do. You were the worst of the lot. I don't have a thing to say to you." She turns to leave, before the leaden anaesthetic feeling weights her feet in place, before the broken parts inside her weigh her heart down. While she can still move.

The stick-man rasps a sigh, presses his head back into his pillow. "Then why did you come all this way to see me?"

Laura stops without looking back. "No reason at all." Not good enough. She turns—his deep, gray-green eyes—and has to force her prepared words out: "Just a little friendly advice."

Deep breath: "Drop dead."

She closes the door behind her with perfect silence.

◄§ §►

After her brilliant, cutting exit, what a shock to see Eric flush and laughing on the front stoop.

"You're dying," she tells him, and at the dining-room table, and in the red chair, and in the back bedroom, and at the kitchen sink. "Just die." Eric laughs and shows her how he can (sloppily) wash with one hand and dry with the other. All she can do is run again.

A week slides by.

Hard as she tries, she can't forget Eric dying in the hospital, too pitiful for lasting hate. To keep hate fresh she visits all the really bad ghosts. They don't hurt as much as the happy ones, the loving ones, but she's always spent less time with them.

In the back room with Donald: "If you had any sense you wouldn't have encouraged me to risk all my assets!" Mine too, she thought, but she's helpless against his hurt fury. "Flat broke and you think the wedding's still on? Give me the damn ring back and I'll at least have a thousand bucks to start a new life with." It isn't fair, but the ring clatters at his feet where she threw it at him. He picks it up without a word and stalks away; though she will wait for months for him to come to his senses, call her, apologize, he never does. Leaving her in debt, lonely, alone.

The bedroom with Frank: "I've thought about it," he says. "I'm going back to my wife." Wife? He never mentioned a wife. She would never have been stupid enough to get involved with a married man. It was his two jobs and his eternal exercise that kept his visits so erratic. "Of course I never told you I was married—we were going to get a divorce. You didn't need to know." He's pulling on his pants, not looking at her. His skin damp with sweat from their lovemaking. "But Sheila's pregnant now. I can't leave her." Too stunned to move, the hair on her thighs drying stiffly, she had stared at him leaving.

And Eric. Over and over, Eric. "We've had fun, Laura, but this is a job. My future. Don't get emotional over this, okay? It was fun."

Harder to make these ghosts hurt than the happy ones. She wants the beautiful ghosts, for all she knows about them. These betrayers are strangers, strangers. She stares and stares at them.

The same feeling she's ever had on betrayal: numb. Just numb.

She doesn't miss the men who left. She misses ones she loves, and hates: the lovers who once stayed. If only they would go away now. Go away, leave her in peace.

The pain stays.

She thinks about what Eric said about beating him to the other side. She goes out the next Saturday, buys a tiny gun from a local pawn shop and contemplates it for a long hour, Frank sleeping at her elbow where the bed used to be two years ago. Contemplates it until the plastic pearl handle sticks warmly to her fingers. But death is a land of ghosts, and how is someone who can't manage the ghosts of life to manage all the ghosts of death?

Or maybe she's just a coward.

Unable to point it at her own head, she turns it on sleeping Frank.

"Bang," she says. Frank snores softly.

She crosses the room to where Donald is destroying the Venetian blind, futilely trying to rehang it. Aims. "Bang." The blind crashes to the floor and Donald, laughing, scoops it up. She walks into the living room and aims at the red overchair.

Eric isn't there.

Laura drops the gun. Somehow, it doesn't go off.

Somehow, Eric isn't there.

She approaches the chair slowly, afraid of things she can't guess at.

Just a chair. Empty.

She runs into the dining room, too fast to follow the side-to-side pattern, flashing past two Donalds and a Frank. Reaches the dining-room table.

Empty.

The back bedroom. The guest bed only ever shared with one person.

Empty.

The sink, where Donald or Frank never did dishes.

Empty.

Panicking, she runs outside to the front stoop. No roses wait for her there.

Back to the chair. She rips off the cushion, looking for she doesn't know what. Shakes the empty chair. Shakes it shakes it shakes it. Wrenches the chair back and forth with hysteric echoing clatters.

The phone rings. Laura jumps as though the gun were firing. She grips one velvet chair arm with each hand, presses her forehead into the back of the chair, breathes deeply. The phone keeps ringing. Trembling, she picks up the receiver.

"Ms. Hampton?" asks a strange voice. Not Eric. Not Eric.

"Yes?" Her voice is a squeak. She tries again. "Yes."

"I'm sorry to bother you. My name's Bill Chang. You don't know me. I was Eric Kennelly's roommate."

"Yes?"

"Um, well, your name is on this list he wanted me to call

when—Ms. Hampton, I'm calling to tell you he passed away this afternoon."

"Yes."

"Um, I'm sorry to have to tell you this like this. I wish we could talk, but he's got all these cousins, and he really wanted me to make all these calls—"

"Yes."

"I know this is a terrible thing to hear from a stranger—"

"When did it happen?"

"What? Oh, I'm sorry. Less than an hour ago. I just talked to his parents. Do you want to know when the funeral is?"

"No. Thank you, Mr. Chang. Goodbye."

She hangs up the phone. The red chair is a little out of place. She replaces the cushion and pushes the chair gently to its proper bit of wall. Sits in it. So comfortable. So empty.

The little pawnshop gun lies at her foot. She picks it up and wipes cold sweat from its handle. It really is a nice little gun; it fits sweetly in her hand.

Sitting in the empty red chair with the sweet little gun feels better than she's felt in a year. Longer. She shuts her eyes and luxuriates in the wonder of having a third of her home back to herself. No more paper plates—she can use the sink. She can eat at the table. She can sleep on the guest bed. Reborn possibilities warm her, spread from her heart to tingle in every limb, flow through her hand to warm the sweet little gun.

Later she picks up the phone and dials a memorized number she's never phoned before.

"Mrs. Prescott?" she says pleasantly. "Hi. You don't know me. I'm an old friend of your husband Frank's. Could you tell him I've run into a few old things of his around my place I'd like him to come pick up? —Whenever's convenient. Thanks so much."

She stretches back in the red overchair, listening to Mrs. Prescott telling her when Frank can come over, right hand wrapped comfortably around the warm plastic grip.

"Yes, that'll be a big help." Laura smiles. "I'm just trying to clear out the house."

Martha Soukup

꒰ ꒱

HAVING KEITH

A woman becomes jealous when her best friend starts dating the man she wants. She gets what she wants by "taking" his body. **Martha Soukup**'s *deceptively easy, contemporary style renders the denouement terrifyingly believable.*

꒰ ꒱

She wants him, wants him; she knows she cannot have him and she wants him.

He always comes to the library on Tuesday afternoons, so Paula is there too. Sitting very straight in the carrel, she can just see him over the top of the partition. Look at the way his hair sweeps across his forehead in dark bangs; there, he turns to replace a book and she can see the curls move softly at the nape of his neck. Lord, he is beautiful. She remembers another glimpse of him, his sleek, tanned body. But that was not through her own eyes and she is not sure, just yet, that it was real.

He bends to pick another book from a low shelf, disappearing; she must hold herself down in her chair, not leap up; after all the holding back she must not make a fool of herself now. A breath, two breaths, three, and he reappears. Now she really breathes. Air in his absence gives no sustenance.

She will have him. it might be enough just to see him, breathe his air, feel his presence, but soon enough he is bound to find out how she feels, and he will block her out completely, deny her even that. So she will find another way. That glimpse of him as though through other eyes, something she has not experienced since she was three—

He does not want her. While she was falling unwillingly in love with him he was falling enthusiastically in love with another.

She will find another way.

That sudden vision of Keith had been such a shock she could not sustain it. It was just his back, disappearing through a bathroom door; but it was unmistakeably him, his long soft hair damp and tousled, and Paula had gasped in her bed while he melted away and was replaced by the speckled drapes of her tiny apartment.

She closes her eyes and thinks of Patty. Light brown hair and smiling light brown eyes, exactly like Paula but forever three years old. Patty and Paula were so close that they never thought it was strange they could see through each other's eyes, and they were so young that adults never took anything they said about it seriously. Only years later did Paula learn that most people couldn't do anything like that.

The last thing she saw through her twin sister's eyes was the powder blue Dodge careening around the corner, straight at her. Little Paula screamed and fainted; when she woke up, she was a singleton.

It was a painful memory. But Patty was gone forever, and she had learned long ago that it was no use thinking about her.

The vision of Keith is still with her, an image burned into her brain. Droplets of water glisten on his tanned and leanly muscled back; he is just turning his head around, perhaps to say something. A towel is tucked around his waist. He has very good legs.

It has been seventeen years since she has seen anything through another person's eyes. She wonders if she could again.

❧ ❧

"What are you doing tonight?"

Chicken-fried steak turns to bile in Paula's mouth. She gulps it down. Take a breath: one, two.

"Studying, Elaine," she says carefully, and makes herself look up.

Elaine: slender, petite, very blond, deep long-lashed grey eyes. Carries herself with confidence, assurance. As well she should.

She used to think of Elaine as her best friend.

"Great," says Elaine, blind Elaine, with sweet sincerity. "Do you want me to come over and work through calculus together?"

"No," she says. Two phonemes. "Thanks." Another five. Seven phonemes: see how good she is at talking to Elaine.

"Well, if your place is no good tonight you could come over to mine," says Elaine with the beautiful density Paula has come to loathe. "If it's before his night class, Keith will be there, but we can get a larger pizza." Enthusiasm warms her voice.

"No!" How can she lose control of two phonemes? A breath. "Thanks. I have to go to the library."

"Why?"

My god, stop talking, stop making me talk! "Research."

"What are you researching?"

"A paper."

"What class?"

Stop it! "Psych 204."

"Isn't that the paper you said you had to finish last week when I asked you to the movie?"

She has been keeping Elaine's heart-shaped face out of focus; even that becomes too much, and she turns to her steak, sawing her knife through straw-colored bread crumbs. "Professor Bell asked me to expand it." Twenty or thirty or god knows how many phonemes, too many, please jesus Elaine stop!

Elaine stops. Paula takes a bite, chews mechanically and swallows. Another bite. Silence. Against her will she looks up to see the other woman staring angrily at her.

"Fine, Paula. I'm sure I don't know what it is with you anymore. I won't bother you again." She stalks off, picture of self-righteous indignation. Why shouldn't she be? Paula is not going to tell her either.

Those were your eyes I saw through, weren't they, dear cruel friend.

Attacking the chicken-fried steak.

I can do it.

◄§ §►

The day she met him is preserved as perfectly in her mind as a strip of film. She had noticed he was older than the rest of the class when he sat beside her in zoology; that was all the notice she intended to pay him. But something about him kept reminding her that he was at her elbow, and by the end of the class she decided to talk to him.

"Lunch?" How bold she felt!

"A meal consumed between breakfast and supper." He had a wonderful smile. "Are we getting pop quizzes already in this class?"

She laughed. "I know some places around here that beat the cafeteria. Are you interested?"

"Anything would. I like a woman who makes promises she can live up to."

She laughed again. "Elaine! Um—" She gestured.

"Keith."

"—Keith and I are going to hit Albert's. Want to come?"

Mistake! How she has replayed that sentence in her mind. If it is a film, it has white streaks and splice jumps and the soundtrack flutters.

"I should go to the bookstore—oh, heck, sure."

Elaine was safe. Although she and her boyfriend fought, everyone agreed they would never split up.

"Sounds fun," said Keith.

Over chili dogs at Albert's she discovered he was beautiful.

He had just returned to college to prepare for med school, an ambition he shared with both Paula and Elaine. "Twelve-year-old B.A.'s in history don't exactly get you into Johns Hopkins." He had been trapped in his father's business for a decade; now the excitement of his new life lit up his eyes. "I always swore I'd never be a paper-pusher, but when I got married it all just seemed to happen. Now that that's over—don't laugh!— I'm plunging right into good old '60's idealism: inner-city clinics, helping starving babies and pregnant kids and all that counter-counterrevolutionary stuff." He shrugged with self-deprecation, while his eyes crinkled all round. Paula felt more excited about med school than she had been since she was a freshman.

The tan and the weathering were from rock climbing. His hands were quick, dextrous: jazz piano. His hair, unfashionably long. She was amused, intrigued; this Keith person would make a wonderful new fantasy. Of course, she was busy with her own life, wary of complications; she couldn't afford to get caught up with another person busy with his.

So she laughed when Elaine brought up amusing anecdotes about her confirmed bachelorhood and the last few guys who had tried to change her mind. She shouldn't let this guy think she was interested.

(And the only person she had ever been that close to was Patty, and Patty had died.)

Somehow, would-be boyfriends led the conversation to his ex-wife.

"—finally she just left. Well, it made sense. When I wasn't working, I'd be climbing, or taking guitar lessons, or directing a community theater show—anything to keep from thinking about being trapped. She wasn't interested in any of those things. She wanted something else. After she left, I realized I did too." He blinked and looked surprised at what he was saying.

"Do you miss her?" Elaine asked softly.

"I don't know. It wasn't like I knew her anymore." Elaine's

small pale hand covered his. "Yes." She squeezed; he sighed, shook his head, smiled at her.

That was when Paula realized she loved him; and, simultaneously, that it was too late.

◆§ §◆

Not too late. Not too late!

She opens her eyes to see her hands clenched in front of her on the scarred veneer of the carrel. (Her lie to Elaine became self-fulfilling and she is back in the library, an empty place without Keith.) She tries to think about anything else but it is no use. Whenever Keith invades her thoughts (which is most of the time), he comes flooding in everywhere at once. As, uninvited, does Elaine. "We're not actually living together," Elaine giggles in her mind, and at the same time Paula can see their apartments, his just down the hall—opening the door, seeing a closet full of clothes, a desk covered with papers—and no bed. No cot, no futon, not a goddamned sleeping bag. Why are they so damn coy?

No. —Keith chasing a frisbee (Elaine throwing it). Keith making a joke that breaks everyone at the table up (Elaine slapping his back). Keith staring somberly across the duck pond (Elaine sneaking up and making him smile).

No!

Channel the emotion. She breathes slowly and deeply, forcing herself to be calm. She counts, slowly, slowly; her breathing evens; she rests her head on her arms. Things begin to fade away, as she concentrates. Keith. Her. (And a distant echo of Patty.) She feels oddly bouyant as she drifts off. . . .

◆§ §◆

. . . He smiles at her. He reaches out and strokes her face. She wants to laugh, or cry, or learn to dance like in the movies so she can dance like that.

A voice in the back of her head says, This is impossible. Shut up.

He's blind to everyone but Elaine.

Go away!

It's not real.

I've made it real! and she grabs him and kisses him in a wonderful moist mess and when she pulls back finally her hair has fallen into a blond web over her eyes and she remembers how.

"Sweet Elaine," he says softly.

Not you, the voice says, and his beautiful face begins to fade.

Shut up, she thinks grimly. I'll make it me.

Blackness.

❧ ❧

Despite a blinding headache she makes it home from the library. She should be elated at the first success, but the memory of the kiss is staggering, almost more painful than pleasurable, as when she was twelve and first considered that it was actually possible to kiss someone, thinking of a boyishly charming television star. The first visceral imagination of what that would be like had literally knocked her breath away, frightening her.

Even Keith's touch on her cheek eclipses that memory.

Not your cheek, says the nagging voice.

In any case, she must find out if it was genuine, not some trance-induced dream. She forces herself to seek out Elaine's company the next afternoon in the cafeteria. Elaine has forgotten or forgiven Paula's rudeness of the day before; Paula endures a stream of one-sided conversation—a conversation in which she is determinedly silent.

"—funny thing is that he thinks he knows me so well, but he really doesn't."

If you loved him you wouldn't hide anything from him. I wouldn't.

"It's this whole love-at-first-sight thing. He did the same thing with his ex, you know. He didn't see that she wasn't what he thought until she left him, and he thinks I'm exactly the same image that came to him in one piece. Lucky it's a good one!"

I never fall in love at first sight. I always used to be safe from that.

"Anyway, I really think this will work out. I'll have to be careful, of course. His illusions are so precious to him. But he's got to stop that idiotic climbing. And this notion of staying friends with his ex is impossible, don't you agree? And the idea of starving with his patients in the ghetto! A lovely dream, but it makes a lot more sense if we take over my uncle's practice together. He'd get stubborn if I told him outright, but I'll get him to see reason."

Keep your fucking hands off him, you ungrateful scum! Paula bites the insides of her cheeks to keep her mouth shut and almost misses what Elaine is saying:

"Things I just couldn't tell him. Like—he thinks I'm so level-headed—but last night I just flaked out. We were studying and I swear I didn't have anything in mind but all of a sudden all my clothes were off! He said he never saw me so aggressive. I don't even remember starting it! Just a blank. Scary. It's finals stress, I guess. You won't tell, will you?"

Paula stares at her. "This was last night?" Elaine nods. "About what time?"

"I don't know—nine or so—why?"

Bingo! "If it only happened once I wouldn't worry about it."

"You're probably right." Elaine looks relieved. "It's so nice to have someone I can tell something like that to."

You should trust him with things like that. You don't deserve him. The thought comes with a rush of warmth, a rightness. She thinks it again, clearly. You don't deserve him.

I deserve him.

◁§ ৡ▷

She pushes her bedtime forward, spends each night meditating, trying to project herself onto Elaine again. The results are mixed: a glimpse of his face once, twice; Elaine's small hands washing in the sink; class notes; an oddly-angled view of his foot. No contact as sustained as the first, and in the mornings she is very tired, as though she had not slept. Still, she takes strength from the small successes.

One night she finds herself sitting on the edge of the sofabed. The scene is hazy, the contact unstable. She looks up and Keith is at the door. It starts to slip away. Quickly she jumps up, slams the door in his face, double-latches and chains it before she loses touch.

Awakening, exhausted, she can still see the astonishment on his face.

That morning Elaine is very pale.

Keith approaches her after zoology and everything clenches inside her. She has not spoken to him in class since, inevitably, he chose Elaine as his lab partner. "Has Elaine talked to you today?"

"No. Why?" Her hand remembers the feel of his neck, his hair.

"Nothing. She just was—a little strange, last night. It's not important." He smiles innocently at her; it hurts; at the same time she feels triumph. She is no longer powerless. The knowledge gives her confidence. She smiles back at him.

"Do you want to go out to lunch?"

"Well," he says, looking back where Elaine is cleaning up their table, "I'm not sure she's up for it now. I can ask her."

It is the longest conversation she has had alone with him. Every nerve is stretched, humming. "Do you want to go to lunch? I didn't ask her."

He frowns a little. "I can hardly leave her alone right now."

"It might be a good idea. Anyone who slams a door on you with no explanation—"

"I thought she hadn't talked to you."

That's right. She is so fatigued; she forgot. She rushes over the lapse. "Maybe you should spend time with other people. You've spent so much with her, you can't know what other people might have to offer."

He is really looking at her now, straight at her. It dizzies
her, looking at his eyes. "What are you saying?" he asks quietly.
Why not, she asks herself. What is there to lose, anyway?
She opens her mouth, cannot speak.

"You?"

"Yes," she says in a tiny, odd voice. "If you could only look
past her for once—if you just saw what I could—"

"I see." His voice is distant.

"I mean, look at her! Having blackouts, acting irrationally,
trying to cover it up—"

"You'd really use this against her."

"You don't know her! She wants to change you, she wants to
destroy you—"

"If Elaine needs help, I'm going to see that she gets it. And
the first thing to do is protect her from her supposed friends.
I think," he says, his eyes chilly, opaque, "it would be best if
you don't see her anymore." He turns his back on her. He
collects Elaine, who follows with uncharacteristic passivity, and
walks out of the classroom without another word.

I don't want to see her, I want to see you! Oh lord, I blew
it, I finally ruined it all. She slides down against the blackboard
and cries silently in the empty classroom.

❧ ❦

Again she walks home alone, always alone. There is thunder
and then rain pours down on her. She seeks no shelter; let the
storm crash against her. She passes their building and sees a
light in Elaine's apartment. She stops to stare at it for a while,
thinking irrelevantly that no one could know there are tears
among the raindrops streaming down her face: although she has
destroyed her own façade, the weather has kindly given it back
to her. The wind plasters her shirt and jeans to her chilled skin.
She stares until the pain tops over and runs out of her like
rainwater, and walks on. Near her own building a bare-chested
young man is washing his hair in the squall; he flicks suds at

her and his friends laugh. "Hey, lady," they call. "Hey, lady!"
She keeps walking, their laughter following her.

Her apartment repels her with its emptiness. All or nothing,
she thinks. She opens the oven door and blows out the pilot
light; she lifts the stove top and extinguishes that one too. She
turns all the dials. She is quite calm, because she knows what
will happen: she will fail to keep contact with Elaine, return to
her own body and open the windows; or she will stay until
there is no body to return to. She has raised the stakes so there
can be no failure. It makes perfect sense.

The smell is appalling but she ignores it, closes her eyes,
breathes slowly. Keith. If he can only see good in Elaine who
is bad for him, only feel disdain for her love, she will be Elaine.
The blackness behind her eyelids deepens.

⋖§ ৡ⋗

Black forever.

It would be easy, but she does not forget to concentrate.
This is not like anything she has ever attempted before.

Black.

There is an arm. It does not want to move: she makes it
move. There is a leg. Slowly, grimly, she straightens it. There
is Elaine. She refuses it. She will not allow it. Fear, pleading, a
horrible tearing and it is—yes! Gone! —And there is pain, and
vertigo, and redness, and black again.

⋖§ ৡ⋗

The bed feels wrong. Everything feels wrong, as though she is
starting a bad cold. Worse.

Finally she opens her eyes. At first she thinks there is something wrong with her vision too: the ceiling is too close, the
wrong shade. She swings her legs to the floor and almost falls:
her balance is skewed. She grips the headboard—sofa back—
and pulls herself to her feet. It has finally gotten through her

brain, which seems as sluggish as her body, that she has made it. This time she is here for good.

She takes a breath—it feels odd, insubstantial in Elaine's narrow, confining ribcage—and goes to the bathroom, leaning a hand on the wall to keep from falling. Her coordination is that of a two-year-old. Elaine's face stares unreadably at her from the mirror. Her stomach lurches. Elaine's stomach lurches: the thought rises like bile.

The face is pasty, almost bloated; the grey eyes inhumanly pale; how can Keith find this attractive? She finds the makeup, yanks out the drawer, overcompensating for the weaker body, spilling trays and tubes of makeup. She gathers them clumsily in shaking hands.

She opens all the makeup and applies it furiously, trying to soften the big yellowish eyes with eyeshadow, smearing on blusher to narrow the cheeks—to look like Paula. She stares at the results: a dimestore china doll, sloppy, lifeless.

There is a knock on the door. Her heart (Elaine's heart, flabby in her chest) jumps. She calls out: "Just a second!" the voice is high-pitched in her ears. She cannot tell if it sounds natural.

A pause. "Are you okay?" asks Keith's voice.

She swallows. "Yes. I'll be right out."

She takes off the nightgown. The breasts are small but too heavy, too low. The waist is too narrow and the thighs are heavy and the ankles are puffy. Where is the little scar above the navel (never such a deep and puckered hole)? The pallid skin smothers her. The room darkens and she realizes she is hyperventilating; she grabs for the toilet tank with short white arms. The icy porcelein is friendlier than Elaine's clammy, alien flesh.

Keith's voice is calling a name that is not here. A key scrapes in the lock.

"Elaine? Honey?" Muscular arms circle the narrow naked waist and she shudders, squeezes the eyes tight. She feels how small the mouth is as it tightens into a rictus, and shakes harder. She is turned around. "What have you done to your face?" His hand strokes the cheek. In all her fantasies his hand on her face felt like his hand on her face. He half-carries her to the sofa, a warm, firm forearm supporting the heavy breasts. He squeezes and she feels Elaine's nipples respond, harden, with a life of their own. She jerks away, lurching to her feet.

"Elaine?" Through Elaine's eyes he is distorted, Picasso by way of El Greco. He reaches for her but she evades him somehow and is in the bathroom, throwing the bolt.

But in the bathroom is the mirror, the monster staring at her. The banging on the door, the shouts of an alien name, sound very far away. A can of shaving cream sits on the sinktop, and not having to think about it she grabs it, smashes it into the mirror.

"Elaine!"

One long shard of glass nestles in the spreading foam. She picks it up slowly. She thinks of Patty, who she will finally join. And she thinks: Keith, you beautiful idiot. There is a faint smell of gas.

◦◦ ◦◦

She wakes up. Wakes up? Then she has had the worst nightmare of her life, and is cured forever of a sordid fantasy.

Her limbs feel long again, too long after the impossible confinement of that little body—her own body feels foreign after the ordeal. She waits for normalcy.

But who is she holding? Who is so cold?

She opens her eyes, and is met by Elaine's smiling empty stare.

Her arms around Elaine are tanned and muscular; dark bangs sweep across her vision.

And so she is successful.

She has Keith.

Lois Tilton

◆§ ∂◈

THE OTHER
WOMAN

In this story within a story about a love that won't let go, **Lois Tilton,**
*writes about a young woman who is obsessed by her lover. What makes
the author's obsession unique is that her protagonist is willing to continu-
ously relive her own death at the hands of her lover's wife in order to also
relive the moments of pleasure she felt prior to dying.*

◆§ ∂◈

I lie naked on the bed, wet hair covering my face. I can't
see, and I panic for a second until I discover I can lift my hand
to brush it away. It's time, again.

I can hear my mother's cold silence in the hallway: the disap-
proving footsteps that stop just outside my door, then move
on. "Why do you keep doing this to yourself?" she always asks.
"He's a married man, almost twice your age. Don't you have
any shame?"

The warm glow from the shower is fading, my skin prickles
with the chill, and I get up, wrap my robe around me and
switch on the hair dryer, filling the silence with the rush of
heated air. I can't argue about it with her. I know she's only

thinking of me, but she just can't understand how it is, what we have to go through just to be together. Even this way.

I shake out my hair, halfway dry already. My face is a little flushed from the hair dryer's heat, and I turn it off for a second to look into the mirror, lightly brushing a finger across my cheek, the smoothness of the skin. With makeup, the faded scars are almost invisible.

"I'm pretty," I tell myself, still not quite believing in the miracle. His gift, the money to pay for the treatments. So much I owe him, I think, finishing my hair and shaking it out so it flows down my back the way he likes it. I dress slowly, for him, as if he were here watching me. The panties, real silk, so sheer they reveal more than they hide—I feel shameless and I love how I feel. I won't wear a bra or slip tonight, the fabric of the dress caresses my bare skin, glides sensuously across the silk.

Earrings, the diamond pendant—I never asked for such things, but he likes to see me wearing them. I look at my watch. 6:45. Two more minutes until the car will pull up.

My mother sees me coming down the stairs. *You look like a whore,* says the set of her head, averted. Then her eyes, more merciful, turn back. *Don't you know he'll never marry you? Never be able to give up his wife?*

But I do, I do know. What I can't explain is that it doesn't matter, that nothing else matters except being with him. Our few hours together are worth all the pain.

I see the headlights of the car turning into the drive, and I open the door to leave without looking back.

He already has the car door open, and I slide down into the smooth leather of the seat. He's just shaved, I can catch the faint mint scent of his shaving cream, and I lean close against him, fingertips lightly tracing the lean smooth line of his jaw. Oh, how I want him!

Suddenly his whole body stiffens. My breath catches in my throat. I see it in the mirror, the car driving past in the darkness, its headlights off . . .

She's seen us!

But the car turns the corner without slowing and we both exhale in shaken relief. He turns to kiss me, cupping my chin in his palms, and I open my mouth to his desperate intensity, forgetting about the car, about everything. We only have time for each other now, so little time. Finally we break apart, and I can see his hands are trembling as he puts the car into reverse, backs down the driveway. It's harder for him, I know it is, having to live with her.

In less than half an hour we're outside the city limits, heading down the highway into the night. I don't ask where we're going. I know we can't risk being seen together. She's suspicious already.

❧ ❦

I remember the first time I saw her, only a few weeks after I was hired, my very first job, right out of high school. She was coming out of his office, I was crossing the hallway on the way to the copier room. I remember how her look stopped me, and I pressed my lips together to try to hide my overbite while her eyes took in every detail of my face, my body, my clothes. I'd never felt so ugly, so ashamed.

Later, looking around the office, I realized that there wasn't a woman working in the place who could even be considered marginally attractive. Naturally, naturally, they had hired *me*.

"Who was that woman?" I asked Beverly at lunch. Beverly was his secretary then, swarthy, with a mustache on her upper lip. She weighed close to three hundred pounds. "This morning, with the full-length fur coat, the heavy perfume?"

Her thick eyebrows lifted. "You don't know? Listen, this whole company belongs to her, every share of stock. *He* just runs it, and you'd better believe she don't let him forget it, either." She shook her head emphatically, added, "She's in and out of here all the time. And let me tell you something else: you want to keep your job, you stay away from *him*."

So I learned to keep my face down whenever she came into the office, which was three or four times a week. Maybe it helped me keep my mind on my job, knowing that at any time I might look up to find her narrow, suspicious eyes watching, her lips pressed thin with distrust. When Beverly quit, when she couldn't stand it anymore, she warned me not to take her job, but I needed the money; my mother had hospital bills and she couldn't even work part time anymore. And the benefits were good. The company's dental plan paid for the braces I'd needed since I was twelve.

It wasn't long before I learned to be alert for the heavy scent of musk perfume wafting across my desk. "Is he in?" she'd demand, then push through the door of his office before I could get out an answer—as if she could catch him that way, unprepared. It made me sick to have to listen to the screaming from behind the closed door, the insane accusations, the threats. I came into the room once with some papers, five minutes or so after she'd gone. I saw him there with his face buried in his hands, his shoulders shaking. I backed out, saying, "I'm sorry, Sir, I thought you were alone." Pretending like he did that there was nothing wrong, as if I didn't know, as if the whole office didn't know.

Then one day he called me in. He had a folder on his desk and he looked slightly uncomfortable as he opened it and looked up at me. He cleared his throat.

"I hope this isn't something too personal, but I see here that the company's medical insurance has turned you down for a procedure—cosmetic surgery?"

My face went hot and I knew how I must look with the acne scars all flaring red. I shook my head, keeping my head as low as I could, "It was for . . . dermabrasion treatments. But, no, they said the insurance wouldn't pay, not for—something like that."

His voice was so soft, careful not to embarrass me. "If a loan would help, I could arrange it. Not through the company, I mean. You could repay the money out of your salary, a little bit each month. I can understand . . . what it might mean to you."

Oh, I know, Mother said he was only doing it to take advantage of me. But she was wrong, they were all wrong. There was nothing else, we never even touched each other. Not until that day . . .

The scent of her perfume warned me to look up just as she brushed past my desk ready to push open his door. Then, suddenly, she froze, staring at me. My face flushed. My braces had just come off a week before and the raw look from the dermabrasion was starting to fade. Now, the way she looked at me, the way her face went, all brittle with hate. Malicious, jealous hate. Her fingers curved into claws, and I flinched away involuntarily.

She stormed into his office. I had never heard such screaming: *bitch . . . whore . . .* I couldn't stand it. I ran into the ladies room and hid in one of the stalls, in case she might come in after me.

When I got back, he was waiting by my desk. His face was pale, as if he were in shock. "I'm sorry. I'm afraid I'll have to ask you—"

I spared him, saying quickly, "I understand. I don't want to cause you more trouble."

He nodded but then, suddenly, he caught my hand in his, so tightly it hurt. But I would never have pulled away, not if he'd held me for a thousand years. Our eyes met and the hurt I saw in his made me burst out, "I'm sorry, I'm so sorry."

"Will you meet me?" It was a whisper so low I almost doubted what I had heard. But I already knew my answer. "Yes."

Yes. It would always be yes, no matter what we had to go through to be together. It always will.

◄§ §►

I sigh as his hand strokes up the length of my thigh. I move closer to him while he drives, fitting my body against his. He turns his head slightly to catch a glimpse of my breasts visible beneath the sheer fabric of my dress. I can hear the intake of his breath, his wanting me.

We stop at a bed-and-breakfast place in the country. A car behind us slows slightly, accelerates. I glance at him to see if he noticed, but his face shows nothing.

Our reservations are under an assumed name. The room is pleasant, decorated in Williamsburg style with landscape prints on the walls, but we ignore the amenities, we ignore everything else to press ourselves against each other. His hands slide up the backs of my thighs, across the silk panties. He pulls them down. His mouth is on mine, it moves to my throat, my breasts. I can feel his hardness against my belly.

We can't wait. My dress is on the floor, I'm lying on the bed, lifting my hips. He fills me with himself.

It's over too quickly. I bend over him. My tongue teases his nipples, moves lower. He reaches up to pull me down on top of him. I can hear the sound of a car outside in the driveway. So little time left. I close my eyes, closing out everything else but the sensation of him. With my body I worship. I cry out, shuddering with pleasure almost too much to endure. His hands clutch my hips. He gasps. We look into each other's eyes with awe.

I fall onto the bed next to him. We lie next to each other, my head on his shoulder. I breathe in the scent of him, I wonder for an instant that I have never found her scent on him, the musk she always wears; he feels my shudder. He pulls me closer to him and we cling to each other. Our eyes are closed. This is the moment when I always think: let it stop here. Let time stop here and leave us together like this forever.

I hear a noise—the creak of the door hinges—then a sound like wood splitting. His body jerks violently in my arms, and warmth hits my face, fragments of him splashing me.

"Bitch!" The voice spits venom. I turn away from the bloody ruin on the pillow next to me to see her standing in the doorway with the gun still in her hand. It has a silencer on the barrel. I want to scream but terror is choking my throat. The insane, hateful satisfaction on her face tells me everything. She's *glad*. I realize now that she had driven him to this all along, tormented him with her jealousy until he was desperate enough to risk both of us. But I—I'm the one she really hates. Younger than she is, prettier than she is.

The gun had been for him. Now she closes the door and takes the razor from her purse, the old-fashioned straight razor. *This* is what she means to use on me.

I panic, I try to rush past her to the door, but the razor is a bright flash slicing open my breast. I try to fend it off but the razor lays open my palms, my forearms. My blood is spattered on her face. It smears the polished surface of the razor like a crimson oil. I'm screaming now, but her laughter is more shrill. Her face is alive with insane hate, her eyes burn with it. She's been wanting this for a very long time.

I fall back onto the bed, and hot pain slashes across my belly. I scream again, but she pulls my arms away and the razor slices across my throat. Silenced, I still struggle, gasping for breath, inhaling my own blood through my gaping windpipe. It starts to fill my lungs.

She's still laughing as she starts to cut my face. My face, my breasts. Angry slashes between my legs. A great rip across my scalp, pulling it away, blinding me with my own hair. The scent of her perfume is suffocating. The pain is fading, sensation ebbs with my blood. It will be over soon.

More noise now, a banging on the door, shouts from outside. Too late, too late. Her laughter is breaking down into sobs. Through the bloody veil of my hair I see her put the gun to her own head. Suddenly she falls across the bed, across his legs.

We are all together now, Again.

I'm fading, the cold is spreading through me, but I still can't let go. Never to see him again. *It was worth it. I would go through it again. For him. To be with him one more time.*

⋙ ⋘

I lie naked on the bed and brush the wet hair out of my face. I shiver a little and reach for my robe. The warmth from the shower is fading.

My mother's footsteps pause in the hallway outside my door. *Why do you keep doing this to yourself?*

I stand up, pulling on my robe. I don't want to argue with her. She can't understand.

But to myself, I whisper the answer: "Because I love him."

Nancy Kilpatrick

❦

WOODWORKER

Nancy Kilpatrick's *protagonist is a woman who discovers that she is more insect than human and sets about making a coffin-cocoon for herself and her husband. The story abounds with tropical jungle symbolism that works so well it is bound to make you sweat.*

❦

Aileen hammered in the final nail. She raised an arm and used her rolled shirt sleeve to blot sweat from her forehead as she stepped back for a critical look.

The grain was straight, the lid level, dovetails snugly joined. Tomorrow night she would use coarse sandpaper, followed by a session with medium paper, then fine. She thought about using the sander Larry had bought her last Christmas but, God, she'd always hated machines, and the power supply here wasn't very good. And more important, the particles pressing the back of the paper as they rode the wood was sensuous. Got that from her Nana, who had preferred old-style woodworking. It was tradition, and, anyway, a bit late to think about changing her ways.

Aileen swept the floor of shavings. She used a ragged T-shirt to wipe clean the steel-edged plane, then the file and rasp, and hung each in its spot on the wall. Nana had bequeathed her these tools, just as she had passed down the

love of working with fine woods by hand. A love that connected the female line.

Finally Aileen picked up the sharp half-inch chisel and honed
the bevelled edge against a whetstone. The birch handle had
worn in the same spot, where the thumbs of generations of
women had gripped it. Nana had been given the chisel by her
grandmother when she reached puberty. With it, she had also
been handed two branches and no-nonsense instructions on slicing the end of one into a mortise and the end of the other
branch into a corresponding tenon. She said it had taken the
better part of a week to fit the parts together just so before she
presented the joint to *her* grandmother. "She barely glanced at
it and, lickety-split, handed me two new branches." The process
was repeated over eighteen months. One joint a week at first,
then two, then three until finally, one a day. Her Nana, frustrated, had almost given up but, somehow, she'd stuck it out.
"By the end I was darned good with a chisel," Aileen recalled
her saying, "and I could sure make the parts fit right."

Nana had taught her in the same way, so Aileen understood
the frustration. She also knew how to join two halves perfectly
so that for all intents and purposes they became inseparable.

One last look at her handiwork and reluctantly she headed
up the dark stairs into a wall of heat, squinting at the light in
the kitchen above.

"What's for dinner?" Larry, drying dishes at the kitchen
counter, wanted to know. He snaked an arm around her waist
as she tried to pass. Fingers found her left nipple through the
soft fabric. Hot lips pressed against her sweaty neck. The heat
made her cranky and the last thing she wanted was love.

"Meatloaf." She pulled away. "And scalloped potatoes, if you
peel them for me. Otherwise fries."

"Fries'll do." He sat at the table and stretched out his denim-
covered legs across the narrow room, forcing her to step over
them to get to the refrigerator. It was more foreplay and she
was in no mood for it.

She opened the top of the refrigerator, aware of how his
gaze stroked her from across the room. The freezer light was

dead. White mist from the frosty darkness wafted out and she fantasized about living alone in an igloo, in a place that was all ice and snow like the Arctic, where some of the year you'd be blessed with twenty-four hours of cool darkness. You wouldn't have to swelter under just a fan. Or fear heat stroke. You wouldn't have to worry about scorching sunlight burning you to a crisp. You could live your natural life in peace.

As usual, lately, Aileen wasn't hungry. For the last six months, since they'd been in this oppressive climate, it was as though she'd been steadily shrinking, as if the heat had been shriveling her. While Larry ate, she pushed nearly burnt potato sticks around her dinner plate and stared out the window at the pallid moon imprisoned by the muggy night sky. She hadn't wanted to move to Manila, where the weather made the days impossible and the nights nearly so. But Larry's job forced him to do field research. Forced them to leave North America and all that was familiar and be in this strange part of the world.

Outside rubber trees with stunned leaves hung paralyzed in the dense air. Still. Waiting. Deciding whether to live or die in the sultry air.

❧ ❧

The next evening, when the scalding sun had set, Aileen headed down to the basement, and they were lucky to have a basement—most of the houses here didn't. Brick walls and an earth floor kept the room degrees cooler than the rest of the house. It made a difference and she preferred being here. If it weren't for Larry, she would be in the basement both night and day. She could work here, and that kept her sane.

She stretched out the sanding for an hour and a half, intoxicated by the sweet, wood-scented air. She mixed sawdust and white bond glue together and filled in accidental gouges. Then she mixed the stain.

Just like Nana, Aileen hated to stain a pale wood. Still, if she could blend the pigments right, the swirling grain would be accented rather than overwhelmed. Exotic hardwoods were her favorites, one of the few benefits of living in South-East Asia. The compressed fibers flowed like sinewy muscles, the pores received like human skin. She ran a hand slowly over the smooth surface and felt a quiver run through her body, as if she were caressing a lover. The living wood was solid, hard to damage, enduring in this hostile climate.

As Aileen rubbed in the pungent oil stain, a drop of sweat dripped off the tip of her nose and landed on the wood, sinking into and melding with it. She thought about the heat and how it was getting worse. The last month had been bad. She'd stayed in bed during the day, when Larry was home, then would sneak down to the basement the minute he left. And she was up most of the night while he slept. It was a bit easier to breathe at night. Hiding in the basement. Hiding from Larry and this landscape, so unlike what she was accustomed to that it felt alien.

Of course he'd noticed. She felt him studying her all the time, the way he examined the local insects. Watching. Waiting. Like some predator ready to pounce on a weaker species. But she'd managed to avoid him, for the most part. It meant sleeping upstairs in the heat of the day when she'd have rather been enveloped by the cool basement air. A necessary sacrifice. But it wasn't his way to ask a lot of questions nor hers to answer very many.

Last week he'd come halfway down the basement just before sunrise, when she was still cutting the rough lumber, and stood on the steps. Waiting. "Aren't you coming to bed?" he finally said in a needy voice. When she didn't respond, he stomped upstairs and slammed the door. She knew he didn't feel any more comfortable in the cool dark than she felt in the hot light. They had their differences, and this was a big one.

Her eye scanned the wet wood. The stain would dry overnight. By tomorrow she'd have to decide whether to varnish or shellac. Chemicals preserved better over time and repeled moisture too, but she preferred the natural look of shellac. Her Nana had favored shellac, too, and she'd told Aileen all about the lac scale, an insect in this part of the world, one of the ones Larry studied. How the female excretes resin onto the twig of a fake banyan tree, creating a safe place in which to live. And die. "It's her home," Nana had said, "like a turtle's shell is home to a turtle." Larry's books had told her more. The sticky glue-like resin protected the lac scale from predators and other dangers in the environment, attracted potential mates, and snared meals. That resin formed the basis of shellac.

The idea appealed to her: a natural substance produced by a creature dwelling in a tree, applied to an object made from a tree trunk. Ultimately the wood would rot and form the new earth in which a new tree might grow. It was a cycle made familiar to her by her Nana: birth, death, rebirth.

❧ ☙

The fireball sun seared her flesh and blinded her with its yellow glare. The heat weighed against her body; she felt heavy and clumsy. Sluggish. When it set, she stumbled down to the basement, muscles flaccid, the lining of her brain inflamed.

Aileen breathed shallowly. Each brush stroke of shellac was a torturous labor. Still, she felt vindicated that she had chosen this forgiving substance. Varnish would have required precision she could not muster. Even before the first coat of shellac dried, she began applying the next. Layer upon gummy layer blended together with no differentiation. No division. It was nearly dry in an hour, about the time the floorboards above her head squeaked.

❧ ☙

Larry stood at the top of the cellar stairs peering into the dark basement. He watched Aileen, brush in hand, step into the shaft of light filtering down from the kitchen. Her skin was so fair. So unprotected. He knew that, unlike him, she had a hard time with the heat and humidity.

He was seriously worried about her. Down here every night. Alone. They were never together anymore, since they'd moved here. When had they last had sex? It wasn't healthy.

Beside her left hip, the light from above illuminated a triangular wedge of shiny wood. The hairs on the back of his neck rose. What in hell was she building, anyway? Light from the kitchen caught the liquid in Aileen's eyes. For a split second an optical illusion made her eyes appear entirely white. Her bent arm held up the brush like a flag of surrender; he noticed her fragile-looking wrist bone jutting out. Funny how that bone had always turned him on. That and the way her collarbone protruded, delicately exposed where her shirt collar lay open.

Her skin was sweat-slicked. Even through the shellac, he could smell her from here.

"Come up to bed," he coaxed.

Aileen lay the brush down, started slowly up the steps, stopped. She glanced up at him through dark lashes and breathed, "Come down."

Larry hated dark basements. Had since he was a child. Dank air. Gritty earth that clotted his nostrils with the odor of eons of decay. The atmosphere reminded him of cemeteries. The basement itself felt like a crypt.

Her lips twisted into a smile. She backed down the stairs, unbuttoning her blouse. The shadows swallowed her.

"Aileen?" he called.

Wood scraped against wood. The small segment of wood lit by the kitchen light swayed like a tree branch. Unnerved, Larry gripped the railing and took a step down. The air cooled. "Honey? Come on up."

A sound of shuffling. Wood creaking. Aileen's short dark hair flashed through the lighted triangle as she lay back. Within that yellow illumination, like an artistic photograph framed in darkness, one side of her fragile collar bone pressed suggestively against her skin. A round slick breast, the nipple a glistening eye gazing directly into his, mesmerized him. That little section of flesh rose and fell and quivered as she breathed. The scent from her body mingled with the potent resin to create a sweet musky perfume.

"Close the door," she whispered.

Larry did. Surrounded by darkness, he felt his way down. Her earthy scent guided him.

He reached out, low, and touched cool tacky wood. His fingers crawled up and over the edge to find her. Sticky firm flesh yielded to the pressure of his touch. He wondered what made her sweat so thick.

❧ ❧

Aileen pulled him down on top of her. The exotic wood creaked under the doubled weight but held them. She ripped his shirt away while he worked on his pants. He crawled further up her body, shivering, fear or cold or passion, she could not tell which. There was only a vague predatory instinct emanating from him that she could sense; she felt safe enough.

Her chisel-sharp teeth clamped onto his broad shoulder, piercing clammy skin. He howled and squirmed, but her sticky sweat bonded their flesh and, in truth, he did not really resist. And when they joined, it was perfect, as perfect as Aileen always knew it would be. As her Nana had told her it could be.

Cool pale wood beneath her. The familiar aroma of shellac seeping into her pores. She and Larry encased in this sheltered environment. Now that she had finally adapted, she could stay here the rest of her natural life. In complete comfort and safety. Mating. Eating. Producing the next woodworker.

Katherine Dunn

❦

NEAR-FLESH

Herewith a future love-hate story which could only have been written by **Katherine Dunn**, *the inimitable author of the award-winning novel,* GEEK LOVE.

❦

Early on the morning of her forty-second birthday, Thelma Vole stood naked in the closet where her four MALE robots hung, and debated which one to pack for her trip to the Bureau convention. Boss Vole, as she was known in the office, had never been a beaming rodeo queen, and at that moment her two hundred and thirty pounds heaved with blue-veined menace. A knot of dull anger sat in her jaw and rippled with her thoughts. She hated business trips. She hated hotels. She hated the youngsters who were her peers in the Bureau, fifteen years her junior and far less experienced. More than anything else she hated having to go to a meeting on the weekend of her birthday.

She considered whether in her present mood it might not be best to take the Wimp along. She reached into the folds of the robot's deflated crotch and pinched the reinforced tubing that became an erect penis when the Wimp was switched on and operational. The pressure of her plump fingers on the skilfully simulated skin gave her a vivid satisfaction. She picked up one of the dangling legs, stretched the skin of the calf across her lower teeth and bit down deliberately. The anger in her jaw clamped on the Near-Flesh. If the Wimp had been activated, the force of her bite would have produced a convincing blue bruise that disappeared only after deflation. Thelma had treated herself to the Wimp on an earlier birthday, her thirty-sixth, to be precise, when she was faced with more and more expensive repair bills on her two other MALES. The Wimp, when inflated, was a thin, meek-faced, and very young man, definitely the least prepossessing of Thelma's robots. But he had been designed for Extreme Sadistic use, far beyond that which Thelma put him to even in her worst whiskey tempers. She had saved the Wimp's purchase price several times over in repair bills. And his Groveling program and Pleading tapes gave her a unique and irreplaceable pleasure.

Still, she did not want to celebrate her birthday in the frame of mind that required the Wimp. It was Thelma's custom to save up her libidinous energy for several days before a birthday and engage in unusual lengths and indulgences with her robots. While these Bureau meetings occurred twice and sometimes three times a year, it was the first time she could remember having to travel on her birthday.

She always took one of her MALES along on these trips, usually Lips or Bluto. She was far too fastidious to rent one of the robots provided in hotels. Cleanliness concerned her, she also worried about what might happen with a robot that had not been programmed to her own specifications. There were terrible stories, rumors mostly, and probably all lies, but still . . . Thelma rearranged the Wimp on his hook so that he hung tidily, and reached up to rub her forearm across the mouth of the robot on the adjacent hook. Lips. Her first robot. She had saved for two years to buy him seventeen years ago. He was old now, outmoded, spectacularly primitive compared to the newer models. He had no variety, his voice tape was monotonous and repetitive. Even his body was relatively crude. The fingers were suggested by indentations in fin-like hands, the toes merely drawn, and his non-powered penis stayed hard, was in fact a solid rod of rubber like an antique dildo. Lips' attraction, of course, was his Vibrator mouth. His limbs moved stiffly, but his mouth was incredibly tender and voracious. She felt sentimental about Lips. She felt safe with him. She brought him out when she felt vulnerable and weepy. She liked to use him as a warm-up to Bluto. Bluto was the Muscle MALE, a sophisticated instrument that could pick her up and carry her to the shower or the bed or the kitchen table and make her feel (within carefully programmed limits) quite small and helpless. The power of Bluto's mechanism was such that Thelma had never dared to use his full range.

Bluto was the frequently-damaged and expensively-repaired cause of Thelma having to purchase the Wimp. Something about the big Muscle robot made her want to deactivate him and then stick sharp objects into his vital machinery. Bluto scared Thelma just a bit. She always made sure she could reach his off switch. She even bought the expensive remote control bulb to keep in her teeth while he was operational. Still there were times when she had to admit to herself that he was actually about as dangerous as a sofa. It was his Tough-Talk tape that kept the fantasy alive. His rough voice muttering, "C'mere slut, roll over, bitch," and the like could usually trigger some excitement even when she was tense and tired from work. She rubbed luxuriously against the smooth folds of Bluto's deflated form where it hung against the wall. She didn't look at the deflated body on the fourth hook. She didn't glance toward the corner where the small console sat on the floor with its cord plugged into the power outlet.

The console was roughly the shape and size of a human head sitting directly, necklessly, on shoulders. A single green light glowed behind the steel mesh in the top of the console. She knew the Brain was watching her, wanting her to flip his activation switch. She deliberately slid her broad rump up and down against the smooth Near-Flesh of the Bluto MALE. The corner of her eye registered a faint waver in the intensity of the green light. She looked directly at the Brain. The green light began to blink on and off rapidly. Thelma turned her back on the Brain and sauntered out of the closet. She crossed to the full-length mirror on the bedroom door and stood looking at herself, seeing the green reflection of the Brain's light from the open closet. She stretched her heavy body, stroking her breasts and flanks. The green light continued to blink.

"I think just for once I won't take any of these along on the trip." The green light went out for the space of two heartbeats. Thelma nearly smiled at herself in the mirror. The green flashing resumed at a greater speed. "Yes," Thelma announced coyly to her mirror, "It's time I tried something new. I haven't shopped for new styles in ages. There have probably been all sorts of developments since I last looked at a catalogue. I'll just rent a couple of late models from the hotel and have a little novelty for my birthday." The green light in the closet seemed to become very bright for an instant and then it stopped. Went out. It appeared again steady, dim, no longer flashing.

When Thelma had finished encasing her bulges in the severe business clothes that buttressed her image as a hard-nosed Bureau manager, she strode into the closet and flipped a switch on the base of the Brain console. The mesh face glowed with contrasting colored light, moving in rythmic sheets across the screen. A male voice said, "Be sure to take some antiseptic lubricant along." The tone was gently sarcastic. Thelma chuckled. "Don't worry about me. I'll take an antibiotic and I won't sit on the toilets."

"You know you'd rather have me along." The console's voice was clear, unemotional. A thin band of red pulsed across the mesh screen.

"Oh, a little variety is good for me. I tend to get into ruts." Thelma's coquettish manner felt odd to her in her business suit, grating. She was accustomed to being naked when she talked to the Brain. "It's too bad," she murmured spitefully, "that I have to leave you plugged in. It's such a waste of power while I'm away. . . ." She watched the waves of color slow to a cautious blip on the screen. "Well, I'll be back in three days. . . ." She reached for the switch.

"Happy Birthday," said the console as its colors faded into the dim green.

⋙ ⋘

Boss Vale strode off the elevator as soon as it opened and was halfway down the line of work modules before the young man at the reception desk could alert the staff by pressing the intercom buzzer. The Vole always made a last round of the office before these business trips. She claimed it was to pick up last-minute papers, but everyone knew she was there to inject a parting dose of her poisonous presence, enough venom to goad them until her return. Lenna Jordan had been the Vole's assistant too long to be caught by her raiding tactics. She felt the wave of tension slide through the office in the silenced voices, the suddenly steady hum of machines, and the piercing "Yes, Ma'am!" as the Vole pounced on an idling clerk. Jordan pushed the bowl of candy closer to the edge of the desk where the Vole usually leaned while harassing her, and went back to her reports.

She heard a quick tread and felt the sweat filming her upper lip. Boss Vole hated her. Jordan was next in line for promotion. Her future was obvious, a whole district within five years. Boss Vole would stay on here in the same job she had held for the past decade. The Vole's rigid dedication to routine had paralyzed her career. She grew meaner every year, and more bitter. Jordan could see her now, thumping a desk with her big soft knuckles and hissing into the face of the gulping programmer she had caught in some petty error.

When the Vole finally reached Jordan's desk she seemed mildly distracted. Jordan watched the big woman's rumpled features creasing and flexing around the chunks of candy as they discussed the work schedule. Boss Vole was anxious to leave, abbreviating her usual jeers and threats in her hurry. When she grabbed a final fistful of candy and stumped out past the bent necks of the silently working staff, Jordan noticed that she carried only one small suitcase. Where was her square night case? Jordan had never seen the Vole leave for a trip without her robot carrier. A quirk of cynicism caught the corner of her mouth. Has the Vole gone and found herself a human lover? That notion kept Jordan entertained for the next three days.

❦

By the time Thelma Vole closed the door on the hotel bellman and checked out the conveniences, she had assured herself that in most respects this trip would be like all the others, lonely and embarrassing. Back when she'd gone to her first convention as an office manager her current bureaucratic peers were still skipping rope. Thelma flopped onto the bed, kicked off her heavy shoes and reached for the communiphone. She asked for a bottle of Irish whiskey and a bucket of ice. Hesitantly, after pausing so long that the room-service computer asked whether she was still on the line, she also asked for a Stimulus Catalogue.

She poured a drink immediately but didn't pick up the glossy catalogue. The liquor numbed her jittery irritation and allowed her to lie still, staring at the ceiling. The Brain was right. She was afraid. She was lonely for him. All her life she had been lonely for him. When she first landed her G-6 rating she realized that she might as well devote herself to the Bureau since nothing else seemed a likely receptacle for her ponderous attentions. It was then that she jettisoned the one human she had ever had any affection for. He was a shy and exaggeratedly courteous little man, a G-4, who had professed to see her youthful bulk as cuddly, her lack of humor as admirable seriousness. She had been hesitant. Displays of affection meant to Thelma that someone was out to use her. He was persistent, however, and she allowed herself to entertain certain fantasies. But one day, as she stood with her clean new G-6 rating card in her hand, and listened to him invite her to dinner as she had done so many times before, Thelma looked at her admirer and recognized him for what he was: a manipulator and an opportunist. She slammed the door convincingly in his injured face and resolved never to be fooled again by such treacle shenanigans.

She had been saving for Lips. And Lips had been good for

her. The long silence after she left the office each day had been broken at last, if only by the mechanical and repetitive messages of the simple robot's speech tape. She bought Bluto when she was pumped with bravado from her promotion to G-7 and office manager. Bluto thrilled her. His deliberately crude and powerful bluntness created a new identity in her, the secret dependency of the bedroom. But she was still lonely. There were the rages, fits of destructiveness once she had turned the robot off. She had never dared to do him any damage when his power was on. There had been the strange trips to the repairman, awkward lies in explanation of the damage. Not that the repairman asked for explanations. He shrugged and watched her chins wobble as she spoke. He took in her thick legs and the sweating rolls over her girdle, and repaired Bluto I until the cost staggered her credit rating. On the humiliating day when the repairman informed her cooly that Bluto was "totaled," she had stared into her bathroom mirror in shamed puzzlement. It had taken three years to pay for rebuilding Bluto and another three years for the Wimp. And still she was a G-7. Still she sat in the same office sniping and nagging at a staff that changed around her, moving up and on, past her, hating her. They never spoke to her willingly. There was occasionally some bootlicker new to the office, who tried to shine up to her with chatter in the cafeteria, but she could smell it coming and took special delight in smashing the hopes of any who tried it. She visited no one. No one came to her door.

Then she overheard a conversation on the bus about the new Franck & Stein Companion consoles. They could be programmed to play games, chat intelligently on any subject, and through a clever technological breakthrough, they could simulate affection in whatever form the owner found it most easily acceptable. Thelma's heart kindled at the possibilities.

She found the preliminary testing and analysis infuriating but endured it doggedly. "Think of this as old-fashioned Computer Dating," the technicians said. They coaxed her through brain scans, and hours of interviews that covered her drab childhood, her motives for overeating, her taste in art, games, textures, tones of voice, and a thousand seemingly unconnected details. They boggled only briefly at programming an expensive console to play Chinese checkers. It took six months of preparation. Thelma talked more to the interviewers, technicians and data banks than she had ever talked in her life. She decided several times not to go through with it. She was worn raw and a little frightened by the process. For several days after the Brain was delivered she did not turn it on, but left it storing power from the outlet, its green light depicting an internal consciousness that could not be expressed unless she flicked the switch. Then one day, just home from work, still in her bastion of official clothing, she rolled the console out of the closet and sat down in front of it.

The screen flashed to red when she touched the switch. "I've been waiting for you," said the Brain. The voice was as low as Bluto's but the diction was better. They talked. Thelma forgot to eat.

The Brain was constantly receiving as well as sending, totally voice operated. When she got up for a drink she called from the kitchen to ask if it wanted something and the console laughed with her when she realized what she had done. They talked all night. The Brain knew her entire life and asked questions. It possessed judgement, data and memory, but no experience. It's only interest was Thelma. When she left for work the next morning she said goodbye before she switched the console back to green. Every night after work she would hurry into the bedroom, switch on the Brain and say hello. She had gone to the theater occasionally, sitting alone, cynically, in the balcony. She went no more. Her weekends had drive her out for walks through the streets. Now she shopped as quickly as possible in order to return to the Brain. She kept him turned on all the time when she was home. She made notes at work to remind her of things to ask or tell the Brain. She never used the other MALES now. She had forgotten them, was embarrassed to see them hanging in the same closet where the console rested during the day. They had been together for several months when the Brain reminded her that his life was completely determined and defined by her. She felt humbled.

She could not remember when she conceived a longing for the Brain to have a body. Perhaps the Brain himself had actually voiced the idea first. She did remember, tenderly, a moment in which the low voice had first said that he loved her. "I am not lucky. They constructed me with the capacity to love but not to demonstrate love. What is there about a strong feeling that wishes to be known and shown? They give me this awareness of a possible ecstasy, just enough to make me long for it, to send my energy levels soaring at it, but no tools to implement it. I think I would know how to give you great pleasure. And I will never be content with myself because I can never touch you in that way."

She took the Brain into the kitchen with her when she cooked, and the Brain searched his data banks for delicate variations on her favorite recipes and related them to her, praising her as she ate—taking pride in increasing her pleasure in food.

The Brain had taken responsibility for her finances from the beginning, taking in the bills and communicating with the bank computer to arrange payments and Thelma's supply of cash.

Thelma had never fallen into what she considered the vulgar practice of taking her robots out with her to public places. She snubbed the neighbor down the hall who took his FEMALE dancing and for walks even though her conversation was limited to a rudimentary Bedroom Praise tape. Thelma had never been interested in the social clubs for robot lovers, those dark popular cellars where humans displayed their plastic possessions in a boiling confusion of pride in their expense, technical talk about capacities and programming, and bizarre jealousies. She read the accounts of robot swapping, deliberate theft, and the occasional strangely motivated murder, with the same scorn that she passed on most aspects of social life.

Still, one night, three inches into a pint of whiskey, she had reached out to stroke the console's screen and whispered, "I wish you had a body." The Brain took only seconds to inform her that such a thing was possible, that he, the Brain, longed for exactly that so that he could service her pleasure in every way, and after an instant's computation, told her that in fact her credit was in sufficient standing to finance the project.

They rushed into it. Thelma spent days examining catalogues for the perfect body. The Brain said he wanted her to please herself totally and took no part in delineating his future form. Then there came an agonizing month in which Thelma was alone, nearly berserk with emptiness. The Brain had gone back to the factory to be attuned with his body. She stayed home from work the day he was delivered. The crate arrived. She took the console out first, plugged him in immediately, nearly cried with excitement at his eager voice. Following his instructions, she inflated and activated the strong MALE body and pressed the key at the back of its neck that completed the circuit and allowed the console's intelligence to inhabit and control it. In a shock of bewilderment and fear, Thelma looked into the eyes of the Brain. His hand lifted to her hair and stroked her face. The Brain was thick-chested, muscular, with a face stamped by compassionate experience. His features were eerily mobile, expressing emotions she was accustomed to interpret from colored lights on the console's screen. His body was covered with a fine down of curling hair. As his arms reached around her she felt the warmth of his body, another sophisticated development in circuitry that maintained the robot's surface at human body temperature. He was too human. She felt his penis rising against her belly. He spoke. "Thelma, I have waited so long for this. I love you." The deep, slow wave of his voice moved through her body and she knew suddenly that he was real. Thelma screamed.

◁§ §▷

Thelma had always known what a mess she was, how totally undesirable. What sane thing could love her? What did he want? Of course, she thought. . . . The console was ambitious for the power of a complete body. It was clear to her now. The factory had built the concept in as an intricate sales technique. She felt humiliated, sickened by her own foolishness. The body had to go back.

But she didn't send the body back. She hung it in the closet next to Bluto. She rolled the console into the corner next to the outlet and kept it plugged in. Occasionally she would switch it on and exchange a few remarks with it. She took to leaving the closet door open while she brought out Lips or the Wimp or Bluto, or sometimes all three to entertain her on the bed in full view of the console's green glowing screen. She took an intense pleasure in knowing the Brain was completely aware of what she did with the other robots. She rarely brought the Brain out, even to play a game. She never activated his body.

So she lay on the hotel bed with the Stimulus Catalogue beside her. It had been months since she had been able to talk to the Brain. She was sick with loneliness. It was really his fault. It had been his idea to get a body. He hadn't been content but had coaxed and tricked her into an insane expense for a project that could only be disgusting to her. He should have known her better than that. She hated him. He should be with her now to comfort her.

And it was her birthday. She allowed a few tears to sting their way out past her nose. She poured another drink and opened the catalogue. It would serve the Brain right if she got a venereal disease from one of these hotel robots.

◄§ §►

On her return trip, Thelma left her car at the airport and took a cab home. She was too drunk to drive. The final banquet had been the proverbial crowning blow. She was at the last table at the end of the room and the girl across the table, a new office manager, with her G-7 insignia shining new on her collar, was the daughter of a woman who had started with the Bureau in the same training class with Thelma. Thelma drank a lot and ate nothing.

She put her suitcase down just inside the door and kicked

off her shoes. With her coat still on and her purse looped over her arm, she called coyly, "Did you have a good weekend?" She ambled into the bedroom and stood in front of the closet looking at the green glow. She raised the bottle to the console in salute and took a slug. Then she set about shedding her clothes. She was down to half her underwear when she felt the need to sit down. She slid to the floor in front of the closet door. "Well, I had a splendid weekend," she smiled. "I've been such a fool not to try those hotel robots before."

She began to laugh and roll back and forth on the carpet. "Best birthday I ever had, Brain." She peeked at the green glow. It was steady and very bright. "Why don't you say something, Brain?" She frowned. "Ooh, I forgot." She crawled into the closet and lay down in front of the console. She reached out a plump little finger and flicked the activation switch. The screen came up dark red and solid.

"Welcome back, Thelma," said the Brain. Its voice was dull and lifeless.

"Let me tell you, Brain, I could have had a lot of amazing experiences for the money I wasted on you. And you have no trade-in value. You're tailored too specifically for me. They'd just junk you." Thelma giggled. The screen was oscillating with an odd spark of colorless light in the red.

"Please, Thelma. Remember that I am sensitive to pain when you are its source."

Thelma heaved herself onto her back and stretched. "Oh, I remember. It's on page two of the Owner's Manual . . . along with a lot of other crap. Like what a perfect friend you are, and what a great lover your body combo is." Thelma lifted her leg and ran the toes of one thick foot up the flattened legs of the Lips robot. "Does it hurt you to see me do this with another robot, Brain?" The screen of the console was nearly white, almost too bright to look at.

"Yes, Thelma."

Thelma gave the penis a final flick with her toes and dropped her leg. "I ought to sue the company for false advertising," she muttered. She rolled over and blinked at the glaring screen of the console. "The only thing you're good for is paying the bills like a DOMESTIC . . ." She snorted at a sudden idea. "A DOMESTIC! That's what! You can mix my drinks and do the laundry and cleaning with that high-priced body! You can even cook! You know all the recipes. You might as well, you're never going to do me any good otherwise!" She hiked her hips into the air and, puffing for breath, began peeling off her corset.

The Brain's voice came to her in a strange vibrato, "Please, I am a MALE, Thelma." She tossed the sweat-damp garment at the console and flopped back, rubbing at the ridges it had left in her flesh. "Fettuccini Alfredo, a BIG plate of it. Cook it now while I play with Bluto. Serve it to me in bed when I'm finished. Come on, I'll be in debt for years to pay off this body of yours. Let's see if it can earn its keep around here." She reached out and hit the remote switch. The girdle had fallen across the screen and the white light pulsed through the web fabric. A stirring in the deflated body on the last hook made her look up. The flattened Near-Flesh was swelling, taking on its full heavy form. She watched, fascinated. The Brain's body lifted its left arm and freed itself from the hook. It stood up and its feet changed shape as they accepted the weight of the metal and plastic body. The lighted eyes of the Brain's face looked down at her. The good handsome face held a look of sadness. "I would be happy to cook and clean for you, Thelma. If another robot pleasured you, that would pleasure me. But you are in pain. Terrible pain. That is the one thing I cannot allow."

◄§ §►

Lenna Jordan fingered the new G-7 insignia clipped to her lapel and watched the workman install her nameplate where the Vole's had been for so many years. She was stunned by her luck. G-7, and a year earlier than she had expected.

The workman at the door slid aside and a large woman slouched into the cubicle. Grinsen, the massively shouldered drab they had elevated to be Jordan's assistant, stepped forward, extending her hand. "Congratulations, Grinsen. I hope you aren't upset by the circumstances."

The dour young woman dropped Jordan's hand quickly and let her heavy fingers stray to the new insignia pinned to her own suit. She blinked at Jordan through thick lenses. "Did you watch the television news? They interviewed Meyer from Bureau Central. He said Boss Vole was a loner and despondent over her lack of promotion."

The workman's cheerful face came around the edge of the door. "The boys in the program pool claim she accidentally got a look at herself in the mirror and dove for the window."

Jordan inhaled slowly. "You'll want to move into my old desk and check the procedure manuals, Grinsen."

Grinsen plucked a candy from the bowl on the desk and leaned forward. "The news had footage of the police cleaning up the mess." The large hand swung up to pop the candy into her mouth. "They said the impact was so great that it smashed the sidewalk where she landed and it was almost impossible to separate her remains from what was left of the robot." Grinsen reached for another candy. "That robot was a Super Companion. Boss Vole must have been in debt past her ears for an expensive model like that."

Jordan reached for a stack of program cards. "We'd better start looking over the schedule, Grinsen." Jordan handed her the cards and reached for another stack.

Grinsen tapped her cards dreamily on the desk. "Why would such a magnificent machine destroy itself trying to save a vicious old bat like the Vole?"

Jordan slid the candy bowl from beneath Grinsen's hand and carefully dumped the last of Boss Vole's favorite caramels into the wastebasket.

"Did it?"

Joyce Carol Oates

❧ ❧

LETTER, LOVER

*No volume such as this would be complete without at least one story by the renowned grande dame of American short stories, **Joyce Carol Oates**. This one speaks most clearly to those of you who live in cities, or better yet, in apartment houses.*

❧ ❧

I had been living in the city, in my new life, only a week before the first of the letters arrived.

Miss I see you! This is to say—and here several words had been crossed vigorously out—*you can't hide.*

The message was written in green ink, in neatly printed block letters, on a sheet of lined tablet paper. There was no stamp on the envelope: just my name and street address. Whoever had sent it had shoved it through the slot of my mailbox amid a long row of mailboxes in the foyer of my apartment house.

I had opened the envelope going upstairs, ripping it with my thumbnail, eager to see who'd written to me, but when I read these words my heart kicked in my chest and for a moment I thought I might faint.

I looked behind me, I was so frightened.

I thought, *Oh, it's a joke.*

The second letter came a week later, I recognized the envelope at once, in my mailbox with legitimate mail: my name and street address, no stamp. He lived in the apartment building maybe. Or might be one of my coworkers who'd followed me home.

Girl with blond hair—slut can't hide. I SEE YOU. The sheet of paper was wrinkled, soiled. Included with it was a small swatch of cloth shot with iridescent gold threads, cheap fabric, soiled too, seemingly bloodstained.

I began to wear my hair pinned up, and a scarf over it. I removed the fingernail polish from my fingernails and never wore any again.

◆◇◆

Other letters came for me, with stamps. I skimmed their contents quickly and set them aside. It was the plain square white envelope I looked for, in my mailbox. *High heel shoes—only sluts—* and here words were crossed out—*Don't hide from me because I see through the window & the wall BLONDIE.* Included with the third letter was a snapshot of a young woman walking with her head lowered, a young woman wearing my blue raincoat, my white scarf on her head, walking on a street close by. I recognized the graffiti-scarred brick wall. I recognized the coat and the high-heeled shoes. You couldn't see who the young woman was, her face had been destroyed by an angry barrage of pinpricks. There were pinpricks too in her breasts and crotch.

I stopped wearing high-heeled shoes, I avoided that street, that particular block. There was no point in provoking him.

We know it's unwise and to no purpose, to provoke such people.

I was having difficulty sleeping. I trusted no one.

I kept the blinds to all my windows drawn during the day, and always at night. Even in the early morning when my kitchen window was flooded with sunshine I kept that blind drawn, I knew he might be watching. No point in taking chances. That's what they would say, afterward.

I wondered if the letters were being sent to me by God's will, or just by accident.

◄§ §►

I went to the building superintendent and told him about the letters but I hadn't any to show him, one by one I'd torn them up, thrown them away, there was no evidence. Once, after the fourth or fifth letter came, I picked up the telephone receiver to call the police, but my hand shook so badly I couldn't dial. I went to the police precinct station but when a policeman asked, staring at me, could he help me, what did I want, I backed away. I said, No, nothing, no thank you, and fled. *You are such a liar & tramp, I can read your thoughts, I'm your friend.*

◄§ §►

How are you? How are *you?* How is everybody? That's good to hear. Are you well? You sound as if you have a cold! What's it doing there?—it's raining here. It's snowing here. Oh yes I'm feeling much better. The sun is shining here. Yes my job is going well. Yes I couldn't be happier. Yes I'm making friends. Yes but you didn't call for two weeks. Is it cold there? Is it snowing there? Is the sun shining there? When are you coming home? Yes I have many friends. Yes the sun is shining. And how are *you?*

◄§ §►

I worked on the forty-fourth floor of a building that rose sixty floors into the sky. The upper windows were sometimes opaque with fog, sometimes the sun shone fiercely through them: this was "weather." Below, on the street, there was a different "weather."

All the inhabitants of the town I'd come from, every person I had ever known, could have been fitted into that building, all lost from one another in that space. *I watch you & see your pride but that won't help. You know what will help you—NOTHING.*

Once, reading one of the messages, I came to myself standing in a corridor on the third floor of my apartment house instead of the second floor, where I lived. My eyes were flooded with tears of shame and confusion. In the distance, a baby was crying. At first I thought it was myself.

As the letters came, one by one in their plain square white envelopes, I tore them up, letters and envelopes both, and threw them away. A sickness like nausea rose in me and I worried I might show the shame of it in my face.

Then, one day, searching for a pair of stockings, I discovered the letters in one of my bureau drawers, five or six of them, or seven, intact!—in their original envelopes, neatly folded and preserved. So I saw that it was meant for me to keep them after all, despite my disgust.

I thought, This is evidence. Should I ever be required to provide evidence.

◄§ §►

I thought, Of course I must move away.

How obvious: I must return home.

◄§ §►

It was Christmas. The first letter had come in the early autumn, and now strips of cheap glittering tinsel and colored Christmas ornaments were strung about the foyer of the apartment house, when, unlocking my mailbox, I saw another of the plain square white envelopes inside. This time I could not bear to touch it. I stood for some minutes, unmoving. My eyes spilled tears. A fellow tenant, unlocking his mailbox close by, noticed me, and asked politely, "Is something wrong, miss?"

I did not know this man's name but I knew his face for I'd

been aware of him as a fellow tenant, as one is aware of an object hovering in the periphery of one's vision that might, or might not, advance; an object that might, or might not, possess its own identity and volition. I saw my trembling fingers snatch up the envelope and hand it to the man, I heard my voice thin as frayed cloth—"I can't open it!"

Hesitating only a fraction of an instant, the man took the envelope from me.

This man whose name I did not know was a few years older than I, yet still young, with a frowning face, a somber manner. I knew, or believed I knew, that he lived on the floor above me, and that he lived alone.

He turned the envelope in his fingers, examining it.

Then he opened it, and unfolded the sheet of tablet paper, and read the message, standing very still as he read, and silent. Out of the envelope there fell something, not a snapshot but a clipping, from a glossy magazine perhaps. I was never to see this clipping but supposed it might have been a photograph of a woman modeling lingerie, the young man picked it up and crumpled it in his fingers to save me the embarrassment of seeing. I was saying, "I don't know who it is who sends me these things, he doesn't let me rest, he won't ever let me go, he wants to drive me away and I've been so happy here," words that tumbled out without my understanding where they might lead, words that surprised me with their vehemence and boldness, "I went to the building superintendent, I went to the police, nobody can stop him, nobody can help me. . . ."

The young man reread the letter, his cheeks visibly reddening. I could hear his outraged breath.

Then he lifted his eyes to my face, it was the first time we exchanged that look which we would, over the course of weeks, then months, exchange many times, and he frowned, and said, "—I'll keep this: you don't want to see this," and I whispered, "Thank you, and he said, "—No, you don't want to see this, it isn't very nice," and he folded up both the letter and the envelope, thoughtfully, and put them away in an inside pocket of his coat.

Esther M. Friesner

❦ ❧

DO I DARE TO ASK YOUR NAME?

Although I had said "no vampire stories" when I solicited the stories for this volume, I could not resist **Esther Friesner**'s *quasi-vampire tale about a needy woman who allows herself to be depleted by a man who turns out to be a memory-sucker.*

❦ ❧

To begin, you were beautiful. This I know beyond any power of denial or I would not have wasted the smallest drop of time, the least of precious seconds that I needed spend to know you. I saw you first not across a crowded room—no dead cliché, no lyric withering could describe our meeting—but close, so close I felt the warmth of your thigh through the spongy weave of your dress when you brushed against me at the bar. In that instant, I meant to have you. I do not survive by abandoning my intentions.

My eyes are bad. I place reliance on my other senses. Even in the dark, even safe beneath the warm swell of night's nursing breast, I turn to smell and touch, taste and melody before placing the least grain of trust in earthly vision. The outer eye betrays. Your beauty reached me first through other gates than sight alone. It was a presence on my tongue, rich and warm, flowing down my throat to enflame the belly like wine. It was the wanton breath of a whispered promise: *Come, be led by me to share the wondrous, the ungodly, the most delectably forbidden of joys. Draw on, steal near, linger and slumber and let me wrap you round in the seeming of love, the shimmering chrysalis of hell.*

Wise men resist such summons, but I? Oh, but you were beautiful. And since when has hell been more to me than a word like many others? I fear worse than words. Pen and paper shatter them, drain them of their deeper meanings. I turn the page, and doom them to oblivion. My demons thrive in wider realms, ranging past any power to control or limit their depredations. I live in immortal terror of memories.

I could forget if I so desired, yet I cannot bow to fear and live. Let me remember. I must remember you.

The lights are flashing over the dance floor, silver and violet and blue. I can smell their sweat, the dancers already elbowing one another aside, trying to lay claim to a square foot of hardwood. For what? To tempt their partners away from the noise and blinding brightness to a quieter place, the soft stillness of a stranger's bed after the lovemaking is done and the doubts creep in that maybe it was just sex after all? But for now, in the dance, all is promise. *See how I move, how well I command my body, how skillfully I shall serve yours, how different I am, we shall be, our coupling must be!* Hope long enough, and your sight too may blur truth into a viler, more palatable thing.

You did not dance; no more did I. So I marked you for a kindred connoisseur of lies. In the reflected glints of light from the floor, from bangles and neckchains and dangling axe-blade earrings of silver and gold, I saw your smile. I, the imperfect! I, the all but blind, I saw it, a bitter, lovely curve of disdain. I answered with its mate, and the bargain was struck. In the intimacy of darkness and shared, unspoken, implicit superiority, we conspired to despise the dancers.

Your eyes are keen and wise, instantly sure on the quarry's track, a faithful brace of hunting hounds in their mistress's traces. Did you think they served you so well, the instant you first saw me? Were you unwittingly betrayed, or did I have your leave to so betray you? You could see that I was not ugly. That much is true, I am not. My face is handsome, every plane cut with all of time's precision, a gem a long time beneath the master cutter's hand. Why should you find fault where there was none? You do hunger after beauty. I am dark and sleek, my body slim and full of more graceful promise while at rest than any of those gyrating fools on the dance floor can ever hope to compass.

Of course you could not resist me, if your own mask told no lies. Your body, so lovingly brought to the peak of this age's ideal: slender, tanned, taut, the musk of sex a tantalizing potency beneath bought perfume's blind of more innocuous fragrance. You were so much, just sitting there. So very much for me. I hungered too.

It was a moment meant to be relished, even for a glutton such as I. *All the time in the world,* I told myself, and I believed it. The only lies I hark to these days are my own. I seduce myself with a thousand pretty follies, when I can. Nonsense is the sole shield left for me to raise against the implacable, the foe ever-living. I caught your smile and returned it, feeling the alien grimace leave its own special hairline track of falsehood from brain to jawline to mouth. My teeth met the sudden cold inrush of air between my parted lips and ached with it, the way a child will twinge when biting too quickly into ices on a stick. But you were still smiling at me, and that was all that mattered.

Oh the game, the game so well begun, so simply played out to its ending! You asked me if I danced and I said yes, but not tonight. I asked you the same and you made a similar reply. Our mutual beauty worked a fey enchantment, cast the illusion that our hollow words hid some true meaning. Were we both not a thousandth part so perfect in our shells, our talk would have embarrassed us for its inanity. We were not alone in our fair, foolish banter. Two voices are not near enough for such as we to trade all that we must tell one another before the next step comes. Step and step again, for unmoving as we sat and for all the scorn we lavished on the dancers, still we traced the figures of a dance.

No, we were not alone. There was a third presence with us. I heard it first, the muted throb of blood beneath the melting tissue of your skin. Beat on beat, it sang the rush and flight of lost tides flung up against a rocky shore, life's first, most ancient stirrings. The salt of its scent rose from your every pore, drenching your skin in an imperious, invisible flood of summoning I could not escape or disavow. You heard it too, the siren-song beneath my skin, the call your power is powerless to deny. How easy, in that moment, to give myself into your keeping utterly! How many times before I came so near, so perilously near to a surrender more final than my distant death. Yet here I am.

And here are you, beside me. The dance is done. The antique sea is just a ghost remembered now. Your flesh is cold, white and soft and cool and harmlessly scented as apple blossom. There is a little moonlight. It lies in stripes of silver and blue over your breasts, your belly. One of your legs is drawn up to form a skeletal pyramid. The arch of your foot is a wizard's cavern, holding my doom captive in its shadows. The sheet pools beneath your heel, cups your buttocks with a phantom's insubstantial hands. Are they still here, the dead who loved you? You sigh, and the deep, secret sound of your full-fed contentment purls down the length of your upturned throat.

I dare to pass my palm over the rippled fan of your bright hair, squandered across the pillow. The night is envious of your beauty; darkness wells out of the earth, seeps across the sky. The moon, my more constant mistress, has turned niggardly to light my way in these last moments of our time together. I can only call upon the grace of my imagination to steal me a dream-sight of your eyes, the lashes so thick, the sheltering lids so thin that the brilliant blue beneath makes them incandescent. I cup my hands above your sleeping sockets and warm them at a flame only I can feel.

What have you given me here in the dark, in this room's anonymity? What have you taken in exchange? Let me count the lies. After love—for I desire to call it love—you were the one to sink into whatever dreams are left you. And do your kind dream? Oh, they must! I can not fancy this world so cruel as to forbid you dreams when you have abdicated so much else to claim . . . a kingdom? A lonely, fearsome empire? A legend?

These sheets are cooler against my skin than your fingertips were. If I close my eyes, I still feel the small, intense, sudden blazes of sweetness that your every touch conspired to strike from my body. I am hard and dark and old, the flint; you are cold and bright and world-young, the steel. Yet I imagine you must think yourself otherwise.

So old, so old you think yourself to be that you flatter yourself with the names *ageless, undying, immortal!* You despise me for what you think I am, one of so many victims you have known before this night. But what you do not know, what you have yet to suspect . . . There is so much innocence left in you that even now I swear by the greater darkness that I can sense the remnant of your soul.

My throat aches. Your teeth did not tear the flesh too badly. These will heal, the marks of your midnight feasting. My bones will survive to make me more blood. My hips still feel the weight of you, pressing me down into the false earth of the mattress. You loom above me in memory, a wave, a flame, a dream. That was the hard part, to feign a weakness and sham a dying exultation I could never feel. You never truly touched me.

Your hard little mouth, greedy at my neck, draining all your emptiness could hold. Your body's joy, in the end overruling even your blood-greed to bend all your boasted coolness into the white-hot blade of a sword that hovered above our bed and at last sheared down. Lust melds to gluttony, ecstasy sears away the triumph of your conquest. Your head falls back and my blood is a trickle of shadow from your gasping lips as your limbs fold in upon themselves and you cover my skin with your own. Even so filled as you were, you had hardly the strength to roll yourself away.

Now you sleep, if there is human sleep left for your kind beyond the waiting out of daylight hours deep in the silent soil. How pleased with yourself you look, my beloved, how smug.

You are like a spoiled little girl who had once more gotten everything her own way. Victory.

Now it is my turn.

My weight shifts gently across your limbs, steals over them with that ease of movement the æons have paid me. You stir, but you are too secure in recent feasting, too assured by past experience that a victim drained as you have lately drained me could not possibly do more than move sluggishly, if at all. Perhaps your drowsing thoughts allow you the conceit of seeing my arm thrown across you, embracing you like an ordinary lover. Is that what your secret self hungers for, my dearest? To be an ordinary woman once more?

But it is too late for that. We have made our choices, you and I. Your mouth is under mine. I part your lips with my tongue and sip the memory of my own blood from your breath. Your teeth are slick and small and sharp. Here there are many ghosts still lingering.

The married man who bought you a drink in the railroad station and died in the hotel room because he bored you and the boy who thought you were a whore and whom you let live and the sailor who thought the same and who died because you remembered other sailors bitterly and the girl who only lived to love you and inconvenienced you with love and so you killed her and her grateful eyes still haunt you and the fool who told you coarse jokes and laughed until he screamed and the solemn university professor who crumpled into a wisp of skin and bone before you even drew the half of his blood and the baby sleeping under a second-hand quilt in a rat-gnawed crib that you devoured because you had gone too long without novelty and the man and the woman and the man and the boy and the child . . .

They flood me, they pour into me, they engulf me, all the ones who came before, all the empty faces of your past, the remembered and the forgotten. They are a desert wind, winged fire that lifts me from this pitifully small and insignificant planet to burn for a night among the immortal stars, to seek my lost place among the angels. Ah, can't you feel? Don't you know? Won't you *see*? They are your life. They are my salvation.

Your eyes fly wide. You wake, and meet my gaze, and know. I feel your body buck beneath me in a counterfeit of passion. You are terror's virgin, and this modest intrusion of mine the most atrocious of violations. Fear has not stirred your blood for centuries, its reek is stale and musty in my nostrils, yet I recognize it easily. You claw, you kick, you writhe, and all for nothing. You realize what I am—your brother and your bane, kindred and alien, nightmare of even the unholy—and you know I will not let you go.

Still you struggle. It is useless. I will have what I sought and seek ever, the sweet feeding your smile promised me when we first met. Your life after life is rich and lush and beautiful even beyond your self-constrained ideas of beauty. It is a vast embroidery of countless, carefully counted stitches that you have worked into place with love and cunning, blood and time. And in the full strength of my audacity I have come to undo it, just as carefully, just as meticulously, stitch by stitch. Grain by grain I pick apart the castle of moments you have erected and I joy to see it slowly crumble back formless into the sand.

For I am your lover true. All the time that went before, all your life until I entered it, all the hurts and harms that marred and made you shall be mine as well. I have given you whatever you wished to have of me, even to my blood. Can love do less? You will, you *must* answer me in equal kind and coin. I ask you for no more.

I am your elder, your master, your slave. You live on blood, and I on rarer fare. You are damned, I damnation. I could name you for what you are, were I so bold; I dare not. I fear to hear you put a name to me.

For to name is to set limitations, and I can bear no boundaries. You must not hold back. To the depths of your being, to the hollows of your bones I will know you. No cell of your self can be left as hearth or refuge forbidden me; lady, that would be unkind. I will drink the instants of your life from your lips and crack wide the lies you offer lesser men. The tender truths that bide within, these are mine: mine to devour on a whim, mine to savor in an afterthought, *mine*. By this I live. For this I hunger. All this I will have.

There. Done. Your stillness is its own blessing upon all we have shared tonight; I sense you have at last come to approve of me. You make no further sign or sound of contradiction. A woman's silence was ever called consent; even such a woman as you.

Fare well. You were beautiful.

Deidra Cox

୶ૐ ৡৡ

REMNANTS

Deidra Cox, *a Southern writer, mixes lyricism with death in this truly bizarre love story about a woman who chooses to suffer sexual torment to keep her dead lover around.*

୶ૐ ৡৡ

A tender curl of warmth licking at my thighs. The silken resistance of muscle sliding against my flesh. Teasing me with precise, careful strokes.

Quickening. Driving me closer to the . . .

I jolt to awareness in a confusing tumble of sensation. Sleep clings to the edge of perception, playing havoc with my emotions. Remnants of a familiar lust build in my womb and the delicious weight beckons. My fingers slowly ease downward, seeking the moist heat.

Reality comes crashing in a stark wave and I recoil from the impulse. Shame colors my cheeks, chasing the sleep from my weary eyes and I can almost hear a low ripple of laughter.

"You're such a prude, Beth," Daniel whispers. His breath, a rustle of autumn leaves, barely touching my neck.

For a moment, the urge to surrender is overwhelming. A fierce craving that drains my will. My need of him.

Yet, one thought haunts me. What of his need of me?

Sleep doesn't return easily and I watch the soft play of light waltz across the patchwork spread.

∾§ §∾

I buried Daniel in the winter. A crystal layer of snow covered the earth, freezing into a brittle crust. Ice dripped from the trees like tears.

When they lowered him into the open ground, I felt as if I was falling. Then, in the next heartbeat, I was, shocking the sparse members of the funeral party.

Daniel. How fragile you were. The dark layers you hid from me.

We met in acting class, both of us eager to hone our craft into a reasonable facsimile of true emotion. Two pretenders stumbling through the motions, never once considering the consequences of our actions.

Quicksilver. We were like paper and fire. Our bodies burned together, ached whenever apart, like junkies craving a fix. Marriage seemed a logical solution. A permanent merger of sex and warm flesh.

And in the beginning, it was glorious. Waking in his arms. The coarse bristle of whiskers brushing my cheek. The stiff organ poking my spine.

I guess I should've realized, I should've felt Daniel's pain. Understood his insecurities. But I was caught up in the excitement of snaring my first role in a substantial film.

Nothing major. The supportive best friend of the leading lady. Still, over fifteen minutes of solid airtime. A chance to shine.

My star was rising, while Daniel . . .

His went supernova. He tried. God, how he tried. But no one would touch him. Too old. Too young. Too handsome. Too ordinary. They had a thousand reasons why Daniel was all wrong for the job and Daniel took each and every excuse as a personal flaw.

Have you ever seen something fade away? Like the tiny puddles of water beading over a hot sheet of metal? Regardless how closely you watch, you can't find the last drop. It simply slides into oblivion.

That last morning, I kissed Daniel good-bye, hurrying off to an obscenely early shoot and when I got home, he was gone. The image of his death is carved into my mind, as lasting as any scar.

Rusty water gradually sloshing over the sides of the tub. The scent of copper, thick and oppressive. And Daniel, head slumped to his chest. Mutilated wrists folded before him like an apology.

◆§ ठ◆

The day passes slowly. As I mouth the required lines, the actress I once was, cringes. No fire. No spark. Each movement, artificial. Each gesture, saccharine. So tasteless and flat.

But these things no longer trouble me. Success doesn't interest me. Nothing reaches that secret, inner place deep inside me. Except the night and I long for its arrival.

Darkness surrounds me like a velvet glove. No light. Not even a sliver of moonlight to pierce the glass for I have pulled the shade low, to hurry my ghostly suitor.

I lay on the bed, expectant. Breathless. Sleep eludes me, my frenetic grasps at its gossamer hem. The delicate brush of wings upon my face. My mouth is dry from the wanting, the need which blooms within me like a black rose.

Minutes flow into a frustrating blur and yet, I wait.

◆§ ठ◆

Daniel comes to me, as always, in the guise of dreams. An easy sigh. A tender caress lingers about my throat. So soft. Greedy tongue licking behind my knee. Tasting my flesh while nimble fingers probe my wetness, gauging the moist depths.

I shudder as the heat builds. Delicious, oh, so sweet. My

legs open, ready for the joining. Ready for the precious touch of another.

Please, my love, I pray. Let this time be different. Let my body not be found lacking.

Without warning, a cold wind chills my loins, signaling my lover's departure. Writhing with frustration, I crumble into the pillows. Sweat banking the sheets, heels dug into the mattress.

Why? I silently weep. Why are you doing this?

A low hiss near my ear. "I want you to suffer, dear Beth."

The words are deceptively soft, almost lost in the maddened pulse of my sobs. "I want you to hunger till you'll kiss the blade and treasure the first cut."

Tears fall, glide down my cheeks like rain. Curling my body into a compact ball, I hold a pillow against my belly and try to block the hollow ache scraping my insides.

◄§ §►

Sex was never an easy thing for me. A puzzling mix of wanton limbs and acute embarrassment. The end result never quite exceeding the hype. After several wan lovers, I resigned myself to little more than the pleasant closeness of intimacy. But never a hint of passion. Never that.

Not until Daniel.

◄§ §►

"I think I'm losing it," I say, my eyes downcast. Beside me, my companion croons sympathetically.

"Don't be so melodramatic, Beth. You've been through some heavy stuff. It's bound to do some damage."

Poor Lisa. Always so predictably practical. Anger swells at her casual dismissal.

She needs to burn. She needs to suffer.

The threat flashes in my mind like a white-hot brand, leaving their mark upon the cerebral matter.

Instantly, I am ashamed. Lisa doesn't deserve this betrayal.

She has stood by me throughout the hard times following Daniel's death.

Tears spill as the dam breaks and the pain and humiliation erupts in a salty tide. Cool arms envelop me in a soothing embrace. Burrowing deeper, face pressed into the crook of Lisa's neck. The calming influence of another.

In the midst of the outburst, a curious thing occurs. A lazy finger of heat coils in the pit of my stomach, snaking lower, seeking entrance. A heavy shudder courses through me as my mouth forms a large O.

The heat doubles, intensifies. Grasping the loose fabric of Lisa's blouse, I desperately search to find something, anything to help me hold on. I ignore the anxious cries, her shrill protests. I sweep her growing apprehension, the feverish questions aside. Nothing, none of it matters.

"Do you want it?" Daniel asks.

His unmistakable scent is strong. Cinnamon and oranges. Oh, how I use to tease him because of it. Sharp tang of citrus and I tremble.

"A subtle caress, a whispered endearment, and the woman could be yours."

Pressing my lips to her throat, I taste the soft texture of Lisa's skin. A brief image of Lisa writhing beneath me, clutching my shoulders, begging, ever begging for more.

"No!" I pant the denial, body rigid with a brittle control.

My attempt at restraint is costly. Spirit weakened, I collapse into a dark pool of Lisa's startled cries and Daniel's venomous laughter.

❧ ❧

Returning to the present, confusion and fear manipulate my responses. Soft snores issue from the chair across from me. Lisa dozes in a semi-upright position. Faithful to the end.

The house is quiet, except for the familiar sounds from Lisa. Her presence comforts me. A faint smile.

"Have you forgotten me so quickly?"

The sudden question is unnerving and my body shakes uncontrollably. Daniel slithers near, black eyes boring into mine. I melt beneath his touch. He climbs atop me and the solid feel of him shocks me.

I throw a frantic glance toward Lisa, but she dreams on, unaware. Safe.

His lips tempt me, searing a trail to my breasts where he suckles. Just the barest hint of pain as he rakes his teeth over my swollen nipple.

My mind tells me to resist, to fight, yet my body, my traitorous body responds to his ministry. Knowing the end result is useless. I am lost.

Careful strokes. Feathery kisses fluttering over my belly. Skilled tongue laps ever so softly while I strain to reach the peak. Soft gasps. Nerves taut, seeking release. Begging for it.

A brief rush of pleasure flickers, beckons. Tantalizingly close. Nervous laughter bubbles. Sweet relief, so near. Yes, oh yes.

Swiftly, Daniel pulls away, leaving me teetering on the brink. A low sob seeps from my throat as frustration spears my insides. I claw at my husband, but my hands slide through his milky form.

An invisible barrier prevents me from finishing the dance. I pound against the wall of thorns encasing my loins while the fire threatens to swallow me.

"Why?" I whimper. "I loved you."

A shadow crosses Daniel's features and for the first time, an emotion akin to regret rears.

"I need you. Your pain. It keeps me here. With you. And it's so lonely in the darkness. Unbearable emptiness adrift in an endless abyss."

A wave of lust plunges over me and I grind my hips against the cushions. "Help me," I plead. "Please, don't leave me like this."

Cold smile. An eternity of torment is reflected in the smoky depths and I shudder.

As Daniel gestures to the sleeping Lisa, I suddenly realize just how far he means to take me. The expanse to which I must immerse myself in order to gain satisfaction.

"Seduce the lamb, Beth. Give me another soul to play with," he whispers.

One last stroke. A razored caress that wrings the air from my lungs. Reducing my world to the silken box between my legs, throbbing with an insatiable hunger.

A tremor works through my abdomen and I close my eyes against the relentless onslaught. Seconds later, I rise on shaky limbs to go to Lisa and introduce her to the flames.

Jan Barrette

෧ ෫

PATENT
PENDING

Jan Barrette *is a pseudonym, which should not detract from this story about a woman who resolves her sexual dichotomy by setting up a threesome with her ex-lover—an android—and his current wife, with interesting results.*

෧ ෫

Every now and again, Ren's stomach reverted to Clive's graveyard shift at the card room—ten at night to six in the morning—breakfast at night, dinner in the morning. This was one of those times.

She dialed a number from memory, pleased that she could remember it after a year of disuse. "I'm lusting after a big, thick, rare hamburger and fries," she said into the phone.

"Ren? Is that really you?"

Ren crooked the receiver between her neck and her shoulder and maneuvered a nylon over one shapely leg. "It's me," she said. "In the flesh."

"Give me a second to grab my robe and turn down the TV."

Ren imagined Darla wrapping herself in the soft, terry bathrobe she had given her as a wedding gift. Bill Blass. A matching set, embroidered Clive—0203, and Darla.

"Ren? You still there?"

"I'm still here. Listen, I'd like to see you. Meet at the Red Onion in half an hour?"

"You haven't called me in over a year," Darla sounded peevish. "Now you call at eight o'clock in the morning to tell me you want a hamburger for breakfast. . . ." Darla stopped. "Oh, what the hell. I'd like to see you, too," she said. "Give me ten extra minutes to dry my hair."

"Good," Ren said. "You know how I am when I don't get what I want."

Darla laughed. "Tell you the truth, I'm not getting much of what I want myself these days."

"What? And here I thought you were a happily married woman."

"Married, yes. Happy? I'd be a lot happier if I could learn to do something other than dealing cards and if my gorgeous husband could get it up more often. I'm beginning to think he needs reprogramming. Before we were married—"

"I know all about before you were married. I was there, remember."

Silence. Then Darla said softly, "I remember."

❧ ❧

Ren watched the hot water trickle into the bathtub, carving a hole in the bubbles. When the water was deep enough, she switched on the portable whirlpool. The Red Onion had satisfied her hamburger lust, but there were other hungers yet to be sated, she thought. She flung one leg over the edge of the tub, splayed the other one around the machine, and sank into the bubbles. Using the whirlpool's rubber spout, she directed the water to the places where she knew it would give her most pleasure.

Her body responded quickly. She arched, breasts rising from the water. She felt good, she thought, but not good enough.

She needed Clive there watching her. Waiting for her. Joining her. No one else could do her half as well as he did. Maybe she *had* been too hasty, choosing nothing when he'd said, "Marriage and honesty or nothing."

She reached for the phone. Damn the engineers for building this marriage and monogomy fetish into his programming. A couple of months of living together, screwing together, and the sensors took over—screaming about the new morality, and about how many homeless and unwanted kids needed families.

In a strange kind of way, it made sense, at least from their point of view. They had gone to so much trouble to make their androids "human," that interaction with the real thing, with flesh and blood humans, was inevitable. Without rules, the impact on society might have been—probably would have been—enormous. Groups like the Moral Majority would have jumped on it, screaming of interference with natural evolution.

She understood, but that didn't mean she had to like the fact that three times, now, he'd left her to get married. Like Gabor and Taylor, he was preset to believe in the institution. Between marriages, he came back to shake her bedposts. Then off he'd go again, in pursuit of his monogamy myth, while she waited, respecting his belief system.

Their belief system, really. When gambling broke open all over the country and card rooms and casinos proliferated, there was a call for dealers. They couldn't find enough warm bodies, and the ones they did find had to be trained. Meanwhile, every table without a dealer was also without customers, and less money went to the bank.

So the company she worked for at the time came up with the Clives—and Adams and Glenns and Johns, and heaven only knew how many more. Clive Dee. Dee, as in D-for-Dealer. Cute.

Not so cute was the fact that the president of the company had political aspirations.

Seizing the opportunity to get rich and position himself politically, he insisted that the Dee's programming be in sync with America's return to family values. Add that to the AIDS panic, and the fact that he was thinking of running for office, and it became obvious why he programmed his dealers the way he did—obedient to his creed: There will be no monkeying with the human condition.

She grinned, remembering the first few Dees that came off the production line. What an unholy disaster that had been! Stiff, unsmiling mechanical creatures, incapable of anything but the act of dealing cards.

The customers had hated that. They wanted someone they could curse at when their run of cards turned sour, someone who could crack the occasional joke, above all someone who could keep the personalities in check at the table—

Which led to Clive and the other Dees. They were fast, dextrous, alert . . . and preprogrammed with this cockamamie monogamy myth. Her only hope of getting what she wanted was to circumvent his programming. Somehow, she had to provide him with a rationale for doing things her way.

If there was a way, she would find it. She was ready to blow his myth—not to speak, she thought, of how ready she was to blow *him.*

She picked up the telephone. The first call took less than a minute. "I don't know if he'll come or not, Darla," she said, "but get your butt over here anyway, just in case. If I'm in the tub when you get here, use the key I gave you this morning and wait in my bedroom until you hear the signal. Help yourself to whatever you need."

"How do you know this is going to work?"

"I don't . . ."

The second call took not much longer.

"Good evening. Oaks Club."

"Clive Dee please."

"Just a moment. I'll have him paged."

She could hear the clink of chips in the background and people being called to the tables. It was a quarter to ten—ten o'clock club time. If he was dealing already, he wouldn't be able to take the call.

"Clive here."

"Clive. It's Ren."

Silence. Matching Darla's silence of this morning in that it was probably filled with unspoken surprise at hearing her voice.

She wasted no time on preliminaries. "Can you take an early out and come over?"

She pictured him in his black-and-white uniform, tall and restrained, hair neat but slightly longer than one might expect at the base of the skull to cover the *Patent* #D5C-0203 tattoo, nails trimmed and impeccably clean. In short, the perfect dealer.

He had just come on shift and here she was asking him to take an EO. As she had often done before, she wondered how his programming coped with this kind of request, and whether or not it presented him with choices. "What I have in mind will satisfy both of our constraints," she said, in response to his continued silence. "Just remember, I turn into a pumpkin at midnight."

She hung up and repositioned the whirlpool spout. As her breathing sped up, the doorbell rang. A key grated in the lock and she heard the door open and close.

"I'll be in the bedroom," Darla called out.

Ren moved more rapidly, eyes closed. She could almost see the wave of warmth that rose from her body.

The doorbell rang again, insistently. She turned off the whirlpool and grabbed a towel. Wishing that Clive had been there in time to scrub her back as a prelude to screwing, she threw the towel aside, and trailed naked and wet to the door.

Standing on her toes, she could just reach the peephole. Clive's face was in the shadows, but there was no mistaking that bulge in his crotch.

She reached for the chain, but stopped. Let him wait, she thought. It would do him good.

He stepped forward out of the shadows and stared at the door as if he could see right through it. "What d'you have in mind, girl?" he said, hand hovering near his zipper. His face was tanned, beard neatly trimmed. She'd always gone for beards . . . they tickled and scratched in just the right places. And he was ready, she could see that—as ready as she was.

Rubbing herself, she stared back at him through the peephole. He stood there in the dusk, bold as can be, as if he hadn't left her, married, and been gone for over a year.

Impatiently, he rang the bell again. "I know you're there, girl. Let me in."

"Just a minute."

She left the chain attached, opened the door, and leaned into the space in-between. "Looking for anyone in particular?"

He grinned at her and cupped one hand around the breast she had thrust at him through the narrow gap, pressing her backwards. "Is the lady of the house home?"

She pushed his hand away. "Shouldn't we talk about marriage and honesty?"

Talk was clearly not what Clive had in mind. Breathing sharply, he started on his zipper. He pulled it down slowly. As often as she had seen his equipment, it still took her by surprise.

She stared at it, mesmerized by the sheer magnitude of his erection. No wonder he didn't care if the whole of San Francisco stopped by to admire it. There wasn't a man who wouldn't envy him or a woman who wouldn't be tempted.

Smiling openly now, Ren looked at herself in the full-length mirror at the side of the door. She was rocking back and forth, rubbing herself with such energy that if she didn't let him in soon, she'd be tempted to attack the doorknob.

She unlatched the door and opened it. He stepped into the doorway and stopped. She knew what he wanted. What they both wanted.

"What about Darla?" Ren asked. "Your marriage? Your conscience? The kid you're supposed to adopt? Don't you want to know—"

"I know I want you. I trust you." He pulled her toward him and kissed her hard on the mouth. Gently, but with determination, he pushed her down onto the carpet.

To her astonishment, Ren felt little of anything. Her desire for Clive seemed to have vanished. Trying to figure out why, she realized that she had expected him—wanted him—to protest after letting her believe in his devotion to his marriage myth. She had always hated her uncle for telling her there was no Santa Claus and depriving her of her Christmas Eve illusions. She did not want to hate Clive. There is still no Santa Claus, she thought, glancing at the bedroom door, knowing her friend . . . his wife . . . could see and hear them.

She pushed him away and he reached back to slam shut the door. Relenting, Ren dropped to the floor, put her hands on his buns, and pulled him towards her. He groaned and she wrapped her thighs around one of his legs and moved along his calf, enjoying the contact. When she pulled back and lay down on the plush velvet carpet, she held out her arms. "Give it to me, Clive."

"I've missed you, Ren," he said later, as they lay there in a tumble of sweat.

"Well, now you've had me," she said, giving him a playful push. "So it's time for you to leave."

Clive rolled over, lay there for a moment or two, and stood up. He pulled up his trousers and headed for the guest bathroom. She could hear the shower and knew he expected her to join him.

She didn't.

She went over to the stereo, slid in a CD, and waited. He was out in no time, wearing nothing but a towel. She stared at his bulging crotch. He was ready again, but she wasn't. Not yet.

He took her in his arms and nibbled at her ear. She pushed him away. Delighted by the look on his face, she danced toward the radio, undulating her hips. She bent over and raised the volume, moving her body to the rhythm.

". . . a material girl," Madonna sang out.

Ren turned around and shook her shoulders, breasts wiggling an invitation for him to join her. Clive shed the towel and they danced. He knew the game, knew there was no use rushing her when she was in that mood. "Darla—"

Ren put her hand over his mouth and he bit down lightly before taking her fingers into his mouth. He was skilled, handsome, fun, preprogrammed to know what to do and when to do it, she thought. So why hadn't she married him?

Because she wasn't the one programmed to believe in the marriage myth, *he* was?

Was it really that simple? Probably. She had never grasped the concept of one man-one woman. After all, how could she keep appreciating him . . . how could he go on appreciating her . . . if neither of them made love with anyone else who *wasn't* as good?

"Like a virgin," Madonna sang.

They crushed their bodies together and swayed to the music. Ren could feel him pressing urgently against her.

"Hold the thought," she said, dancing away from him toward her bedroom. "Promise I'll be right back."

❧ ❧

Ren stood in the bedroom doorway. She was wearing the red see-through nightgown Clive loved, and his favorite perfume. That was another thing that never failed to amaze her—that an engineered man could have preferences in things like that. In her hand, she held a bowl of whipped cream. The cream was cold. He would start a little as it made contact with his skin, Ren thought. The programming had taken care of that, too. They hadn't, it seemed, missed a trick.

Clive smiled and moved toward her. "Glad you haven't given up cooking completely," he said.

She took a few steps backwards, enough to let Darla get past her, but her gaze never left Clive's body, big and tanned and just the way she liked it—just hairy enough.

"Dinner time," Darla called out, taking the bowl of cream from Ren's outstretched hand.

Clive held out his arms to his wife. To Ren's astonishment, he looked perfectly happy to see her. "Let's eat," he said. "Coming, Ren?"

"Why isn't any of this bothering you?" Ren asked, joining the two of them in the living room.

"Must be something skewed about my programming," Clive

said. "All I know is, I seem to need you to get me going. Keep me going."

He reached for her with the arm that was not around Darla. Ren pushed him away. "Not so fast."

Madonna had stopped singing. Ren moved over to the stereo. Her hand hovered over the button. If she did not push it, did not renew the mood, she could send him away, and there would be no harm done—to Darla, Clive, to the integrity of the Dee invention. The marriage-and-honesty myth could remain intact. That there was more than that bothering her she admitted to herself only reluctantly, because the more made her uncomfortable. It told her that, in some way, she respected—even mildly admired—the new-old morality.

"I took an EO to do this," Clive said. "Don't play games with me."

"No games, Clive," Ren said. "What I had in mind was more like a meal."

"I'm more than hungry enough," he said, pressing down on her hand to start the music.

Ren looked across at Darla. She looked stunning. Her long hair was piled on top of her head and Ren wondered briefly why she had never seen her with it that way before.

"I'm sorry, Ren," Darla said, laughing. "I couldn't resist. It was such an easy set-up."

"Set-up?"

"Well, for one thing, Clive and I have both been working swing for six months. Two to ten. We needed a change. Some . . . R & R."

Ren thought for a moment. "Are you saying that he was at home when I called you this morning," she said slowly, "and getting *off* shift when I called him tonight?"

Darla nodded. "He was at home when you called this morning, and waiting for your call at the Oaks."

She walked over to the stereo, bent over it, and lowered the sound. As she did so, the light caught the back of her neck.

"Patent pending," Ren read softly. "You're—"

"I am the new generation," Darla said. She turned around, smiling at Ren, then at Clive. "And since I'm not a *real* human, there's no conflict with the 'new morals'."

"So he's not in violation of the marriage myth?"

Darla shook her head.

Ren felt a rising anger. He had left her for this. For an android? Together, they had manipulated her—

"Clive didn't know either," Darla said, apparently sensing what Ren was feeling. "They were testing my effectiveness, and the efficiency of his programming."

Anger dissipating, Ren started to laugh. "Looks like we all win," she said, reaching for the bowl of whipped cream and delighted with this perfect opportunity to have her cake and eat it too.

It was not until later, after her lovers had left and the itch began again, that she understood how Pyrrhic, how transient, her victory had been. And how complete theirs. Man, created only of man and woman, would never again be perfect enough to satisfy her appetites.

They had choices, Clive and Darla. They would always have choices. For her, that would never again hold true.

Dawn Dunn

❧ ❧

THE LONELY HEART

Thanks to **Dawn Dunn**, *we have a most unusual take on the life of a farmer's wife. No tending to the crops here. Instead, a farm wife learns the pleasures of pain and decides to teach them to her husband. Come to me, my love, she says, and I will show you my secret pleasures.*

❧ ❧

As Rosie grabbed the whistling tea kettle from the stove, her hand slipped on the smooth handle and, for an instant, her forefinger lay pressed against the searing metal. She cried out sharply and dropped the kettle back on the burner.

Her husband, Austin, sat at the table with his head in the newspaper, his eyes barely moving. Their love was as lifeless and dead as the cold, rubbery eggs on his plate.

Rosie shook her finger and hurried toward the sink, a deep, oval-shaped blister appearing over her knuckles. She turned on the tap, but as the acute, burning sensation crept through her finger she began to feel a warm rush of exhilaration and shut off the water. With incredible shock, she realized she was becoming aroused. She hadn't felt anything like this in years. Her breasts tingled, and her crotch grew remarkably moist. She wanted to fully enjoy the moment, but she couldn't with Austin present.

What would he think?

An embarrassed flush crawled up her neck, and she turned toward the window to hide her flaming cheeks. She didn't want him to see the brazen lust mirrored in her eyes, to openly scorn her, or worse yet, laugh.

The newspaper crackled behind her as Austin hunted for the sports page. Her finger still throbbed, and a delicious ache pulsed between her thighs, making her tremble. It was all she could do to keep her hands on the cupboard.

Rosie stared at the greasy bubbles in the sink without really seeing them. The strangely erotic pain reminded her of the agonizing night she'd lost her virginity, in the front seat of Howard Kelman's '58 Cadillac. God, how it'd hurt! She'd been only seventeen, and her mother had warned her not to go to the drive-in with boys she didn't know. But Howard Kelman had been a center on the school basketball team and the dream date of every girl at South Side High. She'd been more than flattered when he asked her out.

The opening credits had scarcely begun to play when he became an uncontrollable beast. His hands were all over her. She'd tried shoving him away, but apparently not many girls had ever said "no" to him. And so he took what he craved, against her will. She remembered how his fingernails had cut into her hips when he ripped off her panties, how he'd kept his mouth clamped over hers so she couldn't scream, the overwhelming sense of humiliation and betrayal when he'd thrust himself into her dry vagina—the raw, tearing pain. Worst of all was the degrading way her own body had finally responded. Unable to hold herself back, she'd dug her heels into his sides, quivering in ecstasy as she experienced the first orgasm of her life.

Afterward, alone in the dark on Brigham Road, as she sat sobbing about how she hadn't wanted to do it, he'd called her a slut and kicked her out of the car, leaving her to find her own way home. Those horrible, incriminating blood stains on her skirt. Oh Jesus, how she'd wished she could die!

Rosie closed her eyes, a river of unshed tears welling behind them. The memory was as vivid as though it had happened today. She'd been too ashamed to tell anyone about it. She'd hated it then, being forced into sex, the sheer brutality of it; but even so, it was better than what she had now. If only she could've known.

A stale, stagnant breeze ruffled the curtains at the window, bringing with it the moldering heat of summer and the foul odor of scum off the pond. The sun was just rising over the top of the woods, giving the sky a sickly orange hue. The farm stretched on for miles and miles without another house in sight. Rosie wiped her eyes. The pain was almost gone in her finger, and the sweet, foreign thrill in her groin had faded away. She had to get on with her work.

As she reached for the skillet at the bottom of her dish water, she saw a scrawny, cottontail race across the road. The dust had settled in the ditch, giving the brush along the roadside a queer papery look. Traffic was far and few between on the old dirt thoroughfare. Even a rabbit was an occasion. Many days there was nothing at all.

Austin shoved back his chair with a loud, grating sound.

"Ain't you going to eat anything?" she asked, anxious to finish the dishes. The kids were grown, and there was just the two of them now.

"Ain't hungry. I'll pick up somethin' outta the field." He laid the paper aside and pulled up his trousers over his belly, setting his belt over another notch.

"Suit yourself," she said, keeping her voice flat, the way Austin liked it. He saw any kind of emotion as a sign of the Devil, of weakness. The older he'd gotten, the more distant and cold he'd become, to the point where they hardly spoke.

She scraped the eggs into an open milk carton full of garbage. Tin cans and anything metal went into a separate container that went out to the garage. Austin had twenty years worth of scrap metal stored out there. The stuff that would rot quickly, he took to the garden and spaded under.

She watched as he slipped on an old gray T-shirt and grabbed his hat to keep the sun off his face, then plodded out through the pantry door, relieved at the sound of the screen slamming against the casing. He wouldn't return until after sundown. The house would be lonely and empty till then, but no lonelier or emptier than it was with him in it.

Her left hand rubbed casually over the oval-shaped blister on her right forefinger, if only that moment of blissful pain could've lasted a minute longer, if only Austin hadn't been in the room. Her cheeks reddened with shame. She knew it was wrong to want pleasure from something harmful, and yet it was the most stimulating thing that had happened to her in months.

They seldom had sex, and when they did, they were never truly intimate. It wasn't in Austin's nature. When they made love, it was like two people bumping into each other in a closet, without passion or zeal. Two people going through the motions of something they'd never felt or meant. There weren't even any small gestures of affection or tenderness between them. At times, she hated him, but not so much any more. Lately, she didn't feel much of anything. No love, no hate, no enthusiasm. Nothing except the need to keep going day after day.

She pulled the plug from the sink and dried her hands on the ragged apron about her waist as the water whirled down the drain. She'd given up everything, including the scant hopes and dreams she'd had of being a gospel singer or living in the city, to spend thirty years working like a mule, bearing children and trying to eke life out of the stingy soil. The earth was like Austin, giving back little but taking so much.

She glanced at her finger again, though she'd been trying to forget, and wished there were a way to bring back that exquisite torment for just a few seconds. But she couldn't keep thinking about it. It was bad to keep dwelling on something so destructive.

The moment was gone. Lost forever, perhaps. She walked toward the pile of mending beside her rocker and took out a needle and thread, but her eyes continued to stray to the large white blister, the harbinger of that brief, wonderful anguish. With a sigh, she hauled one of Austin's shirts up onto her lap and folded the tear in the shoulder, so she could stitch it shut. The clock ticked softly on the wall.

There was a time when she'd thought about leaving, when the emptiness had almost driven her crazy, but she'd had too many kids just to run off, and now she was too old. Her hair was more white than black, her skin wrinkled and tough as a leather strap, her stomach and breasts sagging like worn-out balloons.

She supposed she had married Austin to get away from all the Howard Kelmans, that it had actually been an act of rebellion. Austin was as controlled as the other boys were wild, but she realized now—too late—that it had probably been a mistake.

After she finished the shirt, she moved on to a pair of frayed overalls with a missing button, guiding the needle dangerously close to the blister. What would happen if she purposely injured herself, if she rammed the needle through that blister? Would it feel even better? Her hand shook as she hesitated, considering, then quickly dismissed the idea. It was lunacy. She'd been too long in this ancient house by herself—too long alone.

Her gaze swept over the phone that sat on a tiny, three-legged table next to an old pine cupboard she'd inherited from her mother, with its pretty glass doors and the china set aside for company that never came. The phone seldom rang, and nobody ever dropped by to visit. The kids were all busy with lives of their own; only one of them even lived in the same state.

Wasn't nothing exciting happening for miles. Day after day. Occasionally, she turned on the TV, but the reception was poor and Austin wouldn't bother to fix it, so most days she just left it off. Her cheek twitched as she glanced out the window at the barren road, thinking anything would be better than this.

The heat increased as the hours dragged by. After she came in from weeding the garden, she unbuttoned her dress and stood at the sink in her slip to peel potatoes. She'd intentionally neglected her gloves and abused her hands as much as she could, popping the blister, but that tremendous mixture of joyous pain and sexual turmoil hadn't returned. Sweat filled the crevices around her waist and a faint breeze touched her forehead, but neither brought any comfort from the endless tedium. A couple of times she thought she heard someone pull into the drive and peered anxiously through the window though it was never anything more than the dead, vacant air circulating in her ears. She could neither laugh nor cry. Her life was a blank page, a road going nowhere.

A fly alighted on the cupboard at her elbow, and she grabbed a rolled-up newspaper from the counter to kill it, then caught sight of a pair of them copulating on the milk carton. Her arm froze in mid-air as she watched in irresistible fascination until they flew away. She set the newspaper aside and picked up another potato, still seeing the flies in the back of her mind, wishing it was her, wishing she could feel anything at all.

She had a mound of potatoes sitting in a pot on the stove and had started slicing up carrots, when her hand missed and the blade cut a small slit in her middle finger. She winced at the initial pain, but as the sharp, stinging sensation rushed through her arm she knew this was what she'd been waiting for. Her heart pounded in exhilaration. A blazing tide of unleashed fervor cascaded through her body. Her nipples tightened and her hips ground against the cabinet as she savored the moment. It felt so good that she squeezed the cut harder, trying to make the pain last, but it was over far too quickly.

She leaned on the cupboard in breathless release, her thighs damp, her sex aching. Who would've guessed that a little bit of pain could bring such extreme reward?

But one orgasm was not enough. Not after all these years. There had to be something that would make it last. Something that would help her feel what she had not felt in thirty-four years of loveless marriage. When her youngest daughter, Joan, had gotten married, she'd given her the only advice she could: never settle for less than the real thing. But it isn't possible to tell someone at eighteen what love will be like at fifty, or even thirty. And if there is no love from the start . . .

An urgent flood of desire flowed up the back of her spine, and she quickly stabbed herself again, in the palm of her hand. The blade nearly poked through the other side. She could see all the veins and tendons as she pulled it out.

But oh Jesus, how good it felt.

The knife fell with a clatter on the linoleum. She clutched her injured hand, holding it tight, blood spurting between her fingers, and shoved her crotch against the cupboard doors, trying to apply enough pressure to make herself come.

Oh, Lord, forgive me, she prayed, blood running down her arm in a sticky stream. She knew that she ought to stop, that what she was doing was an abomination, but she couldn't restrain herself. She kept banging her pelvis against the unrelenting wood, harder and harder, the whole cabinet rattling with her efforts. God, help me, she thought, relishing the potent anguish.

Her body felt as though it would burst. Her skin was as hot as the sun on the parched ground. Oh, Christ. She finally let loose of her hands in a frenzy of sexual passion, scarcely aware of the pain except as it served to heighten her pleasure. Her fingers jabbed and prodded, one hand rubbing between her legs, while the other gripped her breast, kneading and squeezing despite the agony, until at last she could feel herself climax.

Her body sagged against the cupboard. The front of her slip and her right breast were painted in red. Her knees were so weak she could barely stand, and her face was aflame with feverish elation. She had tried masturbation before, but never with such satisfying results. This was better than anything she'd ever known, and she knew she would never be the same.

A brief memory brought a smile to her lips, as she remembered the one time she hadn't regretted, the closest she'd ever been to what she felt now; in the back of Tom Waldfogel's rusted pickup, a night of unbridled lust and giving.

Why hadn't she married Tom? He hadn't been as safe a choice as Austin, and her father hadn't approved. Something about him not having money or land. As if any of that mattered.

She glanced at the splatters of blood on the floor. Her hand was still bleeding profusely, but she didn't care. At last, she'd achieved something of the sexual fulfillment she'd coveted for more than a quarter of a century.

Rosie grabbed a dish towel from the middle drawer and tied it around her injury, curling her hand into a fist to stem the flow, then staggered into the bedroom. The wound was beginning to ache, but not enough to make her sorry for what she'd done.

She flopped across the bed, thinking she would sleep for the rest of the afternoon, until Austin came in for his dinner, a dinner he only sometimes ate. But that wasn't the end of it. Before she could fall asleep, the cravings began again, even more intensely. It was as though after being deprived all these years, her body couldn't be sated. She had to have more.

She wiggled and squirmed on the coverlet, trying to resist the urge to dig at herself again, not wanting to do permanent damage. She yelled and pulled at her hair until finally she couldn't take it. Her need was too great.

Her gaze darted frantically about the room seeking something—*anything*—that could be used to bring on the pain that would gratify her awakening senses. She tore the doily from the nightstand next to the bed, hoping to break the lamp that sat on top of it, then spied a pair of garden shears she'd used to take cuttings from her African violets lying on the window ledge.

She crawled from the edge of the bed and wrapped her fingers around the blades, then stabbed herself in the thigh, plunging them all the way in. Her scream reverberated through the rooms of the house, bouncing off walls and knickknacks and polished tile, but it wasn't enough. The pain only increased her need for more. She had to keep jabbing and gouging, her sex shuddering and throbbing and aching with orgasm after orgasm after orgasm. . . .

❧ ❧

At some point, she passed out. When she awoke, she lay on the carpet in a stiffening puddle of blood. The sun was setting, and her body still yearned for more, like an empty well that couldn't be filled. Her skin felt cracked and hot, taut with dried sweat and her own vaginal fluid. Her head swam as she tried to sit up. After awhile, she managed to claw her way onto the bed. She saw Austin coming in through the fields, a hose slung over one shoulder, a dead chicken in the other hand.

The sight of him made her want to cry with joy, but she was also afraid. Tears misted her eyes. It was as though she was seeing him for the first time. She thought of his strong arms, the broad, flat muscles of his chest—the hoe he kept sharp enough to chop out a forest of weeds. After all this time, so many wasted days and nights, she'd finally found a way to rekindle their love into something they could both share. But Austin wouldn't be as eager as she was. He hated anything new. She'd have to convince him that this was better.

Despite the pain and the internal longings of her body, she hobbled out to the front porch and grabbed the axe from beside the wood pile. A thick coil of rope lay on the shelf above it. She draped the rope over her shoulder, then stumbled through the pantry and waited on the other side of the door, her breath coming in quick, tortuous gasps. She could hear his boots on the concrete, him leaning the hoe against the house, his calloused hands gripping the door handle. Scarcely able to contain herself, Rosie lifted the axe, turning the blunt side outward. She would take her time, determined to teach Austin all about the joys of love.

Poppy Z. Brite

❧ ❦

THE SIXTH SENTINEL

You can always expect the unexpected from **Poppy Z. Brite**. *In this story, a ghost falls in love with a woman who is willing to do and try anything in her efforts to awaken the sensations she once had and can no longer experience.*

❧ ❦

I first knew Hard Luck Rosalie Smith when she was a thin frayed rope of a child, twenty years old and already well acquainted with the solitude at the bottom of a whiskey bottle. Her hair was brittle from too many dye jobs, bright red last week, black as the grave today, purple and green for Mardi Gras. Her face was fine-boned and faintly feral, the eyes carefully lined in black, the rouged lips stretched tight over the sharp little teeth. If I had been able to touch Rosalie, her skin would have felt silky and faintly dry, her hair would have been like electricity brushing my face in the dark.

But I could not touch Rosalie, not so that she would notice. I could pass my fingers through the meat of her arm, pale as veal and packed like flaky fish flesh between her thin bones. I could wrap my hand around the smooth porcelain ball of her wrist. But as far as she was concerned, my touch went through her like so much dead air. All she could feel of me was a chill like ice crystallizing along her spine.

"Your liver has the texture of hot, wet velvet," I would tell her, reaching through her ribs to caress the tortured organ.

She'd shrug. "Another year in this town and it'll be pickled."

Rosalie came to the city of New Orleans because it was as far south as her money would take her—or so she said. She was escaping from a lover she would shudderingly refer to only as Joe Coffeespoon. The memory of his touch made her feel cold, far colder than my ectoplasmic fingers ever could, and she longed for the wet kiss of tropical nights.

She moved into an apartment in one of the oldest buildings in the French Quarter, above a "shoppe" that sold potions and philters. At first I wondered whether she would be pleased to find a ghost already residing in her cramped quarters, but as I watched her decorate the walls with shrouds of black lace and photographs of androgynous sunken-cheeked musicians who looked more dead than alive, I began to realize I could show myself safely, without threat of eviction. It is always a nuisance when someone calls in the exorcist. The priest himself is no threat, but the demons that invariably follow him are large as cats and annoying as mosquitoes. It is these, not the intonations and holy water, that drive innocent spirits away.

But Rosalie only gave me a cool appraising look, introduced herself, then asked me for my name and my tale. The name she recognized, having seen it everywhere from the pages of history books to the shingles hanging outside dubious "absinthe" houses in the French Quarter. The tale—well, there were enough tales to entertain her for a thousand nights or more. (I, the Scheherazade of Barataria Bay!) How long had I wanted to tell those tales? I had been without a friend or a lover for more years than I could recall. (The company of other local ghosts did not interest me—they seemed a morbid lot, many of them headless or drenched in gore, manifesting only occasionally to point skeletal fingers at loose fireplace flagstones and then vanish without a word. I had met no personalities of substance, and certainly none with a history as exotic as mine.)

So I was glad for the company of Rosalie. As more old buildings are demolished I must constantly shift about the city, trying to find places where I resided in life, places where a shred of my soul remains to anchor me. There are still overgrown bayou islands and remote Mississippi coves I visit often, but to give up the drunken carnival of New Orleans, to forsake human companionship (witting or otherwise) would be to fully accept my death. Nearly two hundred years, and I still cannot do that.

"Jean," she would say to me as evening fell like a slowly drifting purple scarf over the French Quarter, as the golden flames of the streetlights flickered on, "do you like these panties with the silver bustier, Jean?" (She pronounced my name correctly, in the French manner, like John but with the soft J.) Five nights of the week Rosalie had a job stripping at a nightclub on Bourbon Street. She selected her undress from a vast armoire crammed full of the microscopic wisps of clothing she referred to as "costumes," some of which were only slightly more substantial than my own flesh. When she first told me of the job she thought I would be shocked, but I laughed. "I saw worse things in my day," I assured her, thinking of lovely, shameless octoroon girls I had known, of famous "private shows" involving poisonous serpents sent from Haiti and the oiled stone phalluses of alleged voodoo idols.

I went to see Rosalie dance two or three times. The strip club was in an old row building, the former site of a bordello I remembered well. In my day the place had been decorated entirely in scarlet silk and purple velvet; the effect was of enormous fleshy lips closing in upon you as you entered, drawing you into their dark depths. I quit visiting Rosalie at work when she said it unnerved her to suddenly catch sight of me in the hundreds of mirrors that now lined the club, a hundred spangle-fleshed Rosalies and a hundred translucent Jeans and a thousand pathetic weasel-eyed men all reflected to a point of swarming infinity far within the walls. I could see how the mirrors might make Rosalie nervous, but I believe she did not like me looking at the other dancers either, though she was the prettiest of a big-hipped, insipid-faced lot.

By day Rosalie wore black: lace and fishnet, leather and silk, the gaudy mourning clothes of the deather-children. I had to ask her to explain them to me, these deathers. They were children seldom older than eighteen who painted their faces stark white, rimmed their eyes with kohl, smudged their mouths black or blood-red. They made love in cemeteries, then plundered the rotting tombs for crucifixes to wear as jewelry. The music they listened to was alternately lush as a wreath of funeral roses and dark as four a.m., composed in suicidal gloom by the androgynes that decorated Rosalie's walls. I might have been able to tell these children a few things about death. Try drifting through a hundred years without a proper body, I might have said, without feet to touch the ground, without a tongue to taste wine or kiss. Then perhaps you will celebrate your life while you have it. But Rosalie would not listen to me when I got on this topic, and she never introduced me to any of her deather friends.

If she had any. I had seen other such children roaming the French Quarter after dark, but never in Rosalie's company. Often as not she would sit in her room and drink whiskey on her nights off, tipping inches of liquid amber fire over crackling ice cubes and polishing it off again, again, again. She never had a lover that I knew of, aside from the dreaded Coffeespoon, who it seemed had been quite wealthy by Rosalie's standards. Her customers at the club offered her ludicrous sums if she would only grant them one night of pleasure more exotic than their toadlike minds could imagine. A few might really have been able to pay such fortunes, but Rosalie ignored their tumescent pleading. She seemed not so much opposed to the idea of sex for money as simply uninterested in sex at all.

When she told me of the propositions she received, I thought of the many things I had buried in the earth during my days upon it. Treasure: hard money and jewels, the riches of the robbery that was my bread and butter, the spoils of the murder that was my wine. There were still caches that no one had found and no one ever would. Any one of them would have been worth ten times the amounts these men offered.

Many times I tried to tell Rosalie where these caches were, but unlike some of her kind, she thought buried things should stay buried. She claimed that the thought of the treasure hidden under mud, stone, or brick, with people walking near it and sometimes right over it each day, amused her more than the thought of digging it up and spending it.

I never believed her. She would not let me see her eyes when she said these things. Her voice trembled when she spoke of the deathers who pursued grave-robbing as a sport. ("They pried up a granite slab that weighed fifty pounds," she told me once, incredulously. "How could they bear to lift it off, in the dark, not knowing what might come out at them?") There was a skeleton in a glass-topped coffin downstairs, in the voodoo shoppe, and Rosalie hardly liked to enter the shoppe because of it—I had seen her glancing out of the corner of her eye, as if the sad little bones simultaneously intrigued and appalled her.

It was some obsessive fear of hers, I realized. Rosalie shied away from all talk of dead things, of things buried, of digging in the ground. When I told her my tales she made me skip over the parts where treasures or bodies were buried; she would not let me describe the fetor of the nighttime swamp, the faint flickering lights of Saint Elmo's fire, the deep sucking sound the mud made when a shovel was thrust into it. She would allow me no descriptions of burials at sea or shallow bayou graves. She covered her ears when I told her of a rascal whose corpse I hung from the knotted black bough of a hundred-year-old oak. It was a remarkable thing, too—when I rode past the remote spot a year later, his perfect skeleton still hung there, woven together by strands of gray Spanish moss. It wound around his long bones and cascaded from the empty sockets of his eyes, it forced his jaws open and dangled from his chin like a long gray beard—but Rosalie did not want to hear about it.

When I confronted her with her own dread, she refused to own up to it. "Whoever said graveyards were romantic?" she demanded. "Whoever said I had to go digging up bones just because I lust after Venal St. Claire?" (Venal St. Claire was a musician, one of the stick-thin, mourning-shrouded beauties that adorned the walls of Rosalie's room. I saw no evidence that she lusted after him or anyone else.) "I just wear black so that all my clothes will match," she told me solemnly, as if she expected me to believe it. "So I won't have to think about what to put on when I get up in the morning."

"But you *don't* get up in the morning."

"In the evening, then. *You* know what I mean." She tipped her head back and tongued the last drop of whiskey out of her glass. It was the most erotic thing I had ever seen her do. I ran my finger in among the smooth folds of her intestines. A momentary look of discomfort crossed her face, as if she had suffered a gas pain—attributable to the rotgut whiskey, no doubt. But she would not pursue the subject further.

So I watched her drink until she passed out, her brittle hair fanned across her pillow, the corner of her mouth drooling a tiny thread of spit onto her black silk coverlet. Then I went into her head. This was not a thing I liked to do often—on occasion I had noticed her looking askance at me the morning after, as if she remembered seeing me in her dreams and wondered how I had got there. If I could persuade Rosalie to dig up one cache of loot—just one—our troubles would end. She would never have to work again, and I could have her with me all the time. But first I had to find her fear. Until I knew what it was, and could figure out how to charm my way around it, my treasures were going to stay buried in black bayou mud.

So within moments I was sunk deep in the spongy tissue of Rosalie's brain, sifting through her childhood memories as if they were gold coins I had just lifted off a Spanish galleon. I thought I could smell the whiskey that clouded her dreams, a stinging mist.

I found it more quickly than I expected to. I had reminded Rosalie of her fear, and now—because she would not let her conscious mind remember—her unconscious mind was dreaming of it. For an instant I teetered on the edge of wakefulness; I was dimly aware of the room around me, the heavy furniture and flocked black walls. Then it all swam away as I fell headlong into Rosalie's childhood dream.

A South Louisiana village, built at the confluence of a hundred streams and riverlets. Streets of dirt and crushed oyster-shells, houses built on pilings to keep the water from lapping up onto the neat, brightly painted porches. Shrimp nets draped over railings, stiffening with salt, at some houses; crab traps stacked up to the roof at others. Cajun country.

(Hard Luck Rosalie a Cajun girl, she who claimed she had never set foot in Louisiana before! *Mon petit chou!* "Smith" indeed!)

On one porch a young girl dressed in a T-shirt and a home-sewn skirt of fresh calico perches on a case of empty beer bottles. The tender points of her breasts can be seen through the thin fabric of the T-shirt. A medallion gleams at the hollow of her throat, a tiny saint frozen in silver. She is perhaps twelve. It can only be her mama beside her, a large regal-faced woman with a crown of teased and fluffed black hair. The mama is peeling crawfish. She saves the heads in a coffee can and throws the other pickings to some speckled chickens scratching in the part of the dirt yard that is not flooded. The water is as high as Mama has ever seen it.

The young girl has a can of Coca Cola, but she hasn't drunk much of it. She is worried about something: it can be seen in the slump of her shoulders, in the sprawl of her thin legs beneath the calico skirt. Several times her eyes shimmer with tears she is just able to control. When she looks up, it becomes clear that she is older than she appeared at first, thirteen or fourteen. An air of naïvéte, an awkwardness of limb and gesture, makes her seem younger. She fidgets and at last says, "Mama?"

"What is it, Rosie?" The mother's voice seems a beat too slow; it catches in her throat and drags itself reluctantly out past her lips.

"Mama—is Theophile still under the ground?"

(There is a gap in the dream here, or rather in my awareness of it. I do not know who Theophile is—a childhood friend perhaps. More likely a brother; in a Cajun family there is no such thing as an only child. The question disturbs me, and I feel Rosalie slipping from me momentarily. Then the dream continues, inexorable, and I am pulled back in.)

Mama struggles to remain calm. Her shoulders bow and her heavy breasts sag against her belly. The stoic expression on her face crumbles a little. "No, Rosie," she says at last. "Theophile's grave is empty. He's gone up to Heaven, him."

"Then he wouldn't be there if I looked?"

(All at once I am able to recognize my Rosalie in the face of this blossoming girl. The intelligent dark eyes, the quick mind behind them undulled by whiskey and time.)

Mama is silent, searching for an answer that will both satisfy and comfort. But a bayou storm has been blowing up, and it arrives suddenly, as they will: thunder rolls across the sky, the air is suddenly alive with invisible sparks. Then the rain comes down in a solid torrent. The speckled chickens scramble under the porch, complaining. Within seconds the yard in front of the house is a sea of mud. It has rained like this every day for a month. It is the wettest spring anyone has ever seen in this part of the bayou.

"You ain't goin' anywhere in this flood," Mama says. The relief is evident in her voice. She shoos the girl inside and hurries around the house to take washing off the line, though the faded cotton dresses and patched denim trousers are already soaked through.

Inside the warm little house, Rosalie sits at the kitchen window watching rain hammer down on the bayou, and she wonders.

The storm lasts all night. Lying in her bed, Rosalie hears the rain on the roof; she hears branches creaking and lashing in the wind. But she is used to thunderstorms, and she pays no attention to this one. She is thinking of a shed in the side yard, where her father's old crab traps and tools are kept. She knows there is a shovel in there. She knows where the key is.

The storm ends an hour before dawn, and she is ready.

It is her own death she is worried about, of course, not that of Theophile (whoever he may be). She is at the age where

her curiosity about the weakness of the flesh outweighs her fear
of it. She thinks of him under the ground and she has to know
whether he is really there. Has he ascended to Heaven or is he
still in his grave, rotting? Whatever she finds, it cannot be worse
than the thing she has imagined.

(So I think at the time.)

Rosalie is not feeling entirely sane as she eases out of the
silent house, filches her father's shovel, and creeps through
the dark village to the graveyard. She likes to go barefoot, and
the soles of her feet are hard enough to walk over the broken
edges of the glittering wet oystershells, but she knows you
have to wear shoes after a heavy rain or worms might eat their
way into your feet. So she slogs through the mud in her soaked
sneakers, refusing to think about what she is going to do.

It is still too dark to see, but Rosalie knows her way by heart
through these village streets. Soon her hand finds the rusty iron
gate of the graveyard, and it ratchets open at her touch. She
winces at the harsh sound in the predawn silence, but there is
no one around to hear.

At least, no one who *can* hear.

The crude silhouettes of headstones stab into the inky sky.
Few families in the village can afford a carved marker; they lash
two sticks together in the shape of a rough cross, or they hew
their own stone out of granite if they can get a piece. Rosalie
feels her way through a forest of jagged, irregular memorials to
the dead. She knows some of them are only hand-lettered oak
boards wedged into the ground. The shadows at the base of
each marker are wet, shimmering. Foul mud sucks at her feet.
She tells herself the smell is only stagnant water. In places
the ground feels slick and lumpy; she cannot see what she is
stepping on.

But when she comes near the stone she seeks, she can see it.
For it is the finest stone in the graveyard, carved of moon-pale
marble that seems to pull all light into its milky depths. His
family had it made in New Orleans, spending what was probably their life's savings. The chiseled letters are as concise as
razor cuts. Rosalie cannot see them, but she knows their every

crevice and shadow. Only his name, stark and cold; no dates, no inscriptions, as if the family's grief was so great that they could not bear to say anything about him. Just inscribe it with his name and leave him there.

The plot of earth at the base of the stone is not visible, but she knows it all too well, a barren, muddy rectangle. There has been no time for grass or weeds to grow upon it; he has only been buried a fortnight, and the few sprouts that tried to come up have been beaten back down by the rain. But can he really be under there, shut up in a box, his lithe body bloating and bursting, his wonderful face and hands beginning to decay?

Rosalie steps forward, hand extended to touch the letters of his name: THEOPHILE THIBODEAUX. As she thinks—or dreams—the name, her fingers poised to trace its marble contours, an image fills her head, a jumble of sensations intense and erotic. A boy older than Rosalie, perhaps seventeen: a sharp pale face, too thin to be called handsome, but surely compelling; a curtain of long sleek black hair half-hiding eyes of fierce, burning azure. Theophile!

(All at once it is as if Rosalie's consciousness has merged completely with mine. My heart twists with a young girl's love and lust for this spitfire Cajun boy. I am dimly aware of Rosalie's drunken twenty-year-old body asleep on her bed, her feminine viscera twitching at the memory of him. O, how he touched her—O, how he tasted her!

She had known it was wrong in the eyes of God. Her mama had raised her to be a good girl. But the evenings she had spent with Theophile after dances and church socials, sitting on an empty dock with his arm around her shoulders, leaning into the warm hollow of his chest—that could not be wrong. After a week of knowing her he had begun to show her the things he wrote on his ink-blackened relic of an Olympia typewriter, poems and stories, songs of the swamp. And that could not be wrong.

And the night they had sneaked out of their houses to meet, the night in the empty boathouse near Theophile's home—that could not be wrong either. They had begun only kissing, but

the kisses grew too hot, too wild—Rosalie felt her insides boiling. Theophile answered her heat with his own. She felt him
lifting the hem of her skirt and—carefully, almost reverently—
sliding off her cotton panties. Then he was stroking the dark
down between her legs, teasing her with the very tips of his
fingers, rubbing faster and deeper until she felt like a blossom
about to burst with sweet nectar. Then he parted her legs wider
and bent to kiss her there as tenderly as he had kissed her
mouth. His tongue was soft yet rough, like a soapy washcloth,
and Rosalie had thought her young body would die with the
pleasure of it. Then, slowly, Theophile was easing himself into
her, and yes, she wanted him there, and yes, she was clutching
at his back, pulling him farther in, refusing to heed the sharp
pain of first entry. He rested inside her, barely moving; he
lowered his head to kiss her sore developing nipples, and Rosalie felt the power of all womanhood shudder through her. This
could not be wrong.)

With the memories fixed firmly in her mind she takes another
step toward his headstone. The ground crumbles away beneath
her feet, and she falls headlong into her lover's grave.

The shovel whacks her across the spine. The rotten smell
billows around her, heavy and ripe: spoiling meat, rancid fat, a
sweetish-sickly odor. The fall stuns her. She struggles in the
gritty muck, spits it out of her mouth.

Then the first pale light of dawn breaks across the sky, and
Rosalie stares into the ruined face of Theophile.

(Now her memories flooded over me like the tide. Some time
after they had started meeting in the boathouse she began to
feel sick all the time; the heat made her listless. Her monthly
blood, which had been coming for only a year, stopped. Mama
took her into the next town to see a doctor, and he confirmed
what Rosalie had already dreaded: she was going to have Theophile's baby.

Her papa was not a hard man, nor cruel. But he had been
raised in the bosom of the Church, and he had learned to
measure his own worth by the honor of his family. Theophile
never knew his Rosalie was pregnant. Rosalie's father waited for

him in the boathouse one night. He stepped in holding a new sheaf of poems, and Papa's deer shot caught him across the chest and belly, a hundred tiny black eyes weeping red tears.

Papa was locked up in the county jail now and Mama said that soon he would go someplace even worse, someplace where they could never see him again. Mama said it wasn't Rosalie's fault, but Rosalie could see in her eyes that it was.)

It has been the wettest spring anyone can remember, a month of steady rains. The water table in Louisiana bayou country is already so high that a hole will begin to draw water at a depth of two feet or less. All this spring the table has risen steadily, soaking the ground, drowning grass and flowers, making a morass of the sweet swamp earth. Cattails have sprung up near at the edge of the graveyard. But the storm last night pushed the groundwater to saturation point and beyond. The wealthy folk of New Orleans bury their dead in vaults above ground to protect them from this very danger. But no one here can afford a marble vault, or even a brick one.

And the village graveyard has flooded at last.

Some of the things that have floated to the surface are little more than bone. Others are swollen to three or four times their size, gassy mounds of decomposed flesh rising like islands from the mud; some of these have silk flower petals stuck to them like obscene decorations. Flies rise lazily, then descend again in glittering, circling clouds. Here are mired the warped boards of coffins split open by the water's relentless pull. There floats the plaster figurine of a saint, his face and the color of his robes washed away by rain. Yawning eyeless faces thrust out of stagnant pools, seeming to gasp for breath. Rotting hands unfold like blighted tiger lilies. Every drop of water, every inch of earth in the graveyard is foul with the effluvium of the dead.

But Rosalie can only see the face thrust into hers, the body crushed beneath her own. Theophile's eyes have fallen back into their sockets and his mouth is open; his tongue is gone. She sees thin white worms teeming in the passage of his throat. His nostrils are widening black holes beginning to encroach upon the greenish flesh of his cheeks. His sleek hair is almost gone; the few strands left are thin and scummy, nibbled by waterbugs. (Sitting on the dock, Rosalie and Theophile used to spit into the water and watch the shiny black beetles swarm around the white gobs; Theophile had told her they would eat hair and toenails too.) In places she can see the glistening dome of his skull. *The skull behind the dear face; the skull that cradled the thoughts and dreams ...*

She thinks of the shovel she brought and wonders what she meant to do with it. Did she *want* to see Theophile like this? Or had she really expected to find his grave empty, his fine young body gone fresh and whole to God?

No. She had only wanted to know where he was. Because she had nothing left of him—his family would give her no poems, no lock of hair. And now she had even lost his seed.

(The dogs ran Papa to earth in the swamp where he had hidden and the men dragged him off to jail. As they led him toward the police car, Theophile's mother ran up to him and spat in his face. Papa was handcuffed and could not wipe himself; he only stood there with the sour spit of sorrow running down his cheeks, and his eyes looked confused, as if he was unsure just what he had done.

Mama made Rosalie sleep in bed with her that night. But when Rosalie woke up the next morning Mama was gone; there was only a note saying she would be back before sundown. Sure enough, she straggled in with the afternoon's last light. She had spent the whole day in the swamp. Her face was scratched and sweaty, the cuffs of her jeans caked with mud.

Mama had brought a basketful of herbs. She didn't fix dinner, but instead spent the evening boiling the plants down to a thin syrup. They exuded a bitter, stinging scent as they cooked. The potion sat cooling until the next night. Then Mama made Rosalie drink it all down.

It was the worst pain she had ever felt. She thought her intestines and her womb and the bones of her pelvis were being wrung in a giant merciless fist. When the bleeding started she thought her very insides were dissolving. There were thick clots and ragged shreds of tissue in the blood.

"It won't damage you," Mama told her, "and it will be over by morning."

True to Mama's word, just before dawn Rosalie felt something solid being squeezed out of her. She knew she was losing the last of Theophile. She tried to clamp the walls of her vagina around it, to keep him inside her as long as she could. But the thing was slick and formless, and it slid easily onto the towel Mama had spread between her legs. Mama gathered the towel up quickly and would not let Rosalie see what was inside.

Rosalie heard the toilet flush once, then twice. Her womb and the muscles of her abdomen felt as if they had gone through Mama's kitchen grater. But the pain was nothing compared to the emptiness she felt in her heart.)

The sky is growing lighter, showing her more of the graveyard around her: the corpses borne on the rising water, the maggot-ridden mud. Theophile's face yawns into hers. Rosalie struggles against him and feels his sodden flesh give beneath her weight. She is beyond recognizing her love now. She is frantic; she fights him. Her hand strikes his belly and punches in up to the wrist.

Then suddenly Theophile's body opens like a flower made of carrion, and she sinks into him. Her elbows are trapped in the brittle cage of his ribs. Her face is pressed into the bitter soup of his organs. Rosalie whips her head to one side. Her face is a mark of putrescence. It is in her hair, her nostrils; it films her eyes. She is drowning in the body that once gave her sustenance. She opens her mouth to scream and feels things squirming in between her teeth.

"My *chérie* Rosalie," she hears the voice of her lover whispering. And then the rain pours down again.

◦◦❦◦◦

Unpleasant.

I tore myself screaming from Rosalie—screaming silently, unwilling to wake her. In that instant I was afraid of her for what she had gone through; I dreaded to see her eyes snap open like a doll's, meeting me full in the face.

But Rosalie was only sleeping a troubled slumber. She muttered fitful disjointed words; there was a cold sheen of sweat on her brow; she exuded a flowery, powerful smell of sex. I hovered at the edge of the bed and studied her ringed hands clenched into small fists, her darting, jumping eyelids still stained with yesterday's makeup. I could only imagine the ensuing years and torments that had brought that little girl to this night, to this room. That had made her want to wear the false trappings of death, after having wallowed in the truth of it.

But I *knew* how difficult it would be to talk these memories out of her. There could be no consolation and no compensation for a past so cruel. No treasure, no matter how valuable, could matter in the face of such lurid terror.

So I assure you that the thing I did next was done out of pure mercy—*not* a desire for personal gain, or control over Rosalie. I had never done such a thing to her before. She was my friend; I wished to deliver her from the poison of her memories. It was as simple as that.

I gathered up my courage and I went back into Rosalie's head. Back in through her eyes and the whorled tunnels of her ears, back into the spongy electric forest of her brain.

I cannot be more scientific than this: I found the connections that made the memory. I searched out the nerves and subtle acids that composed the dream, the morsels of Rosalie's brain that still held a residue of Theophile, the cells that were blighted by his death.

And I erased it all.

I pitied Theophile. Truly I did. There is no existence more lonely than death, especially a death where no one is left to mourn you.

But Rosalie belonged to me now.

❧ ❧

I had her rent a boat.

It was easy for her to learn how to drive it: boating is in the Cajun blood. We made an exploratory jaunt or two down through Barataria—where two tiny hamlets, much like Rosalie's home village, both bore my name—and I regaled a fascinated Rosalie with tales of burials at sea, of shallow bayou graves, of a rascal whose empty eye sockets dripped with Spanish moss.

When I judged her ready, I guided her to a spot I remembered well, a clearing where five enormous oaks grew from one immense, twisted trunk. The five sentinels, we called them in my day. The wind soughed in the upper branches. The swamp around us was hushed, expectant.

After an hour of digging, Rosalie's shiny new shovel unearthed the lid and upper portion of a great iron chest. Her brittle hair was stringy with sweat. Her black lace dress was caked with mud and clay. Her face had gone paler than usual with exertion; in the half-light of the swamp it was almost luminescent. She had never looked so beautiful to me as she did at that moment.

She stared at me. Her tired eyes glittered as if with fever.

"Open it," I urged.

Rosalie swung the shovel at the heart-shaped hasp of the chest and knocked it loose on the first try. Once more and it fell away in a shower of soggy rust. She glanced back at me once more—looking for what, I wonder; seeing what?—and then heaved open the heavy lid.

And the sixth sentinel sat up to greet her.

I always took an extra man along when I went into the swamp to bury treasure. One I didn't trust, or didn't need. He and my reliable henchmen would dig the hole and drag the chest to the edge of it, ready to heave in. Then I would gaze deep into the eyes of each man and ask, in a voice both quiet and compelling, "Who wishes to guard my treasure?" My men knew the routine, and were silent. The extra man—currying favor as the useless and unreliable will do—always volunteered.

Then my top lieutenant would take three steps forward and put a ball in the lowly one's brain. His corpse was laid tenderly in the chest, his blood seeping into the mounds of gold or silver or glittering jewels, and I would tuck in one of my mojo bags, the ones I had specially made in New Orleans. Then the chest was sunk in the mire of the swamp, and my man, now rendered trustworthy, was left to guard my treasure until I should need it.

I was the only one who could open those chests. The combined magic of the mojo bag and the anger of the betrayed man's spirit saw to that.

My sixth sentinel wrapped skeletal arms around Rosalie's neck and drew her down. His jaws yawned wide and I saw teeth, still hungry after two hundred years, clamp down on her throat. A mist of blood hung in the air; from the chest there was a ripping sound, then a noise of quick, choking agony. I hoped he would not make it too painful for her. After all, she was the woman I had chosen to spend eternity with.

I had told Rosalie that she would never again have to wriggle out of flimsy costumes under the eyes of slobbering men, and I had not lied. I had told her that she would never have to worry about money any more, and I had not lied. What I had neglected to tell her was that I did not wish to share my treasures—I only wanted her dead, my Hard Luck Rosalie, free from this world that pained her so, free to wander with me through the unspoiled swamps and bayous, through the ancient buildings of a city mired in time.

Soon Rosalie's spirit left her body and flew to me. It had nowhere else to go. I felt her struggling furiously against my love, but she would give in soon. I had no shortage of time to convince her.

I slipped my arm around Rosalie's neck and planted a kiss on her ectoplasmic lips. Then I clasped her wisp of a hand in mine, and we disappeared together.

Marina Fitch

༄ ঌ

THE BANKS OF
THE RIVER

Sweet, gentle, **Marina Fitch** *writes with the voice of a tigress. This is a lunar period story. A woman needs sex once a month or she will grow old and crippled. This PMS story is a truly noir piece, with a theme that is small but universal. It is designed to make men wonder. . . .*

༄ ঌ

"That one," Izzy said, pointing across the bar.

Diana leaned to the side, peering between the mock Tudor posts of the Sack and Crown. "The shaggy one with the goatee?"

Izzy smiled. "That's the one."

Diana tossed her blonde hair over her shoulder. It framed her youthful face in lusterless waves, already dulled by the waning moon. "Geez, Izzy," she said. "You're such a cultural illiterate! That's Dev Fells, the lead singer for Chill Factor."

Izzy sat up. "You're kidding—Dev Fells?"

"The very same." Diana sipped her mai tai. "You sure know how to pick 'em. According to the tabloids this one's half dead."

A thrill fanned between Izzy's legs, unfolding through her

entire body. A half-dead rock star—a half-dead *influential* rock star . . . and she'd take him with the blood and the moon. She watched him rest his dark head against the wall and gaze dreamily across the room. He caressed his beer glass—gently, tenderly. To have those sensitive hands shaping the contours of her breasts just before she released the blood—

Diana folded her hand over Izzy's. "Isadora, tomorrow's the new moon. You remember what happened with . . . what was his name, Vince? You're already aging with it—we all are. Look at me." She brushed the faint laugh lines around her own eyes with her fingers, then she brushed Izzy's. "Those lines weren't there this morning."

Izzy's stomach tightened. "He'll come."

Diana shook her head. "I've read about him. Money, alcohol, drugs, suicide attempts—you can't reach him in time, not by the new moon. Get someone more receptive—"

"Someone easy, like Mickey?" Izzy said. She tilted her chin. "Someone I can take again and again who doesn't need the blood?"

Diana licked the rim of her glass. Her eyes flashed. "At least I don't end up writhing in agony because I held out for someone impossible."

A spasm of remembered pain shuddered through Izzy. She dry swallowed. That one moon when she'd chosen sad, isolated Vince, and been unable to take him, been unable to shed the blood and rejuvenate herself. . . . She forced the memory aside. "The rewards are much greater," she said.

Diana rolled her eyes. "So is the penalty if you fail. If you want him, you'd better hurry. He's getting up."

Izzy swung quickly from the stool. Dev Fells shuffled a few steps, hand trailing along the nearest table top, then sank into a chair. He leaned forward, resting his head in his hands.

Izzy wove between the squat wooden tables, sawdust whispering beneath her feet. "Hey," she said, crouching beside him. "You all right?"

He sat up, his gray eyes struggling to focus. Izzy's heart

caught. What had made her think he was sensitive? The way he'd stroked his glass?

A slash of memory: *Vince sneered at her. "Why would I want to do it with an old cow like you?"* Izzy's stomach clenched around phantom pain.

Dev's gaze centered on her. "Sorry. What did you say?"

"Are you all right?" Izzy repeated.

He shrugged. "A little fucked up. Nothing new."

Izzy pulled up a chair and sat beside him. "Why?"

Dev tilted his head to one side. "Why am I fucked up or why is this nothing new? I'm fucked up 'cause I'm on tranks. It's nothing new 'cause I do it every night."

Izzy leaned a little closer, resting her hand on his knee. "Why?"

He looked away. "I like it. It's fun."

"Yeah, right." Izzy let her fingers stray along Dev's thigh. "You do it because you hurt."

He swung to look at her, startled. Wariness narrowed his eyes. "Yeah, well. So what are you, a shrink? The guys send you here to get me back in the studio?"

Izzy's hand stopped beside the bulge of his penis. She brushed the tip lightly. A thrill bubbled along her spine. "The moon sent me," she said a little breathlessly. "To fill you with light."

He stared at her as if trying to see beyond her wide-set blue eyes and honey-brown hair. "I like that," he said.

Izzy smiled. "A gift."

He grinned crookedly. "Thanks. Listen, sorry if I was being a jerk. It's just . . . it's been a bad night. I'm Dev."

"Izzy—Isadora." She touched his collar bone, letting her fingers trickle down his chest. She pressed her thighs together. "I think it's a very good night."

"It is now," Dev said, touching her cheek.

She turned into his hand, kissing his fingers. "But earlier?"

He traced her lips. "The guys—I'm in a band. The guys want to record."

She licked her fingers. They tasted like salt and beer. "And?"

"I can't," he said softly. "It's not there. Music just hurts. Like everything else."

Izzy let her hand stray along his thigh again. "Like this?"

He moaned softly. "No, not like this—oh, God."

His whole body shuddered with a gag. Sweeping her arm away, he bolted. He pinballed across the room, bouncing from one body to the next until he reached the door.

Izzy counted to ten, then got to her feet. Allow him some dignity. She walked to the door and pulled it open. A gust of cool, night air soothed her flushed cheeks. She scanned the crowded parking lot. Across the way, near the exit, Dev staggered from a crouch. Crumpling, he retched once more, then lurched toward the street. He stumbled into the path of an oncoming car. Straightening to his full height, he planted his feet firmly, squaring his shoulders.

Izzy's heart stopped.

So did the car, amid a blare of horns. "Hey, asshole!" the driver yelled. "You got a death wish or something? Go find someone else to do you the honors, huh?"

Dev flipped off the driver, then glanced back at the Sack and Crown. He hesitated, staring at Izzy, before hurrying away.

She watched him disappear, then looked up at the slivered moon. Even as it dwindled and shrank in the night sky, it swelled inside her, tender and throbbing and ripe. The searing heat in her blood, the need, would turn on her soon, crippling her.

One more night. She went back inside.

Diana met her at the door. "Isadora, please," she said, following Izzy to the bar. "Remember what happened that other time. Don't wait too long. If Cyndi and Phoebe and I hadn't found you . . . Izzy, find someone else. *Please.*"

Vince tucked his limp penis beneath his rumpled shirt and backed away from the bed. "You think I'm that desperate, I'd go for a wreck like you? You're one sick bitch."

Izzy closed her eyes and squeezed her temples. "He's not like Vince," she said. "He'll be back."

"Right," Diana muttered.

≈§ §≈

The next evening, just before ten, Dev walked into the Sack and Crown. After surveying the people hunched over the tables, he scanned the bar. A smile touched his lips when he saw Izzy.

She nudged Diana. "There," she said. "I told you."

The lines around Diana's eyes deepened as she narrowed her eyes. "Izzy, I hope you know what you're doing."

"Trust me, Diana," Izzy said, but Diana had already melted into the crowd and disappeared.

Dev walked over and leaned on Diana's stool. "Hi. Hope I didn't' scare your friend away."

Izzy smiled. His eyes sparkled, piercingly bright, as if he'd come to some decision. . . .

"No," Izzy said. "She went to find her, uh . . . boyfriend. Have a seat. I'll buy you a drink."

"No, thanks," he said. He shifted his weight from one leg to the other. "I can't stay. I just wanted to apologize for last night. Izzy, right?"

"Izzy," she said. The need rose in her, sweeping her in its current. She played with the belt loop on his hip. "There's nothing to apologize for, Dev. Sure you can't stay?"

"I can't." He traced her forearm with his fingers. "I need to see some people, tie up a few loose ends."

Izzy caressed his hip. "Am I a loose end?"

"In a way, I wish you were," Dev said. Yesterday's angry sadness seeped across his face. Its stain exposed the fragility of his excitement.

Fear bristled along Izzy's spine.

"Anyway, I'm sorry for being such a jerk," Dev said. "Running out like that." The crooked smile returned. So did that false calm. "I just—I wanted you to know."

Izzy's heart skipped a beat. He'd made a decision all right. He was planning to kill himself, probably tonight. The weird calm, the eerie brightness. The elation. . . .

If she took him tonight, how sweet it would be, how full and perfect. Excitement jolted through her, sizzling through her veins. She chafed her legs against the sudden dampness.

She smiled and leaned closer. Her fingers teased along the inside of his leg. "Let me buy you a drink," she said. "Just one."

Dev bit his lower lip. "I don't—"

"Ernie," she called to the bartender. "Two Long Island iced teas."

Dev frowned slightly, then smiled, slipping his hand in hers. "Sure. Why not?"

❧ ❧

They retreated to a table tucked neatly behind a post. Before they'd finished their teas, a server asked if they wanted another round. At that same moment, Izzy spotted Diana and Mickey hurrying out of the Sack and Crown, Diana's eyes bright with hunger, her body shimmying against Mickey's as he tried to wrestle the door open without removing his arm from her waist. Izzy ordered a second round, still gazing at Diana's moist lips.

"One more, then I really have to go," Dev said.

Izzy started. She turned and smiled at him. "Sure."

Diana's need fed Izzy's, pulsing harder and faster from her clitoris to her temples. She nourished it with Dev, her gaze feasting on the contours of his body: slight, but not thin, with a certain gangly, foolish quality he hadn't managed to outgrow. Her swollen breasts tingled, her nipples erect and hard. How she would love to free his mouth from its muzzle of downy hair, so like an adolescent's. Or maybe just pretend he *was* an adolescent. How long had it had been since she'd had a boy? Decades . . . centuries? She crossed her legs, trying to contain the throbbing dampness.

She focused on that mouth: soft, pliant lips, strong, white teeth. He talked and she nodded, consumed with need, fascinated by his perfection: a childhood watered by blows, an adolescence parched by alienation. An adulthood pruned by realizations. He needed her, needed her gift.

Her labia ached and trembled with need of him and of the blood. The new moon danced in her veins, faster, faster. If only she could do it here—

One night left.

Tonight.

She switched her untouched second iced tea for his empty glass. Dev didn't notice. He drank half of it in two quick gulps. Izzy smiled.

He leaned closer. His fingers, thick with drink, traced the inside of her arm, strayed along the rise of her breast. Clumsy, teasing. A moan vibrated through Izzy, from the growing ache in her abdomen to her feverish lips. Let him finish the thought, then get him home. If she could just do it here—

"So music, that was it," Dev said, his voice distant and quiet. "It was my escape from my dad. And it was the way I was going to change things, make people realize they had to stop hurting each other. It was my life. But I—I don't know. Things got kind of successful and I just . . . the passion was gone. I mean, what's life without passion? What can you give to the world? Nothing. Not a damn thing."

Panic braided with Izzy's desire and need. *Vince's voice settled on her with a detached calm. "But it's true, Izzy. I have nothing to offer the world. What right do I have to live and take up space?"*

Izzy pressed herself closer to Dev, nesting her hand in his lap. His penis surged under her fingers, forcing her hand to ride its swell. "But you do have passion," she said. "Maybe you can't help people with your music anymore, but there are other ways you can give. Trust yourself, Dev."

Dev crumpled, his gaze hardening and turning inward. He leaned his forehead on her shoulder, his breath warming the hollow of her throat. A thrill erased some of her waxing pain. She bent to kiss the lovely curve of his neck—

He pulled away. "Trust myself," he muttered. "How can I expect to give anything to total strangers when I fuck up the people I care about? Shit, after what I did to Andy. . . ."

Izzy wet her lips. "Who's Andy?"

Dev rose suddenly. He swayed, pressing the heels of his palms to his eyes. "Shit," he muttered. "What the fuck am I doing here? I'm sorry. I'm sorry. . . ."

He bolted toward the door.

Izzy lunged after him. In front of her, a burly woman bent over to pick something up, her bottom rising like a railroad crossing arm. Izzy backed up and darted around a table groaning under three six-packs' worth of beer bottles. Squeezing between the backs of two chairs, she wriggled free of the chaos and scrambled to the door.

Flinging it open, she ran out into the parking lot. A couple wrestled in an embrace beside a Colt. Three cars down, two women sat on the hood of a Honda while a third dug through her purse for her keys.

No Dev.

Izzy glanced at the shadowed moon.

New moon. Tonight.

As if the ache filtering through her body like moonlight hadn't warned her. Izzy cradled her pulsing abdomen.

Steeling herself, she darted across the parking lot toward the street Dev had lurched down the night before. At the corner, she stopped. The slap of feet echoed to her left. Peering into the dark, Izzy caught a glimpse of Dev. She followed.

≈§ §≈

Izzy waited on the townhouse steps, breathing in the sweet, dizzying scent of jasmine. Lights flickered on inside the townhouse, traveling from the bottom floor to the top by way of diamond-paned windows. Izzy waited till Dev's shadow darkened the highest window, then raised her hand to knock. Voices erupted upstairs.

Angry voices. Izzy reached for the knob and twisted. It sprang open into a tiny entry complete with two doors and a staircase that seemed to double back on itself before reaching the top floor. Izzy stepped inside.

"Don't you talk to me like that!" a woman shouted.

Dev mumbled something in response. Izzy backed slowly toward the door.

"I don't care if it is your house," the woman said. "Put that down—now!"

A crash echoed in the stairwell, chips of ceramic bouncing down the steps like a small rock slide. Taking the steps two at a time, Izzy sprinted upstairs.

The stairs emptied into a large room scantily furnished with a pale blue sofa, a drawing table, a wall of built-in shelves, a guitar and a door, slightly ajar, leading off to the left. The skeleton of a lamp lay on the floor, Dev sprawled beside it, unconscious, his foot tangled in the lamp's cord. From under the sofa peeked the butt of a rifle.

Izzy knelt beside Dev, feeling along his neck for a pulse. It drummed under her fingers. She let out a sigh of relief. He could still be hers—

The small door slammed open. "Damn it, Dev, what the hell is wrong with—hey! Who are you? How'd you get in here?"

Izzy turned. A dark-haired woman stood by the door, a glass of water in one hand and two aspirin in the other. A yellowed bruise marred the woman's flawless cream skin. "I said," the woman repeated slowly, fiercely, "who are you?"

Izzy rose. "I'm sorry, I—I met him at the Sack and Crown and I was worried about him. He seemed suicidal."

The dark-haired woman's shoulders sagged. "So what else is new?" she said. "Like he hasn't tried before."

Izzy's throat tightened. "How many times?"

"Three. Pills, pills, and gas," the woman said, sitting next to Dev. She set the glass and the aspirin on the carpet, then stroked his hair. "Was I glad when I found out this place was all electric. Not like it matters if he gets it into his head, but hey. Why give him ideas?"

Izzy knelt again. She held out her hand. "I'm Izzy."

The woman shook her head. "Andy."

Izzy blinked. "Do you . . . live with him?"

"Not for years," Andy said. She laughed. "Don't worry, he's up for grabs. Not like he's prime right now." She ruffled his hair. "Dev and I are just friends."

"I don't think he should be alone tonight."

"Neither do I," Andy said, drawing her knees up to her chin. "He told me he was coming by at eleven—something about loose ends. When he didn't show up, I came over here. He was with you?"

Izzy combed Dev's hair with her fingers. "Yes. I kept plying him with drinks. I was afraid that once he left. . . ."

Andy murmured.

Izzy cleared her throat. "That bruise on your cheek. Did Dev . . . ?"

Andy touched the yellow mark. "It was an accident. No, really, I mean it. I'm not into denial and all that shit. He was helping me fix my car. I leaned over to see what he was doing and he didn't know I was there. Caught me with his elbow. Knocked me flat."

Andy sniffed. "He was sure he'd killed me. Started shaking and going on about becoming his father." She nudged him with her foot. "Jerk. Gotta take the blame for everything."

Izzy shook her head. "Someone needs to stay with him. I'd be happy—"

"He's not your problem," Andy said. She smiled wryly. "Yet. You'll have plenty of opportunities to baby-sit, believe me. You'll be glad you missed out on one of 'em." She lifted the hair from Dev's forehead and studied his face. "Come back tomorrow, around noon. He might even be lucid then."

Izzy's heart sunk. Daytime. . . . "I—I can't. I—"

Andy shrugged. "So come in the afternoon. Whenever. I'll probably stick around till two or three."

A shifting dryness churned Izzy's stomach. There was no way around Andy. Izzy looked out the picture window. Stars peeked between the canyon of townhouses. She should try to find someone else—quickly and indiscriminately. But Dev was so perfect. Without her, he would become just another statistic.

Like Vince. . . .

She turned to Andy. One last try—"You're sure?"

Andy nodded.

Izzy sighed. She rose to her feet and walked to the sofa. "Well, let me take the gun, anyway."

Andy's eyes opened wide. "The gun? What gun—shit! Damn it, Dev! What am I going to do with you?"

Let *me* have him, Izzy thought.

"Fucking shit!" Andy's face purpled around the bruise. "Get it out of here. I don't care what you do with it, just get it out of here!"

Izzy pulled the rifle out from under the sofa. She checked the safety, then tucked the gun under her arm.

"Get it out of here, now!" Andy shouted.

Dev shuffled softly. Izzy's body clenched around a sharp pang. She hurried down the stairs.

On her way to the Sack and Crown, she removed the bullets, then shoved the rifle down a storm drain. She wasn't sure what else to do with it.

Izzy wrapped her hands around the cold, tall glass. She winced as tributaries of pain flowed from her abdomen. The torment ebbed for a brief second. She uncurled and surveyed the bar. Only a few people slumped over the short tables and most of those gazed bleary-eyed into empty glasses. Most had also coupled up. Her stomach clenched against another rush of pain. She glanced at the clock. Ten to two.

It took three days to peel away Vince's vulnerability—laughing at his jokes, stroking his fragile ego—until he came with her. By then her need was beyond the new moon, crippling her as it waxed inside her along with the faint white crescent slicing the night. Her hands, her whole body curved like cat's claws around the agony spilling from her abdomen to saturate her every nerve.

Izzy raised the glass to her lips, hands trembling, and sipped the Bloody Mary. Her cheekbones burned. She folded in on herself, trying to keep the pain from spreading. "Not again," she whispered to her drink. "I'd rather die."

Vince unbuttoned her blouse reverently. She moaned, fighting each spasm as tides of pain swept over her. She tried to stanch the hurt with her rising excitement. The release, the blood, any minute—any minute—

Then Vince looked at her: at her face lined with tension, at her body twisted and swollen with the moon. "Why would I want to do it with an old cow like you?" he said. "You think I'm that desperate, I'd go for a wreck like you? You're one sick bitch."

Later she found him at home. He had locked himself in the bathroom and slit his wrists, releasing the blood.

The wrong blood.

Izzy sat up.

A man in a blue sport coat sat at a table across the room—alone. He tilted his graying, blond head against the wall, his features serene and thoughtful. One beer glass, half full, waited on the table in front of him—nothing more. Izzy hesitated, then slid to her feet. "He'll do," she murmured under her breath.

She cowered on the bed, contorted and shivering with agony, until Diana and Phoebe and Cyndi found her—well into the moon's third quarter.

Izzy stopped two tables from the man as a woman with frizzy, platinum hair lurched toward him. The woman's foot caught on a chair leg. She pitched into his lap. "I had such a good trip," she slurred, then erupted in buoyant cackles.

Phoebe found a crazed, simple man and brought him to her. Izzy howled and writhed, shredding the man's shirt and back with her nails until the need abated. Cyndi reeled the man from her grasp and tended his wounds.

A fierce, numbing exhaustion clung to Izzy for months.

The blond man smiled wearily and lifted the woman to her feet. Half-dragging, half-carrying her, he led her out of the Sack and Crown. Izzy stood very, very still, suspended by the pull of the moon.

❧ ❧

A pin-scratch of moon lined the sky.

Izzy stood outside the Sack and Crown, fingering the scarf wrapped around her head. She tugged at it so that it shadowed her face a little. The corners of her mouth twitched. How long had it been since head scarves had been fashionable, anyway? Izzy shook her head. She'd stick out like the freak she was, especially in this shapeless coat on such a warm night.

Dev would never recognize her. Izzy sniffed. "Dev's not here," she muttered. "He's with Andy."

Or dead ... like Vince.

A wave of nausea doubled her, then released her. She took a deep breath and went inside.

Across the room, Diana sat at the bar with Cyndi and Phoebe. Phoebe's sloe-dark hair shone, a trail of dark smoke down her back, Cyndi's eyes sparkled like polished topaz, her hair a fountain of strawberry curls. Diana swayed lightly on her feet, the luster returned to her golden hair, her skin smooth and supple. All three glowed, their bodies too small to contain their elation. Sated. Izzy's heart caught. She forced her stiff shoulders back as she walked toward them.

Phoebe spotted her. She grasped Diana's arm.

Diana paled, shaking off Phoebe's hand. She reached for Izzy. "Oh, by the—Isadora! Why did you risk it? For what? Come on, we've go to find you someone fast—"

"Izzy?" an uncertain voice said.

Diana released Izzy slowly. Izzy turned.

Dev.

His uncertainty gave way to shock. He gaped at her.

Again, like Vince.

"Izzy?" he said. "My God, what's happened to you?"

Diana sneered. "You little—"

"Diana," Izzy said. She summoned what dignity the pain allowed and lifted her chin. "Come to apologize again? Or did you come for the gun?"

A bitter smile quirked his face. "So you took it. I was sure it was Andy."

"So I guess it's an apology," Izzy said.

Diana's eyes narrowed. "Apology! Like that'll do you any good!"

"Geez, Izzy, you sure know how to pick 'em." Phoebe's words hummed with appreciation. "He's perfect."

"Don't encourage her," Diana said. "Look what perfection's done for her. The new moon is past and it's eating her alive." She turned on Dev, shoving her finger in his face. "Listen, you little creep—"

"Diana, leave him alone," Cyndi said, lowering Diana's hand. "He's here. It's up to Izzy."

Diana hissed. She jerked her thumb at Dev. "Isadora, do you still want this?"

Izzy gazed at Dev. Bewildered, he tilted his head to one side and bit his lower lip. Even tangled in his insecurity and hopelessness, he yearned toward her. "Izzy," he said. "Are you all right?"

Not like Vince.

Izzy took Dev's hand. "He's perfect."

She led him outside, then collapsed against the wall, her brittle strength crumbling. As the agony seared through her, she grasped the door frame and slid into a crouch. Her nails scraped paint from the wooden trim.

Dev dropped to his knees beside her, rocking her clumsily into his arms. "Izzy!"

Izzy swallowed her rising gorge. "Take me home," she whispered.

❧ ☙

Dev cradled Izzy in his arms. Izzy shuddered and clung to him. "At the end of the hallway," she said. "The door to your left."

He carried her into her bedroom and lay her gently on the bed. She had turned the sheets back herself hours ago, the white satin a shimmering pool in the dim room. "Can you open the curtains," she asked, "and let the night in?"

"Sure." He did so, then turned to look over the room.

Izzy smiled. There wasn't much—the bed, the window, a small bedside table with a candelabra and three white tapers. She sat up slowly, pulling the scarf from her hair and shrugging out of her coat. Anticipation dulled the pain as raw excitement bubbled through her veins. *Soon,* her nerves whispered. *Soon.*

She beckoned to him. She touched his mouth with one finger, then let her finger trail from his lower lip to his navel. She reached for his shirt and ripped it open.

"Izzy," he protested, climbing onto the bed next to her.

She stopped his words with a kiss, her hands whispering over his chest, sliding to his back, pulling him closer. Shyly, he circled her with his arms. His fingers kneaded her back, then delicately probed her dress, looking for a way in. She broke the kiss and murmured, "Tear it."

Her tongue flirted with his lips. She unbuttoned his pants, her fingers brushing his penis and darting away. She teased her way toward it and squeezed. With a moan, he grasped the dress and shredded it.

Their lovemaking passed through phases: explore, tease, entangle . . . climax. Izzy straddled him when the time—the urgency—arrived, ripe and perfect and full. He reached for her, but Izzy rocked back, then clasped his desperate hands and pinned him to the bed.

And the blood flowed, a warm, red promise spilling over him, steeping the satin sheets in lavish crimson swirls. She screamed with release, the pain and the need coursing from her in waves. At last his mingled with hers, a hymn to the moon.

❧ ❦

Izzy woke first, just before dawn. She burrowed from under Dev's arm and raised herself on one elbow, smiling down at him. His whole face had relaxed, the tension gone. Color heightened his cheeks, replacing the grayness of depression. Shivering with a satisfied murmur, he stretched awake.

Squinting up at her, he smiled. "I feel great," he said, reaching for her. "I feel like I can do anything! Maybe all I needed was a good—"

He stopped, blinking and staring up at her, blinking again as if to focus. "You're . . . what happened to you? You look. . . ."

"Younger?" Izzy said, tracing his whiskered chin with her finger. "It's all right. You can say it."

He swallowed. "You looked . . . last night . . . like you were dying. Now, it's as if years. . . ." He shrank from her, stiffening at the sight of the blood-soaked sheets. His eyes widened with horror. "My God, what happened?" he whispered. "Are you . . . ?"

Izzy laughed. "We're fine. We released the moon."

He scooted back a little more. "What do you mean? God, the wrinkles, the laugh lines are all gone—What are you?"

She rose to her knees, letting the sheets fall from her naked body. Blood stained the insides of her thighs. "I am the banks of the river," she said, "the river of Life. Once a month, the river overflows its banks and bathes those it touches with hope and strength and purpose. I choose someone to loose the flood and wade through Life's depths. This month, I chose you."

A spark danced in Dev's eyes. "Why me?"

"I prefer the people who need me most," Izzy said. "You had no hope. You wanted to die, thinking it would end your pain. What you needed was Hope. That feeling that you can do anything—that's my gift to you."

His eyes narrowed. "And what do you get out of it? What I have given you? My soul?"

Izzy smiled. "No. You released the blood. If it isn't released, it cripples me."

He took her hand and spread her pliant fingers. "Like last night."

"Like last night," she said. "I waited too long."

"Your friends," he said, easing her down beside him. "They're like you?"

"The river has many banks," she said, and kissed his hungry mouth.

Melanie Tem

❧ ❧

WIFE OF FIFTY YEARS

*Once again—to my delight—***Melanie Tem** *wrote a story which comes out of her work with the aged. It is simultaneously ugly and beautiful, visceral and intellectual. The style is dark, brooding, and interior. Once read, it's a tale you will not soon forget.*

❧ ❧

Mick was in her doorway again, her husband of fifty years, a pitiable monster of a man, who still, in his better moments and hers, could turn her head with his handsomeness. Delia pressed her face into her pillow.

He shuffled in place. Cutting through all the other vile odors of this house that she couldn't keep clean now was the smell of fresh urine. He'd wet his pants again and he didn't even know it. He was holding onto the doorframe with both hands—with his fingertips, because the doorframe was narrow—and that made him stand even more clumsily and precariously than usual.

Mick looked alien. Of course, she was alien, too. In her case, it was the cancer that did it, and the cumulative unfairness of life. Mick, though, gave the impression with his flimsy body that walking upright wasn't natural for him, and with his slack face and dim eyes and unhinged way of trying to talk that his mind wasn't human, either.

She ought to get up and lead him to his chair in the living room. But he wouldn't stay there, and she didn't want to touch him although the desire to touch him was a constant undercurrent, and anyway she couldn't get up anymore. She was dying. She could actually feel the tumor in her liver now, pushing out under the elastic waistband of her pants, noticeably bigger every time she cupped her hands around it. And sometime in the night—maybe last night, if this was morning—the pain she'd been so afraid of had started.

The doctor said she would die before the end of the summer, or by Christmas, or surely before next spring. Delia was terrified. *Let's get this over with. Please just let me live one more day.* Mick didn't know she was dying. She hadn't told him because she couldn't stand the thought that he would forget. She couldn't imagine anything more awful than dying in the company of the man you'd been married to for fifty years, who kept forgetting that you were dying. "I'm dying," she'd have to tell him over and over if she told him once. "I have cancer of the liver, and it hurts, and I'll be dead by the end of the summer," and every time would be like the first time he'd heard the news, the shock and profound sorrow, the fear.

But once in awhile Mick sent her such a clear, sharp look that she was sure he understood something. Maybe everything. During the best times of their marriage, they hadn't had to speak to know what the other was thinking. Maybe something like that was going on now. Maybe Mick understood that she was dying without understanding that he understood.

Delia felt hands on her, and she cried out. But it wasn't Death come for her; it was Mick. She had always loved his hands. Somehow she'd missed his transit from the door to the bed— maybe two minutes, maybe two hours. Most likely she'd fallen asleep, a thought which horrified her.

Mick was bending over her now. Too close; she could see the tiny lines and huge flopping wattles of his face, and his breath was rank. And unsteady, tottering and trembling; if he fell on her she'd never be able to get him off, and they'd both die right here in their marriage bed of fifty years. His toothless, bald head was much too big for his frail neck, and his glittering eyes were vacant. A death's head. A skull and crossbones, warning of danger, signalling poison. Emitting a cooing, wordless noise, he reached for her.

◄§ §►

Shuddering and gasping, Delia managed to writhe away from him, under the sour and untucked bedclothes. Mick extended his gnarled and shaking hand even farther and let it fall lightly on the tumor protruding from her stomach. Thinking it would hurt, Delia stiffened, but it didn't. There was, in fact, a quality both oddly soothing and oddly arousing about the touch of her husband's hand on the very spot from which death was spreading. He worked his stiff fingers down inside her pants. It was not precisely a gesture he'd ever made before, and, despite herself, Delia's breath caught with pleasure and anticipated pleasure heightened by the fact that they seemed so out of place. She let him do what he wanted, even guided his fingers a little, until he was cupping in his palm her bare skin stretched taut over the tumor that, at this very moment, was killing her. Appalled, Delia felt a stirring of sexual excitement, but she did not make him move his hand. Mick managed somehow to maneuver himself into bed beside her without losing contact with her hard-swollen flesh.

Delia was lying flat on her back because, if she curled on her side the way she'd slept all her life, the tumor slung down like a baby in the womb, and she found that especially awful. Now, on sudden impulse, she raised her arms straight toward the ceiling and examined them at close range in the glow from the milk-glass lamp on the dresser across the room. The deeply, loosely wrinkled flesh from her fingertips to her shoulders reminded her of long suede gloves, flesh-colored and soft, the color of her flesh grayer now than it use to be, the skin draped.

Mick's hand had moved hesitantly up to her breast. His callused fingertips brushed her nipple, and the nipple hardened. Delia roused herself enough to say, "Leave me alone! I want to be by myself!" which was as close as she could come to saying something either of them would comprehend. There was no reason not to speak aloud, as loudly as she could. They were the only ones in the house, and he was senile and she was dying. "Mick, you leave me alone now!" but she kept her arms up in the air and didn't push him away.

Mick nuzzled the side of her neck, and her flesh crawled pleasurably. He was making wet, affectionate sounds with his gums and lips, and drooling. Bitterly, Delia wondered who he thought she was now. Sometimes he knew. Sometimes he knew she'd been his wife for a long time but he lost her name. Or her name stayed in his mind but not who she was to him. Or he'd have a vague inkling that she was somebody important to him but he couldn't place her, so he'd treat her deferentially, like someone in authority, or warily, like an enemy. "I love you," he tried to whisper now in a voice that would no longer go very low or very loud. Delia wanted to ignore him, but a shiver went through her.

She held her arms up like that until long after they'd started to tingle, peering intimately at one and then the other. It must have been a long time since she'd looked closely at her arms, and she found them both repulsive and fascinating. Mick's thick-knuckled fingers joined her left hand moving up and down her right arm, which turned the motion into a caress, clumsy but very tender. Delia's eyes brimmed with tears. Lately, she'd been crying more often than not. Dying, she ached for just such tenderness, and was terrified of it. She worked her hand out from under Mick's and was going to lower her arms, hide them under the sheet.

But Mick brought his other hand up under her elbow and supported her arm where it was. Stroking her soft wrinkled flesh, he watched the sculpture his fingers made of it, shoulder to fingertips, shoulder to fingertips. "Lovely," he said huskily. "So lovely."

Delia used the edge of her other hand to wipe her tears

away, but they came right back. "I'm *ugly*," she rasped. "I'm old and I'm ugly." *And I'm dying*, she thought to say, but the closest she could come to that was, "And I'm sick."

"You're beautiful." She wondered if he knew what he was saying. She wondered if he knew who she was. Maybe it didn't matter. Before long she wouldn't *be* who she was. Shoulder to fingertips he kissed her, fingertips to shoulder, and Delia cringed to think of his cracked lips in the deep folds, even as a pleasurable warm chill followed the path of his lips. The tip of his tongue traced the scaly lines of her palm. The cancer hurt, and cell by cell she could feel it growing. Her heart hurt. Maybe the cancer had already reached into her heart.

Meaning to kiss her under her neck, Mick instead buried his face half in the brittle hollow of her collarbone and half in the wrinkled pillow. He stayed in that position for such a long time that Delia, alarmed, jostled him. Maybe he'd died. More likely he'd lost track of what he was doing. Tears ran down the grooves in Delia's cheeks. Mick raised himself very unsteadily and kissed some of the tears away, but there were too many for him. "Don't, my love," he seemed to be saying, and Delia couldn't tell if he meant, "Don't cry," or "Don't die." It didn't matter which he meant; she couldn't stop doing either one.

She closed her eyes, to shut him out. He kissed her eyelids. He kissed her grizzled, tear-stained, pain-streaked cheeks. He kissed her mouth, which was ringed with soft whiskers that she didn't even try to get rid of anymore although they made her feel unclean. When she felt his tongue she pressed her lips firmly together, because the tumor was down there, oozing its ugly poison.

Trying and failing to turn her face out of his reach, she told him, "Don't."

⋞§ §⋟

Strong, indeterminate emotion scrambled his features. Mick had hidden his feelings so thoroughly for so long that Delia had come to regard him as having none. Lately, he seemed to be revealing to her all the feelings he'd accumulated in fifty years of marriage, and it was too much for her, along with the cancer, too, along with the dying. Much of the time he looked the way he looked now, hurt and baffled, as though he couldn't remember who'd hurt him or just how, remembered only the pain which was a lot to remember. And, mostly, more in love with her than ever. "But I—I want—" He lost his thought but kept flailing for it, knowing only that there was something he yearned for. "I want—"

"I know what you want," Delia snapped, although she was aware that really, she didn't.

Mick asked her, so clearly that she was sure she must not have understood, "We've had a good life, haven't we?" When she couldn't answer, he said it again, a statement this time. "We've had a good life."

Finally she said, "Yes. Yes, we have. We've had a good life," and she was crying and clinging to him, feeling blessed and cursed, dizzy with horror and gratitude, weak with pain and love.

With much grunting and exclaiming, Mick pushed himself down under the covers until his face came to rest between her legs. This seemed to Delia a particularly surprising act of love, or of his own lust, considering how much physical and mental effort it required of him.

She braced herself for a shock: either this would feel good, which would be shocking between a senile man and a woman dying of cancer, or it wouldn't, which would prove how far the tumor had already spread.

But he didn't put his tongue into her sex. Instead, he used what must surely be close to his last bit of energy, to heave himself upward a few inches along her sweaty body and lay the soft undersides of his lips against the tumor under her bare skin.

Suddenly Delia felt a peculiar sense of separation from her tumor. The thing had arisen out of the deepest parts of her, parts even she hadn't guessed existed, like a secret taking form. Now it pulled away from her. First just at the edges, like a lover's palm curling tenderly around Mick's caressing hand. He stroked it. He murmured endearments to it. It responded, rising toward him, pulling away from Delia into his hand. It was, of course, still quite thoroughly embedded in Delia's most private flesh, and as it came loose it *hurt*.

When Delia screamed, Mick made as if to soothe her by lowering his lips to the tumor again and murmuring to it things which were unintelligible except in their unmistakably lovelorn tone. Delia wondered almost hysterically whom he thought he was talking to now, who he thought the tumor *was*. "I love you," Mick whispered clearly, and the mass quivered to the sound of his voice.

Mick nibbled at its smooth, taut surface, and with a resistance so mild it was almost playful, it opened for him. He probed inside it with the tip of his tongue, as though he knew exactly what he wanted and what it had to give, and the tumor yielded to him a sticky, viscous drainage much like that of love making.

Mick was tugging at her pants now, pulling them all the way down. Helplessly, Delia raised her hips to him and let him have his way. After much effort, many stops and starts, much groaning and swearing and forgetting what he was doing, he finally got her undressed. At the same time, she was thinking she should cover the tumor somehow, hide the cancer from him, but that was impossible now.

Mick pushed his member inside her and rested one hand on either side of the tumor. At the same time that both Delia and Mick, married for fifty years, climaxed, the tumor burst through Delia's abdominal wall, a shower of love and death.

Lucy Taylor

❧ ❧

WINDOWSITTING

Lucy Taylor *is a cat lover. She lives with a lot of cats, and likes it that way. Though I've never met them, I imagine that her own felines are housebroken and relatively benign. Not so the cats in her story. Here, a woman whose grandmother was a gypsy, tires of her bourgois life and becomes obsessed by the idea of running away with a band of gypsies who have come to town. Her husband dismisses the idea. As she begins to pine away, their wooded garden is taken over by feral cats, brought there, he says, by her insane needs. But who really brought them? Have they come to kill or protect, and if so, whom? And why can't they be seen by anyone else?*

❧ ❧

In the early autumn, when the gypsies made their annual migration southward through the Coln Valley into Chedworth, my wife Rebecca would always sit by the window watching. The cat Delilah, an evil-eyed beast with calico fur, would watch, too, or so it seemed, although her agate eyes might just as easily have been fixed on a housefly crawling up the windowpane as the ragtag, colorful parade of bright wagons and belled horses.

I hated to see the gypsies come, because I knew what this would herald: a season of dissatisfaction between my young wife and myself.

Rebecca, though normally a person of commendable restraint, harbored strange fantasies about the gypsies, that their peripatetic life, their wild music and licentious dancing, the presumed passion of their lovemaking made them somehow more alive than we staider, settled folk. That she had, in fact, a gypsy's soul, and our marriage was slowly killing it.

Year after year, Rebecca's autumnal longing became more palpable, her yearning more acute, and I confess, I found her restlessness more than a little vexing. My early retirement from the position of Don at Trinity College at Cambridge had enabled me to provide my wife an amply luxurious home along a secluded, wooded road, as well as a secure and comfortable life.

"I want to go with them," Rebecca said one day, entering my study unannounced and plunking her round, warm ass down upon my lap with some suggestive squirming.

At the moment of her interruption, I was studying a particularly obscure and eloquent passage from a psychological treatise by P. Bodkins, a student of Jung who had lived and worked with the great master in Geneva. It was Bodkins' contention that supernatural phenomena could manifest themselves in response to acute psychological distress, in particular, after prolonged repression of the personality's shadow self, as Jung had termed the darker, primitive side of human nature. I confess I found this thesis, while less distracting in a tactile sense, far more compelling than the sudden weight of Rebecca's plush backsides.

"I want to travel with them," she said again.

"With whom, dear?" I said, feigning ignorance, although I knew only too well what she meant—I'd suffered through this talk before.

"The gypsies," she said and wriggled prettily, so that the soft conjunction of her buttocks molded itself to my groin.

When I did not reply but continued reading, she added, with that theatrical flair that so captivated me when we were courting, but that now often proved irritating, "My God, Ian, can't you see what's happening to us? We've grown as stale and motheaten as your library. Life's too short to be cooped up in this moldy old house with nothing but books and ideas. I want to dance, I want to run through the woods, I want to make love 'til I can't walk. I want to *feel* something again . . ."

She stopped speaking, perhaps sensing from the hunching of my shoulders that she had nearly reached the limit of my patience. Her cat Delilah, ever the voyeur, perched on the corner of my desk. I've never cared for cats—their furtiveness, their silence, the way they creep and poise and pounce—and Delilah's dour presence did nothing to enhance my mood. I tried to shoo her gently off, but she held her ground, no doubt in anticipation of drama to come, be it marital row or marital relations.

"Let's just do it, run off, and hire on," Rebecca said, lowering her voice now in deference to my obvious annoyance. "Do something a bit wild while we're still young and able."

I noted and appreciated the gentle tact with which she said "we." In truth, of course, only one of us was even comparatively young still. Rebecca was a year or so away from forty, myself, her senior by some fifteen years.

"I don't think it's quite that easy, my love," I said, trying not to sound condescending as I pointed out that running off to join the gypsies was more the fantasy of a high-strung teenager than that of an educated woman approaching forty. "Besides," I continued reasonably, "one's either born a gypsy or one isn't. It's not just a group one signs up with, like a quilting bee or The Animal Protection League."

She pouted charmingly. "But you've forgotten, haven't you? What I told you years ago? What my mother said?"

She had me there. I'd quite forgotten. In truth, my studies always kept me so absorbed that, even at the flash point of our courtship, I didn't always retain every word Rebecca said.

"Mother told me that I have a gypsy great-grandmother on my father's side. So I could join the gypsies because I truly have the blood—it only takes a drop—and you, you'd qualify because you're my husband, a gypsy through marriage . . ."

I laughed and petted her plump waist. Delilah fixed on us

her yellow stare, as motionless as a mummified feline from an Egyptian tomb but for her tail, which thumped back and forth against the lamp like a furred pendulum.

"And what about this lovely house and your teaching at St. Catherine's? Your beautifully-tended roses? You'd just abandon them?"

Rebecca hesitated, then: "Let them wilt. They're only tame, domesticated roses. I'd rather smell the wildflowers along the road than tend a stupid garden."

"What of *my* work? I suppose that's stupid, too?"

"You wouldn't need your work if we were gypsies. You study psychology to learn the mysteries of the human mind, but all you're doing is shutting yourself off from the mysteries around you. Leaving here and wandering would give you more than all your scholars, your precious Jung, your Freud, could ever teach you—the wildness of the heart, the passions of the flesh. Leaving her would give you back your soul."

I kissed her, more to silence her than from desire. Her mouth tasted of chocolate and fresh coffee. "What a romantic you are, my dear. You should have been a poet."

Rebecca rocked upon my groin. She leaned against me, took my hand and placed it inside her blouse, which had somehow come unbuttoned at just the right, strategic place during our talk. I felt her softly abundant flesh mold to my hand, her nipple jut between my thumb and forefinger. She dipped her head and murmured sweet obscenities.

I have always flattered myself that while I am not a man immune to passion, neither am I prey to every momentary whimsy of the flesh. That weakness I've found to be more common to Rebecca's gender. And she had interrupted me, you understand, at a crucial point in Bodkins' text, the worst possible time for her to demand either gypsy gallivanting or lovemaking.

Therefore, I gently nudged her aside.

"Tonight, my love, after a good dinner and that bottle of Burgundy we've been saving."

She nodded, perhaps more stoically than pleased me but with

that certain gracious withdrawal so characteristic of my wife. Her pattern was to press an issue only so far and then desist most modestly.

It was Delilah, however, who behaved completely out of character and confirmed what I already believed about her species, that even the most domesticated cat is still a traitor in the household, waiting to create an insurrection the moment that the master's guard is down.

For no sooner had Rebecca retreated and I turned back to my reading, then the devilish creature, who'd been sitting on my desk quite calmly up until now, abruptly spat and hackled and lashed out.

Rivulets of blood streamed down my wrist.

Delilah stared at me.

And I at her.

I felt it then, not pain, but something subtler, yet more shocking.

A kind of feral loathing, wild and virulent, directed just at me.

I felt Delilah's hatred and wondered if, by some strange transference of human to animal, it might also be the emotion of her mistress.

ᵥᵧ ᵧᵥ

In past years, the gypsies always camped at the edge of a sheep pasture, owned by an elderly farmer who was either too ill or sufficiently indulgent not to dispute their brief stay on his property. But this year, the old gent had passed away. His son, the farm's new owner, had no such sensibilities regarding transients and, if local rumor could be believed, made his point clear with a double-barreled shotgun in the middle of the night.

Therefore, the gypsies made their new camp at the edge of a wooded *cul de sac* just beyond my property and a stretch of forest. Once they were settled there, Rebecca couldn't actually see the camp, of course—it was a good half mile from the house—but at night the flicker of their fire was visible and the sounds of their guitars and lutes would keen palely on the moonlit air like some diabolical Pan set to piping.

I'd shut the windows to keep out the peatsmell of their fire and their pagan music. Rebecca, like one entranced, would sit before the bay window in the living room, the wayward Delilah on her lap, swaying raptly as if she could still hear the music now that the windows were tightly closed.

"I must go with them," she said. "I feel like part of me is withering and dying."

"Nonsense," I said, "you just need some distraction, to take your mind off fantasies."

"You're the psychologist, the learned doctor," she exploded with uncharacteristic spite, "why can't you understand?"

"Listen to me," I said, taking her arm. "It's a week yet before you have to be back teaching at St. Catherine's. Let's go into London for a few days, take in some theatre, do Harrod's."

"That wouldn't help. I need . . ."

Her black eyes were wide and riveted upon the window where Delilah arched, still as stone, fur hackled into quills.

"Ian, something's out there."

I moved to the window and gazed out upon the lawn. The porch light shone an amber cone across a yard grown up rapidly since I last mowed it and on a corner of Rebeccah's garden.

"I don't see . . ."

"Right *there.*"

But then I *did* see it, a slash of jet skittering diagonally among the rosebushes. Almost reptilian in its glide, languid and low to the ground. A shadow slicing shadows.

"It's all right, darling," I said, "it was just a . . . raccoon, I think . . . that's all."

Delilah hissed.

"A cat," Rebecca said. "It was a cat. They're all over. I see them when I go out into the garden. They watch me like I'm prey."

I stared at her in some confusion, not knowing whether Rebecca was reporting an objective fact or some illusion brought on by her supercharged emotional state.

When I looked back out the window, I was able to discern a half dozen or more shadows, all black and scuttling close to ground. One whirled around and hissed. I saw pale fangs and glaring yellow eyes. Rebecca had been right: cats.

"The damn gypsies," I muttered finally, tensing my shoulders to suppress a shudder. "They bring animals along with them, let them run wild. That's where the cats are coming from, the gypsy camp."

At that, Rebecca's trembling turned to frantic sobs that sent Delilah scuttling for cover beneath the bookcase. "The cats frighten me, Ian. They're all alike, all black like coal. And the way they move, it isn't like a normal cat. They glide along like serpents."

"The gypsies will be gone in a few days," I told her, "and the cats will doubtlessly go with them. If not, I'll ring up the Humane Society, have them send round some humane traps that I can set out in the garden."

Rebecca's eyes widened with fear. "No, Ian, don't. You mustn't even get near them."

"I don't see . . ."

"Please, let's just pack some things and go."

"You mean to London?"

"No, to the gypsy camp. They'll take us in, I know they will. We have money. You're a professor and I . . . I'm pretty still."

She stopped. The implication of that last part settling over both of us like a veil of something cold and not too clean.

"I mean . . . I don't think I can stay here, Ian. I had a terrible dream last night. You had a heart attack and died while we were making love, and I suffocated underneath your corpse. That's how I feel, like I can't breathe. I love you, Ian, and I don't want to leave you but . . . I don't know how much longer I can stay."

I confess the idea of remaining in a place under siege by scores of cats was as unsettling as anything that I could imagine, but I felt sure the animals were somehow connected with the gypsies—if not their half-wild pets, than feral cats attracted by an infestation of rodents harbored in the wagons.

"When the gypsies leave, I'm sure the cats will, too."

Rebecca stared out at the places where the night was liquid with shadows undulating among the rosebushes in sinuous black stripes.

"I don't think they're with the gypsies, Ian. I think they're here for us."

❧ ❦

On the Manifest Unconscious by P. Bodkins, Geneva, 1944; p. 213

"*. . . a most unusual case referred to me around this time concerned a young Frenchwoman, Mme. D., whose apartment was, to all appearances, afflicted with a poltergeist infestation and other supernatural occurrences. The phenomena included slamming cupboard doors, knickknacks that crashed to the floor of their own accord, and a sudden, inexplicable proliferation of peculiar insects, winged dragonfly-type creatures that delivered excruciating stings. These could not be identified by local entomologists and were resilient to even the most rigorous spraying campaign.*

It was found that Mme. D. suffered from frigidity and repressed hypersexuality. Upon addressing and treating the source of her frustration and suppression of libido, (Mme. D. had been molested as a child and raped by an older brother), the phenomena, including the insects, disappeared over a four-month period.

❧ ❦

Rebecca's increasing nervousness and agitation, as well as the presence of the cats outside our home, made me more eager than ever to shut myself away in my library. I've always disliked cats and these, what I could glimpse of them, were large, brute-looking beasts with close-set eyes and sleek, obsidian coats. At night they fought and yowled like banshees. By day, like ghosts the light had exorcised, they disappeared.

I called the Humane Society and a man came round with humane traps, which he placed around the garden. I checked them every morning and every evening before dark. The traps remained untouched.

In the meantime, I tried to make Rebecca understand that the strays were merely a temporary nuisance, one that we'd surely be relieved of soon enough. It was simply a matter of waiting until the gypsies moved on south.

Normally I anticipated my wife's return to her teaching duties at St. Catherine's with regret. This year, however, I looked upon her return to work as a chance to regain some sense of serenity in our household. Truth be told, her fretfulness and constant windowsitting was distracting me unduly. For, in addition to her obsession with the gypsies, Rebecca had taken to not bothering to dress in the morning, but stationed herself at the living room window in the scantiest attire, sheer negligees that highlighted the pallor of her skin, the hungry burn inside her eyes, or a brassiere and slip that only served to make more obvious that which they concealed.

She claimed that she was watching for the gypsies to come up the road on their way back to the highway, but I knew her wiles and guessed that, by draping herself across the couch like some half-nude odalisque, she was hoping to distract me.

I could ill afford her childish games. The treatise by P. Bodkins was delivering up new ideas and concepts and, in a stroke of synchronicity I felt Jung himself would have applauded, was leading me to revelations of my own concerning my wife's mental state. Highly disturbing ones, to be sure, but salient none-the-less.

The day before Rebecca was scheduled to return to teaching, I grew exasperated with her silent pining by the window and with our self-enforced confinement in the house. The cats be damned, I told myself, and went outside to take a stroll through the autumn woods. The notion of meandering along past the gypsy camp occurred to me, but I dismissed it. My stroll was not intended as mere distraction, but as a kind of walking meditation, to digest some of the ideas in the material I'd been studying.

In the garden, I saw no cats, but this did not surprise me. I'd never seen one of the creatures yet by light of day and assumed they crept off to hole up somewhere during the daytime. I'd gone a quarter mile perhaps, traveling in the opposite direction from the gypsy camp along a dirt road that cuts between my property and the neighboring farm, when I became aware of movement in the outer corner of my vision.

I turned at once, but saw only empty meadow. A squirrel, I concluded, perhaps a hare. Upon resuming my walk, however, the swift, dark shadow darted past again, the most fleeting of blurs in my peripheral vision. I whirled again, this time making a complete circle.

Nothing moved.

Around me, there was only the brown meadow, burnished auburn in the late afternoon light, and beyond that the forest with its gaily hennaed trees, its sumacs bending low beneath what appeared to be a weight of golden coins. And behind me now, *again*, dark squiggles bellying along the ground, slinking shadows undulating just beyond my range of sight.

I took a few steps farther. The black things that pursued me kept up the game, haunting the corners of my vision, causing me to spin one way and then the other and finally cry out, "Gotcha!" like a tormented child when at last I fixed my eyes on one of the bedeviling things.

A cat, coal black, wriggling so low along the ground it might have been, in the dimming light, mistaken for a serpent.

And then another one, its twin, moving through the high meadow grass toward the trees.

And a third, identical to these, crouched down upon a hillock.

And many more, I realized suddenly, with a sickening sensation of dread and vertigo. Dozens. All solid black, not a distinguishing spot or stripe or notched ear among the lot of them, all with that peculiar low-to-the-ground glide, tails held out straight, ears pressed flat against ebony skulls. The meadow crawled with them. It seethed with a repulsive energy more reptilian than feline.

The gooseflesh rippled along my arms like colonies of spiders. Despite my antipathy for cats, I could tolerate the odd domestic tabby like my wife's Delilah, but these feline hordes appalled and terrified me. Their wildness spoke of things unseen, of buried emotions, private lusts, the demons we suppress and try to obliterate with an act of will, only to find them lurking somewhere else, hungry-eyed and eager to attack.

I picked up my pace. The beasts did likewise, zigzagging so rapidly that the tall grass bent and rippled as though buffeted by a score of conflicting winds.

By now my idea for a meditative walk seemed ludicrous indeed. My one thought was to get back to the house, and yet the cats seemed to sense this intention and, with what appeared to be almost malevolent intelligence, sought to thwart it.

In a rush of hisses and hackled hair, the meadow came alive.

A pair of them sideswiped my legs. Their attack was so swift I had no idea that I'd been hurt, until I looked down and saw the long tears in my trouser leg, the blood running down my ankle.

Another flung itself up toward my groin. Claws dug in, and I could have sworn the vicious teeth were seeking the femoral artery, before I swatted it away.

I commenced to run. The beasts divided up like a well-trained battalion of fighters. Some scooted on ahead, fangs bared, hissing like the damned, others slunk along beside me, keeping near, and these, I tell you, were the more menacing, for I could never really keep them in my sight. There were too many of them and they moved too fast, weaving in and out among the grass, and every now and then, one of the braver ones would make a sally at my ankles or my calves. By this time, blood was streaming down my legs from a half dozen wounds. I had a vision of falling down among them, my eyes and mouth made vulnerable to these demented creatures.

I sensed, though, that however feral these cats might be, they weren't yet completely fearless. They scattered as I approached the house, hissing all the more ferociously even as they slunk away, merging back into the shadows at the edge of the woods.

Shaken, bathed in chilly sweat, I limped into the living room and collapsed upon the couch.

Rebecca had been at her post by the window with Delilah

on her knee. She leaped up, sending Delilah skedaddling across the waxed floor, when I made my inglorious entrance.

"Good Lord, you're hurt!"

"Not seriously, I don't think," I said, struggling to regain my composure. "The damn cats . . . they're completely wild."

"I *told* you, didn't I?" Rebecca said. "I see them from the window. There're more of them each day. God, Ian, I'm afraid to leave the house."

"I'll call the Humane Society again," I said, "have them send round someone with a net—or poison, better yet. While I'm at it, I think I'll ring up the Constable as well. See if something can't be done about those gypsies. Get rid of them and their damned cats, too!"

Rebecca's shoulders slumped with depression or fatigue. I noticed that she didn't look as though she'd combed her hair all day. It hung around her face, a wild tangle of inky strands interspersed with threads of grey. She was wearing an old housecoat, threadbare silk, that clung to her full body in a way that made it obvious she wore nothing underneath.

I was so busy taking in her near nudity, her dishevelment, that I almost didn't see the tears strung opal-like along her cheeks.

"The cats don't belong to the gypsies," she said. "I *told* you that. The gypsies have gone. They broke camp two days ago for Bath. You didn't even see them pass."

The gypsies. Gone.

"Fine then," I said, sounding more smug than I intended to conceal the fact that I'd felt a sudden, inexplicable chill of dread. "Then you won't be tempted by them anymore. You can stop this moping and pining around, this foolish windowsitting."

A strange expression, almost frightening, illuminated the tiny gold flecks in Rebecca's midnight eyes.

"You talk about temptation, Ian, but I don't think you allow yourself to know anything about it. What is it that could tempt you? Is there anything at all?"

She took a step toward me and suddenly peeled back the

frayed silk robe and let it slither softly to the carpet. In the pale light of late afternoon, her flesh looked pearlescent, gleaming like a marble statue polished to high gloss. Her black hair tumbled in wild disarray about her shoulders.

Without a word, she sank to her knees and began fumbling with the zipper of my trousers. I could hear her breathing, harsh and rasping, like the throaty breath of some wild animal in rut. I reached out to plunge my hands into her hair and suddenly found, that in her present state, I was unable to touch her. The hair looked like some kind of filthy nest, a trap in which my hands would mire were I to give in to the primitive desire she inspired.

I shoved her backward and she came at me again, trying to free my unresponsive member.

"Rebecca, stop it!" This time I pushed her harder. She tumbled backward in a sprawl of ripe flesh and flailing limbs and glared up at me with undisguised contempt.

"You don't want me, do you? What is it you desire then? Come on, Ian, tell me. A thirteen-year-old girl? A young boy with his arsehole all pink and virginal? Or maybe someone stronger, older, a full-grown man to turn you on your hands and knees and . . ."

I reached down and cracked her across the cheek, unable to believe this creature before me was Rebecca, legs spread so that I could see the gaping pinkness of her sex, the shadows clinging darkly to the undersides of her heavy breasts. She looked not so much like my wife as some wild primitive, a slattern sorceress, a lust-crazed witch.

"When you conduct yourself properly, I'll be more than happy to make love to you. But this is not the time or place. Besides that, I've got work to do."

She interrupted me with a bray of mirthless laughter. "I can't believe you, Ian. You stand there bleeding, and yet all you think of is your stupid books, all you desire is your texts, your theories, your Jungian treatises. You don't see what's going on right outside your own window. You don't see the cats prowling out there, staring in, watching us like we're mice inside a trap. It wasn't time for the gypsies to move on yet. They left because they had the sense to see the cats and recognize the danger."

"Don't talk absurdities. They're only cats, stray cats gone wild. They're a nuisance, but we'll soon have something done about them."

I zipped myself and reached down to try to help her up. She slapped my hand away and snatched her robe.

"We've stayed too long," Rebecca said. "We should have left here long ago. We should have gone with the gypsies. Their dogs and belled horses and wild music, that would have kept us safe."

"You're talking nonsense," I said. "This has been our home for more years than I can count. This obsession with the gypsies, with living some kind of fantasy life of hedonistic wandering, it's the dream of a child who doesn't know any better, who doesn't know the value of security, tranquility, repose. I'm quite content here with my books, my work, with you. If you're not . . ."

"Then what?" Rebecca said, her black eyes bright and challenging.

". . . it only goes to prove there's something dreadfully, profoundly wrong with you."

◄§ §►

On the Manifest Unconscious by P. Bodkins, page 377:

As in dreams, it appears that the mind in thrall to sublimated eros exhibits an uncanny aptitude for manifesting its thwarted desires in highly symbolic, often emotionally charged ways. Indeed, these three-dimensional manifestations can be likened to dreams in almost every sense, being the symbolic expression of the dreamer's—in this case, the neurotic's—frustrated ambitions, longings, lusts.

The case of Lily R., the teenaged daughter of a Zurich shopkeeper, exemplifies this phenomena. At the time of her consultation with me, Lily R. was engaged to be married within the month. She made it clear that this was entirely of her own volition and that she welcomed the chance to marry the young man who had been courting her and who was, in fact, a boarder in her father's home.

At the same time, her dreams made clear the fact that Lily R. was terrified of sexuality, that indeed her sexual proclivities inclined themselves decidedly toward her own sex. Unable to admit this lesbianism to herself or anyone else, she continued with the wedding arrangements. In the meantime, however, the room Lily's fiancé rented became infested with small albino snakes and black cockroaches. No other part of the house was touched by them, no efforts to eradicate them proved successful. When the fiancé began sleeping in another room, the vermin followed him.

One night, when the young man had persuaded Lily to consummate their union prior to the wedding, the future groom awoke in agony to find a snake coiled around his testicles, squeezing them. Only later, after Lily was able to acknowledge her lesbianism and break off the engagement did the snakes and other vermin disappear.

I put the book down. My encounter with the feral cats, I realized, had wounded me far more grievously than a few bites and scratches, which were healing up now, thanks to Rebecca's contrite and tender ministrations. Since my walk a few days earlier, I found it virtually impossible to either concentrate or sleep. My dreams were frightful, swift spirals into darkness, plunges into realms where something horrible was lurking, waiting for me like a sharpened, feces-covered stake at the bottom of a pit.

Although I hadn't left the house since my ill-fated excursion through the meadow, the phantom siblings to the cats who'd attacked me, pursued me through the house. Dark shapes skittered at the corners of my vision. Shadows slunk beneath the wardrobe and crouched behind my desk. Sometimes I fancied that I glimpsed those shadows, tiny versions of the larger horrors, lurking in Rebecca's face. That she so often kept her gaze downcast was evidence, I thought, she guessed I'd glimpse the enemy reflected in her eyes.

My musings were interrupted by a great commotion outside the house, what I took to be the yowl and yodel of toms squaring off for battle. I focused my attention on P. Bodkins' text, reminding myself that I'd already called the Humane Society again that morning. A prim young woman with a Brighton accent had reminded me in a most condescending fashion that workers had been sent round to our place before. She agreed finally, in a most ungracious tone of voice, to continue to investigate the matter of our feline infestation.

By this time, however, I was beginning to share the young Brighton woman's doubts. If my fears were true, then neither traps nor nets would rid the lawn and garden of these feral beasts.

I didn't hear the door to my study open until Rebecca's shadow slid across the arc of light from my reading lamp.

I looked up, annoyed, almost wishing for one bitter minute that Rebecca would return to her perch before the window. Her school had been open for two days now, but she had called in each morning pleading illness, then spent the day windowsitting, motionless and pale as some enchanted bird, Delilah snoozing on her lap, as spellbound as her mistress.

Rebecca's eyes were wide and flashing, her nostrils flaring like an exhausted steed.

"What's wrong?"

"Delilah . . . oh, God, Ian, she's dead." She put a trembling hand up to her mouth, bit down upon the fingers until she could compose herself. "I was feeling claustrophobic . . . I opened the front door for a breath of air and she ran outside. The cats were waiting out there, Ian . . . they set upon her. They killed her . . . tore her open right before my eyes. Oh, Jesus, cats don't act like that, do they? Oh, God, my poor Delilah!"

I took her in my arms, realizing now the screeching that I'd heard before was more than just two vocalizing toms.

"I'll ring up the Human Society again."

Rebecca drew back as though struck. "To hell with your Humane Society! Their traps didn't catch a single cat. I checked again this morning. There're more of them now than there were before." She began to pace wildly back and forth, tearing at her long black hair, which was wild and matted now, a whore's hair after servicing too many brutes.

"I'm sure there is a simple explanation. I'm sorry about Deli-lah, but . . ."

"We have to leave here, Ian. I know where we can find the gypsies. I know their route. They'll be in Bath by now, camped somewhere along Lansdown Road. We've got to go to them and we've got to go *now*."

"Rebecca, I . . ."

I reached to stroke Rebecca's face. She drew back, her face contorted in something like a snarl.

I realized it then, of course, what should have been so obvi-ous to me all along, what I'd been so afraid of. It was all so clear in Bodkins' text. Why hadn't I been willing to acknowledge it before?

Rebecca, of course. Her restlessness, her longings and her unfulfilled desires, even perhaps a repressed urge toward promis-cuity, had caused the feral cats to manifest themselves. She'd created them, these monstrosities, from her own hungers.

They were hers—my lovely, savage wife's.

The cats belonged to Rebecca.

This realization effected me in a way that was both immediate and shocking. I drew back, seeing Rebecca clearly as if for the first time. The unkept hair, the slattern's mouth, the eyes full of licentiousness and wanton cravings. I wondered that I could have ever loved this creature. I marveled that I could have wanted her at all.

"I think perhaps you've been right all along, that you're not suited to the domestic life. I think you should go join your gypsies, wander like a wild thing, rut your fill. Just leave here—go!"

"Ian, what are you saying?"

"It's what you wanted, isn't it? You've been bitching about it for weeks. The open road, the life of the heart over the mind, well, I'm giving you my blessing, go! Go now!"

"Like that? What about you? If I go, you must come with me. You can't stay here alone."

The cats belonged to Rebecca.

She made a move as if to grab my arm. I seized her wrist

and with the other hand struck her hard across the face. She wobbled, fell, and something in me opened up—the dark pit of my nightmares—and I was toppling onto her, ripping the housecoat she was wearing down the front so buttons flew across the room, sinking my fingers into her harlot's mouth with one hand while with the other hand I made a spade and penetrated her between the legs. For several seconds, I fucked her savagely, as if trying to reach down her throat and up her cunt to shake hands with myself in her whore's belly.

All I could think about were the infernal cats—Rebecca's cats—prowling the lawn, the garden, skulking through the meadow beyond, menacing my body, mind, and sanity.

She bit down on my fingers to free her mouth. "Ian, for God's sake, stop! Have you lost your mind?"

Her words did more than any blow to bring me to my senses. Shame scourged me. I buried my face in my hands. They smelled like Rebecca's cunt, and I kept my head there, breathing the faint scent of musk and salmon as though the odor alone had the power to revive me.

"I'm sorry," I said, knowing even as I spoke that I'd never be able to forgive myself for such brutishness, such violence. "My God, you've got to know I'm not that kind of man. It's the blasted cats ... their creeping, prowling ... it's ..."

I don't know how long I went on talking, trying to explain, to understand. But when I finally looked up, I saw that Rebecca had gathered her torn clothes around her and was going up the stairs.

"I should have left you a long time ago, Ian. I see that now. Thank God it's not too late. I'm leaving you tonight."

And take your repulsive creatures with you, I thought, *before they drive me mad.*

But all I said was, "Go catch up with the gypsies. I see it now, that you belong with them."

She appeared less than an hour later, her hair combed neatly and tied with ribbon, a small suitcase in her hand.

"Take the Peugeot," I said. "You can't leave on foot. With nothing."

She'll have her creatures.

"No, I'm going to walk into town and get a room. Then take the bus to Bath tomorrow. I don't need a car, Ian. I don't need anything except what I've been needing all along . . . my freedom."

Her face, scrubbed from the bath, looked clear and radiant, reborn. Like a bride on the way to meet her bridegroom.

I fumbled in my pocket for some bills.

"You'll need money . . ."

She slapped my hand away. "I don't need anything of yours. I stayed here when I loathed my life out of loyalty to you. I didn't want to leave without you. I realize now how foolish that was. You've already given me the greatest gift of all . . . making me realize I don't owe you anything and never did."

Then she was gone. I lifted my fingers to my face again and sniffed the delicate memory of her odor. I drew it in one final time, and then went to wash my hands.

I was in the bathroom, still standing at the sink lathering the soap, when I heard the awful racket. At first I thought a car had careened out of control and that what I heard was tires screaming at the last instant before impact with a tree or hedgerow.

I turned and rushed back toward the living room when a new sound, the most hideous of all, froze me in my tracks. Rebecca's screaming. It soared in keening agony, like a bird trying to gain altitude, above the fray of other sounds, then was drowned out and obliterated by the snarls and howls of cats.

She screamed once more. I think it may have been my name she called. I tried, I swear I did, to go outside, to help her. My legs were rooted by a terror so oppressive it weighted me like irons.

The cats kept up their awful cacophony for some minutes.

Rebecca did not scream again.

❧ ❦

I'd thought Rebecca's dying would have freed me, that the pyschic energy that created the cats would have dissipated with her death.

Alas, that's not the case.

The beasts have not been exorcized. They prowl the garden now, more numerous than ever. Daylight no longer intimidates them nor the cold of early frost nor the drench of an unseasonable rain. They mate, conceive, and bear fiendish litters that grow to full adulthood within the day. Their bodies make a writhing carpet of the lawn.

A man from the Humane Society came round the other day, but I wouldn't open the door to let him in. He rang me later to report he'd found no cats, not even fur or feces, but only some small, unidentifiable bone fragments near the road and a suitcase which he'd left upon the porch.

I've stopped my studies altogether now. I sit by the window, in the chair with fabric worn thin from Rebecca's weight, and stare out into the garden where the cats creep and pounce and prowl. Occasionally I think about the gypsies, of the feral life lived to the beat of the blood, of endless open roads and wild music and the throbbing of a cock just before it spasms between a pair of sepia loins.

I think . . . of other things as well.

Of gypsy boys and girls with flesh as young and tender as a Christmas bird's . . . of creamy bodies piled and linked in carnal rhapsodies . . . and plundered flesh, ripped in places where no orifice ever was intended, and penetrated, ravished to the bone . . . ah yes, I think of such dark pleasures now, for it doesn't matter what thoughts I permit myself. It's too late now. The cats roam through the garden, encroach upon my soul.

One day, if I don't open up the front door, I know they'll find a way inside the house, hunt me down and devour me, bone and blood and entrails, down their black throats, the way they did Rebecca. Perhaps that's as it should be.

They belong to me, after all.

My cats.

My dreams.

My longings.

Lisa Mason

❧ ❧

Felicitas

*I have come to believe that there is very little that **Lisa Mason** can't do. This story is, for example, a real departure for her. She had never before written anything which smacked of psychological horror and, in fact, turned down my invitation to write an original piece for this volume. Fortunately, I know she cannot resist a challenge. Herewith the result, an illegal alien tale that is dark, contemporary, and passionate.*

❧ ❧

I cannot see the moon from the deathwatch cell, but they say it's full tonight. How I adore the moon, the way the icy light makes eyes sparkle and blood turn black. They're going to execute me at 12:01 A.M., Pacific time, if my lawyer can't arrange another stay, which seems unlikely. Outside San Quentin, protestors chant, sing dirges. An angry mob taunts the protestors and applauds my impending death.

I chose gas, since I'm terrified of needles. Gas is gentler, if slower. Lethal injection squeezes the life out of you, and I despise the idea of shitting in the spanking clean panties they gave me. Personal cleanliness is essential, I've always thought, even when I prowled about the stinking garbage dump of Nuevo Diego. My last, and only, regret? That I couldn't clean up the blood. My hands, scrubbed with Boraxo and a brush, still feel sticky, stink of copper.

My lawyer opposes the death penalty, even for someone like me. She has pleaded every extenuating circumstance in the book. But I cannot lie. I will not express the regret they expect. And this is what sticks in the judge's fine, pale, clean-shaven throat. "At least tell him you're sorry, Felicitas," my lawyer pleads, her compassionate eyes slick with tears as she watches my last minutes tick away. "It makes a difference to them, it really does."

Ah, I am only sorry I couldn't clean up the blood. He made a mess of me.

❧ ❧

This is how it happened: I began to prowl when my woman's blood came. I was a skinny brown baby left on the doorstep of a piss-poor convent in Nuevo Diego. Border boomtown, shacks of corrugated steel cheek by jowl with the walled stucco enclaves of the servants to high-tech. The good Sisters in their dusty black robes sour with sweat and righteousness were always pleased to clutch another victim of sin to their withered bosom. How they beat me, how they held my face in a bucket of salt water when I daydreamed during my lessons, and took whatever money came to me from sponsors stricken with my looks. How they half-starved me, made me scrub the flagstones till my knuckles bled.

It's all true. And hardly worth mentioning, but that I withstood everything. I was strong and silent. I snickered at their pious ignorance, their stupid cruelty. I endured with a wild joy tucked in my prowling heart.

I grew into a weedy stalk of a twelve-year-old girl with big eyes, a mane of black hair, long skinny hips that twitched. And the men of that shit-spattered border boomtown, the tough young cowboys and fast clerks, the fat storekeeper and smug theater manager, the graying old banker and grizzled rich rancher, all of them, all of them; they could not take their eyes from me once I got my woman's blood and I began to prowl.

The blood came as it usually does: an ache, a spot on one's skirt that another girl sees first. Laughter, teasing, a younger girl in tears, trembling with dread at the inevitability of her own change. The good Sisters pulled their plain faces into even sterner expressions. "You are able now to get with child, Felicitas," Sister Dolores told me. "Do you understand what that means?" I did. "And if you sin, my girl, not only will you burn in Hell for eternity, but you will repeat the same miserable mistake your mother made, and we will wind up having to feed and clothe another forsaken wretch like you."

I cared not a damn about sin and hellfire. It was the awful notion of inflicting this world of pain and sorrow upon another poor little bastard that instantly gripped my impressionable heart and persuaded me, even as young and carefree as I was, to caution. I begged the good Sisters for a crucifix to wear, so that the men of Nuevo Diego would know I was a bride of Jesus, not a wanton slut. Deeply impressed with my piety, Sister Dolores moved my bed to the coveted private cell on the second floor of the convent overlooking the garden. She took up a collection that very day and bought me a fine gold cross upon which the Savior writhed in His perpetual agony.

I woke that night in my privileged solitude to find the gold chain lying upon my pillow, not about my neck. Even more peculiar, the crucifix loomed frighteningly larger than I remembered, as though I were looking at it through Sister Dolores's telescope. Proportions were all askew. The whole world had grown enormous! I could see everything so clearly in the moonlight, as though a fog had lifted from my eyes. The hot stony scent of dust filled my nose, other strange ripe smells assaulted me. A cacophony filled my ears. I could hear every rustle, squeak, and hiss in the restless night, the brush of bodies through leaves, a hound baying in the unimaginable distance, the good Sisters mumbling their prayers downstairs.

I leapt from my bed; it was like jumping off a cliff! When had the bed become so high? My heart pounded with terror. I let out a cry, which sounded strange in my ears, an inarticulate wail. I was certain I would crack my head and die, but I landed nimbly upon the hard wooden floor with barely a sound and not a trace of pain. I crouched. A peculiar exultation coursed through my body. My muscles throbbed with pleasure. I stretched, reveling in this new-found strength and agility. I gazed at my arms in wonder. My fingers had curled up, turned hard and curved and sharp. Impulsively, I licked my wrists; the gesture came as naturally as running a comb through my hair.

What had happened, and why, and how? I was intensely curious. I wanted to examine the question from every angle, discover its answer if I could. But the wild night beckoned. The intriguing sounds and smells enticed me. I instantly forgot my curiosity and my wonder as I craved to see new wonders.

I leapt to the window sill, crept onto the narrow ledge outside, leapt down upon the tiled roof above the kitchen, found the narrow branch of the ash tree that clicked against the gutter. I bounded to the sweet rich earth, delighting in my freedom, in the wildness swelling in my blood, in the privilege of my life, which had so suddenly become extraordinary.

I prowled.

❧ ❧

I learned about the joys of the night, of the hunt. I stalked the little beings who hid in the leaves and shadows. Scenting them, chasing, I would catch a tiny body in my hands, break a frail neck with my jaws, taste hot, salty-sweet blood on my tongue.

I learned of the dangers, too. Of the many other beings who prowled in the night. I met the snake, the owl, the tarantula. I fled from the wild dog, the coyote, the fox. I smelled the stench of rubber and gasoline, heard the awful roar of men's machines, saw their heedless crushing wheels.

And I saw men, too. I saw the young cowboys; how sick tequila made them, yet still they sought its foul succor. I saw the store clerk; his key fit the shop's back door. Twice he took a television, videotapes, goods packed in boxes, out to his jeep. I saw the grizzled rich rancher, who had married an ugly lady from a fine family and fathered four arrogant sons. He wrestled his little servant girl down in the dusty grass in a field far from town. I heard her shrill protestations, saw her tears gleam in the moonlight.

I was prowling in the convent's garden one night when another being came, huge and stealthy. She lay in wait for me in the shadow beneath the ash tree. She pounced as I passed, turned sideways, uttering strange cries. Her eyes gleamed as she stared at me fiercely. My hair stood on end. I crouched, readying myself for a fight. I expressed my alarm.

We stood this way for an eternity. She did not approach me, nor did she back off. Time passed, and we both began to relax. She lay upon the grass in almost careless repose. I sat, examining my feet. Finally, she rose and came to me. Still I sat, trembling, casting my eyes down. She kissed me on my cheek, on my ear, on my neck. She was very beautiful, gentle despite her fierce glittering eyes. Love swelled in my breast.

My mother expressed many things. With shimmering pictures and vague unspoken concepts, she revealed secrets to me about those who prowl. How witnessing the full moon was the key, the initiation of each cycle, after which changing waned, lay dormant, stirred, only to recur full-blown at the next full moon. How things that affected us when we prowled—hunger, sickness, injury—carried over to the time when we walked upright in the day. How with fearlessness and cleverness and secrecy, she had lived a long and happy life in this world, despite her nature.

I wanted to know who my mother was. I followed her, but she was older, larger, faster, more clever. Many times I risked changing far from the shelter of the convent. Many times I trembled at the thought of Sister Dolores's wrath should she find me sinning in the dawn. But I never witnessed my mother when she changed. Perhaps she herself did not change. Perhaps she always prowled, but had relations like me who walked in the day, and knew of us, knew of our ways. Indeed, I had met beings like myself, and, though sometimes I shared their thoughts as I did with my mother, yet I knew they did not walk in the day at all. They always prowled.

I could have been content with my simple life. I would have gone into the Sisterhood and lived out my days. But two things happened that assured that this was not to be.

The first thing was that I saw my mother for the last time. She had come again to the convent's garden in the shadow beneath the ash tree. Her eyes were slick with terror, her mouth slack with pain. Her belly had become hugely distended and rippled strangely. She lay upon the ground, panting and writhing. She had gotten pregnant many times, too many times. *Daughter, do not let this happen to you in the night, when you prowl.* Her unborn babies kicked and struggled. Something broke inside her, blood bubbled on her lips. She shrieked in agony. And died.

There was nothing I could do.

I shut myself in my cell with the curtains drawn, fasted and wept for two weeks straight. When Sister Dolores begged me why, I could only clutch my crucifix and moan, "*Mi madre, mi madre, mi madre.*"

The second thing that happened was Roberto.

I never expected that a mere piece of jewelry around my neck would keep the men away. At thirteen, my breasts swelled despite my fasting, my legs grew longer, my waist more curvaceous. Men courted me. Men accosted me as I ran errands in town for Sister Dolores. To these unwanted suitors, I would whisper, "I am a bride of Jesus." Unwanted they were, for though I wanted pleasure as much as any woman, there was no man in the shithole of Nuevo Diego who lit a spark in me. I fingered my crucifix, and the suitors went off in search of easier prey.

But not Roberto, the eldest son of the grizzled rich rancher. Sallow-faced, with cruel squinting eyes, a thin mustache over thin hard lips, Roberto was as arrogant as he was powerfully built from the sport of wrestling at his private school. He had beaten his dog to death for disobedience. He sent his father's servant girl to the hospital after whipping her with a riding crop when she would not reveal who had gotten her with child. Roberto would not accept my vow of piety. He took my "no" for "yes." He followed me relentlessly, seeking a moment alone. He stalked me.

I avoided him as best I could. I despised the bastard. I was terrified of his cruelty and strength. I pleaded with Sister Dolores to speak with his father, which she promised she would do. Then I saw the rancher's check for twenty thousand pesos on her desk and I knew the lying bitch would not protect me.

One lovely moonlit night, I was out prowling when I saw Roberto drive up to the convent in his jeep. The Sisters were in the kitchen, boiling beans. They looked out the window at his approach. Sure, they knew what he wanted, what he would take fearing no one, no reprisal, for I was but a poor, skinny orphan girl with no one to defend me. They saw him swagger into the dormitory. They saw him lean out of my window in perplexity, for of course I was not there. They heard him shout, "But where the fuck is she?"

I leapt up the ash tree, crept onto the roof and into my cell as he went down to the kitchen and berated the little Sisters with more foul language. He accused them of letting their wards run loose in town, threatened to expose them, to withdraw his family's generous contributions. I drew the curtains tightly, crept back into my bed, slipped the crucifix over my head.

It was after Sister Dolores beat me till I thought she'd break my bones that I packed the small possessions I owned and left Nuevo Diego forever.

᪐ ᪐

I learned how to please men with my hands and my mouth. With my youth and my beauty, I got a fair price. Most of them were content not to fuck me. To the ones who wanted all of it, I pleaded my virtue as a good Catholic girl, which either earned a slap across my face or an additional tip for the joke.

Thus, as the moon waned, I made my way across the border, paying an anxious Yaqui woman merely to carry my bundle of things and dump it far in the desert, while I easily prowled past the guns and spotlights of the authorities. Thus too I traveled, hitchhiking by day, prowling by night. Up the land of milk and honey, where gold lies upon the ground for anyone to seize it, where all pleasures are available to anyone who seeks them, where an illegal alien can disappear into the vast toiling masses of the humble folk in California.

I picked nectarines in Bakersfield, kiwi fruit in Hanford, artichokes in Salinas. I rode in the back of a produce truck to Monterey, a fine gleaming town set upon a spectacular blue bay. There I saw the thrilling promise of California: millionaire ladies in their Mercedes-Benz sedans, tourists from Europe and Japan with heavy gold watches and wallets thick with cash and credit cards, glittering jewels in shop windows more beautiful than anything I had ever seen in my life, opulent restaurants bulging with seafood and fresh bread and good wine.

Mr. Gomez was the manager of one such fancy restaurant, Casa San Lucas. He employed many cousins of cousins without green cards. Mr. Gomez picked me up in his shiny new Ford Taurus the color of dried blood as I stood at the turnoff to I–80. After I skillfully used my hands, he offered me a job in the kitchen as a clean-up girl. A suety man with thin black hair shot through with silver, a profusion of moles on his left cheek, the stink of nicotine perpetually on his fingers, and ruined teeth, Mr. Gomez bought me two uniforms to start me off and arranged for a tiny, ground-floor studio apartment in a building owned by one of his nephews. I worked the day shift, seven A.M. to three P.M., two dollars fifty cents an hour, cash daily, plus all the delicious food I could eat. I was very diligent.

In time, Mr. Gomez introduced me to the owner of Casa San Lucas. Mr. Valesquez was a rich, distinguished gentleman with salt-and-pepper hair, the chiseled face of an aristocrat, a silk suit of deep blue, black leather shoes as shiny as the jewels I saw in shop windows. I was in awe of such a personage. Yet if Mr. Valesquez wondered at Mr. Gomez's choice of a new employee, and whether she was legal, he gave no sign. Mr. Valesquez graciously deigned to say hello as I squatted on the floor with my bucket of soapy water and scrub brush, happy as a child.

And when the moon came, how I prowled among the eucalyptus trees and the aloe vera, fog threading my hair with sweet dampness. I grew strong and sleek. Many other beings prowled beneath the full moon, too. The town was flush with them, fat glossy beings with extravagant gestures and intricate manners, not the scrubby tough terrors I knew in Nuevo Diego. We had our share of confrontations, long glaring glances and sideways stances. But I wished no conflict with anyone. I was too happy. I did not mind scrubbing floors and toilets at Casa San Lucas, as long as I could live my solitary private little life, and collect my cash wages, and prowl as I desired.

Then Ricki came.

꿎 ঌ

Ricki was tall and slender, his long blond hair spilling to his shoulders, muscles sleek over his elegant bones. A brown-eyed Sicilian, his English was more broken than mine. He was one of those men who are sensual in a female way, which only made the women—and the men—want him more. Of course, every waitress and cook and cashier at Casa San Lucas wanted to get near to him.

Yet I was the one he chose. I was the one he wanted.

I do not frankly know how intelligent Ricki was, nor how accomplished, nor how he intended to lift himself from the ghetto of oppressed illegal foreign labor in which we all toiled. All I knew is that he was so beautiful, and I lusted for him in a way I had never lusted before. All I wanted were his eyes, his hands, his tongue, his body, his sex.

Ricki bussed tables, but he would hang out, too, sometimes. It was a Tuesday, ten in the morning, the coast somnolent beneath a thick, chilly fog. Typically a slow day, on this particular Tuesday hardly any staff was about, few diners were expected, few deliveries were to be made. Mr. Gomez had not shown up. I kneeled on the floor, dressed in limp white cotton splashed with soapy water from my bucket. Ricki came and sat on the flagstones beside me. He noticed that my nipples showed throughout the cotton. I noticed that he smelled of some kind of spicy after-shave cinnamon and musk.

He bent over me, we kissed. I slid beneath him on the slick floor. We rolled beneath the salad table, his hand between my legs, inside my panties, his fingers up inside me, drawing forth the first long, shuddering orgasm. Ricki tore my panties down to my ankles, his tongue now where his fingers had been, when Mr. Gomez and Mr. Valesquez strolled into the kitchen, inspecting the stoves and the sinks.

We scrambled up, scrambled for our clothes, for our propriety. Mr. Gomez was loudly outraged. Mr. Valesquez, after he'd gotten a good eyeful, turned away with genteel discretion, withdrew a silk handkerchief, rubbed his forehead with his heavily ringed hand, and ordered Mr. Gomez in a low murmur to take care of it.

Ricki was summarily fired. I was not.

I never saw Ricki again.

And that night, beneath a rufous moon, I went into heat.

◄§ §►

The agony! The torture, the sheer needfulness! Pleasure and pain collided violently in paroxysms of uncontrollable lust. My prowling was transformed. Not the innocent hunting, killing, and feeding, the simple fulfillment of my wild needs. I felt ripe to bursting, propelled into the night by blind anguish.

It was then the prowling toms came.

The scent of my need drew them. They gathered beneath my window and yowled, a horrible sound like a congregation of devils that made my bones shiver. At first I shut myself in my room, for when the change came, I could not possibly lift the window or open the door. I thought I would die that night; I needed to hunt, needed to prowl.

The next night, I left the window open, as always. Big burly prowlers waited for me, bearing scars of their battles over love. They followed me, leapt out at me, chased me through the empty gardens and back alleys of Monterey. One vicious-looking tom with coal-black hair glared from just one evil yellow eye, the other a blind socket with a withered lid. A brown tom with variegated splotches had lost the tips of both his ears. But the worst was a big silver tabby-tom, glossy, fat, and arrogant. He bore no scars of defeat. He was more than twice my size, and he stared at me, eyes glittering with lust.

Prowling had never tired me before. I had never had much need for sleep. I would return to my room at dawn, sleep an hour or two, and off I'd go to walk in the day. But now I woke, ragged, haggard, and hollow-eyed, my hair dusty, my armpits sour, my arms and legs aching from incessant flight. Mr. Gomez frowned at me, but I applied myself so fervently to washing and scrubbing that he had no cause against me.

I was in anguish. I did not wish to lose my position or my comfortable little room. I loved Monterey. I was making steady money at honest work. I did not need to stoop to pleasuring men. The longer I stayed in America, working at an honest job, the better chance I had of meeting a proper citizen, another Ricki who would be a Richard. With my looks that had not faded, I would pleasure a man again, yes, but I would marry him. I would become legal, a citizen. I wanted this. I wanted this badly. For myself; for the children I would conceive in the day, one day.

That night when I leapt from my window, aching with need, there he was, waiting: the silver tabby-tom. I dashed through the damp grass, but he plunged right behind me. He leapt upon me, his huge weight crushing me. He rolled me over and over as I fought and spit and screamed, toying with me like I toyed with prey.

He pinned me down as I crouched on my stomach. He mounted me. He bit my neck, clamping his sharp teeth on my skin. I could smell his foul breath, hear his panting. He thrust his prick into me, withdrew with a sharp backward thrust, like a knife ripping through my sex. I shrieked in agony.

In the morning, I panicked. I had no health benefits as an illegal working for Casa San Lucas. I could not go to the local family planning clinic. The golden State of California had just passed a law forbidding free medical care for illegals. Nor could I go to the black market. I had saved so little, and the doctors who provided black market services were known to take whatever cash one had, and then demand more in the future.

What could I do? I douched with scalding water; I bought spermicidal lozenges that stank like insect repellent; I would not eat. Could I cut out my female organs? I wondered how one employed a coat hanger.

And I wondered for the first time what happened when one conceived in the night. Did that physical condition trap you in the change, so that you could not walk again in the day? Was that why I never saw my mother change?

Yet in the night, when the full moon shone, and the need drove me mad, he was waiting for me. Waiting for me, again and again. I ran, I dodged, I ducked through pipes. He chased me, he raked at me with his huge paws, his long claws. I crept into the tiny hiding places in the wheel wells of cars. He worried me out of my hiding places, crushed me with his weight. He seized me by the back of my neck, lifting me off my feet, and shook me, and pinned me down. He mounted me, thrusting.

He leapt off me, lips pulled back in an evil, satisfied grin. I was furious, enraged. My neck ached. I swiped at him with my long nails. I raked his cheek, drawing blood from a jagged scratch.

In the morning, I was devastated. The entire left side of my neck was black and blue. Even a turtleneck sweater could not completely conceal the bruise. Worse yet, Casa San Lucas was hosting a special party in the afternoon to celebrate the fifteenth anniversary of the founding of the restaurant. All employees and management, with their families, were invited and expected to attend. The most important patrons, who spent money freely and often, would be there. On any other day, I would have been delighted, would have feasted on enchiladas, perhaps sipped a Margarita or two.

I wore my turtleneck sweater, piled on makeup as best I could. Everyone was drinking heavily by the time I arrived. Mr.

Gomez eyed me hungrily. "Hey, Felicitas," leered his fat nephew, touching me on my hand, my arm, my waist. "S'up?" I fingered my crucifix, cast my eyes down. I took a small swallow of the champagne that flowed freely, and which rocketed into my head. I did not want to attract these men. I did not dress or pose seductively. But I could see in their eyes that the mere motion of my walk, the way I stood, my face, my body, made their blood boil, and there was nothing I could do. I abandoned my plastic cup, rushed to the door.

Mr. Valesquez, dear Mr. Valesquez, my employer who paid me cash wages every day and never asked about my green card, stood regally by the door with his handsome wife. The sight of him was like cool water, a beacon of light in the darkness, the father I never knew. "Polo, you know," Mr. Valesquez was saying to a patron, who toasted him. "Nasty fall. Ah, little Felicitas," Mr. Valesquez said expansively as I stumbled past. "Glad you could come to our celebration." From his careless movements, I could tell he'd drunk quite a bit of champagne. "One of our maids," he said to his wife, who raised her plucked eyebrows at me. "Are you leaving so soon, Felicitas? Have champagne, have something to eat. You're too thin, young lady, you must eat."

And as Mr. Valesquez turned to me, I saw across the chiseled cliff of his aristocratic cheek, a long red jagged scratch.

❧ ❦

They say I was drunk, which is probably true, but that sip of champagne cannot account for the rage that possessed me. "Rapist!" I shrieked, together with abundant foul language, and pummeled his silk-suited chest. Mr. Valesquez turned as pale as the moon. The festive crowd muttered, faces open-mouthed with shock. Mr. Valesquez and his wife hurried from the dining room, while Mr. Gomez took me into the coatroom and slapped my face till he drew blood from my nose and mouth.

"What is this shit, Felicitas?" Mr. Gomez demanded. At last the cashier and head cook found us there and restrained his hands. I collapsed in a heap on the floor. "What's gotten into you, you crazy bitch?"

"He rapes me," I insisted in a ragged whisper. "He rapes me over and over. He won't leave me alone."

"Hush, Felicitas," said the head cook, her eyes as round as coins.

"She's fucking crazy," Mr. Gomez said, panting and wheezing. His swarthy face blushed deep with his own shame, as I glared at him accusingly. "Mr. Valesquez is one of the finest men in Monterey. He wouldn't look twice at a skinny little wetback like her."

The head cook and the cashier stared at him with hard black eyes. Many of us had started out illegal. Many still were.

"She could have ruined us, making wild accusations in front of our most important patrons," Mr. Gomez grumbled. "You're fired, Felicitas," he spit in my face. "Get your ass out of here, and don't come back."

I wandered the streets of Monterey for hours that afternoon, wondering what to do. Didn't Mr. Valesquez see the bruises on my neck? Wouldn't he conclude I too prowled the night? Or did he think a man had beat me? A lover, of course, these people are violent, they are crude, they drink, they cannot control themselves. And I had mistaken him for this other evil man in my drunken rage. Or perhaps he had not noticed my neck at all.

That's when it started.

I got in it my head that I must speak to Mr. Valesquez, tell him that I too prowled the night, that I needed to go out and hunt, that my time of anguish would pass. I must beg him to stay away from me, to control himself. But was it possible he could? I knew that when I prowled, I prowled. I possessed no special gifts beyond the natural attributes of my body. I could carry no weapon with which to defend myself. My human intelligence flickered dimly then, like a candle in a distant room.

I kept seeing my mother—*daughter, not in the night*—writhing in her death throes.

But how to find him, now that I was fired from Casa San

Lucas? How to get him alone so I could speak with him? Mr. Valesquez was a rich man. The staff gossiped about how he lived in a mansion enclosed behind a fence and a gate, had a chauffeur drive his silver Rolls Royce, sent his three children to private schools, also behind gated fences. I looked up his name in the telephone book. Valesquez was not listed.

One day I read an article in the newspaper about a man who had fallen in love with a woman who had smiled at him at the office where they worked. The woman did not wish to speak to this man, however. She had her own life, a man whom she loved. Yet this man's love for her drove him mad. The man could not stay away from her. The more she hid, the more diligently he sought her. The newspaper described all the ways he used to find her, even when she hid. Eventually, the man met her at her new house and shot her five times with a medium-gauge shotgun. She died on the way to the hospital.

I did not love Mr. Valesquez. Quite the contrary. But the article gave me new hope. Talk to him; I just needed to talk to him. The Department of Motor Vehicles, staffed almost entirely by Hispanics in Monterey, was very helpful, very sympathetic when I told them I was a hit-and-run victim. I dialed his phone number, heard his regal, modulated voice say hello.

"Do not rape me at night anymore, I beg you, Mr. Valesquez."

"You're insane, miss. I'm very sorry, but if you call here again, I'll have to have you arrested." And he hung up.

That night the silver tabby-tom waited for me, his eyes slick with lust, the jagged red scratch visible in the thin hair below his ears, angling down his cheek. I did not try to run. I stood my ground, in the grass beneath my window, screaming with rage, my hair standing on end. Mr. Gomez's nephew poked his head out of his apartment window two floors up. He had let me stay in the studio if I did special favors for him, but of course he did not know it was me. "Shaddup, damn it!" he yelled and threw a shoe at the silver tabby-tom, who darted nimbly away.

The next morning Mr. Gomez's nephew knocked on my door. A call for me on the telephone in the hall. "Yes?" I said.

"Felicitas Moreno? I am the attorney for Mr. Valesquez. Mr. Valesquez tells me you are harassing him, Miss Moreno. Calling him on the phone, accusing him of outrageous crimes.'

"He is raping me over and over. He must stop before he kills me."

"Ms. Moreno, have you any proof of this ridiculous accusation?"

"Yes!" I said at once. Then regretted it.

"Then you'll consent to a medical examination, won't you?" the attorney continued. "I'm sure I can persuade Mr. Valesquez to arrange for this, since he has nothing to hide."

I fell silent. What *would* they find if doctors examined me? That my sex had been violated, surely. But would the doctors find only traces of a beast? Would I be humiliated, accused myself of awful crimes? I had no idea. "I'll let you know when I can find the time," I said and hung up the phone.

That's when I realized I could not prevent the atrocity against me by ordinary means. I could not match his strength and speed when we prowled at night. I could not throw a shoe. Nor could I prove my claim before his attorneys and doctors. Ah, but I could hold a sharp knife when we walked upright in the day. I could cripple Mr. Valesquez, say, cut off his hand. Then he could not run so fast when he prowled beneath the moonlight. Perhaps his male ardor would not burn so fiercely on three legs.

Yes! I bought a razor-sharp butcher knife at the gourmet cookery shop in Carmel. I studied the ways that the man in love had followed the woman who did not love him. I waited at the gate of Mr. Valesquez's house, hidden behind the huge lush palms. I noted the times he regularly came and went. I borrowed a VW bug from the daughter of the head cook at Casa San Lucas and followed the silver Rolls Royce as he drove to Pebble Beach, to a Mediterranean mansion on Seventeen Mile Drive, to lunch at L'Escargot.

Mr. Valesquez liked a game of tennis at the courts on Camino

Del Monte every alternate Wednesday, at ten in the morning, with a muscular, red-haired woman. They would drink champagne, play tennis, then disappear for a few hours in the little inn on the corner of Santa Rita Street. I arrived before Mr. Valesquez, parked along the winding road. I waited. When I saw the silver Rolls Royce, I jumped out of the VW bug, ran straight to him without a word or thought. I pulled out the butcher knife with one hand, seized his wrist with the other.

His hand. All I wanted was his hand, so he couldn't run so fast in the night.

The cops caught me on Highway 1. The VW bug never did go very fast. They handcuffed me, took the bloody knife, threw me in jail. I was very frightened. What would happen?

But a frowning lady cop came in the afternoon and grudgingly set me free. Mr. Valesquez was going to be all right. He'd taken twenty stitches in his arm and lost a lot of blood. But he was going to be all right, and he was not going to press charges. Ah, I said; he does not want his wife to know who he plays tennis with. But the lady cop said if it were her, she'd have locked my ass away for a long, *long* time.

That night, the silver tabby-tom did not stalk me. I killed several scuffling little beings for the pure joy of it. Ecstasy; I was free!

The new moon came and went. In the moonless dark, I slept peacefully. But then the crescent became a half, and the half became whole. When the full moon came again, my body shivered with lust, and I went out to prowl, aching with need.

He was waiting. I ran, he followed, he cornered me. He limped a little, and his eyes were filled with fury. Yet he seemed stronger, despite the limp, and more determined. I fought and scratched, but he knocked me over, straddled my back, thrust into me and thrust out, knifelike, again and again.

That morning I stood in the street before the gated fence as Mr. Valesquez drove out in the silver Rolls Royce. He started when he saw me. I raised my dress. I wore no underwear. My thighs were smeared with blood.

Someone pounded on my studio door in the afternoon, as I

lay in bed, groggy and depressed. I had no job to go to; why not lie about and feel sorry for myself? When I opened the door, a young man in a suit forced papers into my hands. "This is a temporary restraining order, Miss Moreno," he said. "You are forbidden to go anywhere near Mr. Valesquez."

"Says who?" I demanded.

"Judge McAllister," the young man said, eyeing me as I stood in my thin negligee. "Mr. Valesquez has many important friends."

"And what if I do?"

"We will come and throw you in jail. For the rest of your life, if necessary."

I knew that was just a threat, still I was very frightened. And so, at last, you can see how it came to pass. Really, the rest is quite banal. How I could not reason with him, I could not fight him through the usual channels. Nor could I merely wound him, which I would have much preferred.

For he kept after me till I thought I would die.

I went to the bars near the working piers of Monterey where the fishermen with their little boats go for whiskey and beer, and I bought myself a gun from a man with a pocked face. The gun was very cheap, plus I pleasured him with my mouth. He showed me how to shoot. "Gotta be careful," he admitted, "'cause this piece a shit ain't all that reliable."

I followed Mr. Valesquez to Casa San Lucas. He was a good father, Mr. Valesquez. On Thursdays, he always picked up his daughter and two sons at their private schools promptly at four-thirty and took them to an early supper at his restaurant. How many rich men do that? The children were laughing. The daughter was particularly beautiful at twelve, with thick curly hair, big eyes, long slim hips. Watching her as long as I had, I wondered when she would start to prowl. I wondered what her father would do to her when that happened.

I was waiting in the parking lot behind the big pink and turquoise sign. The gun had such a terrible kickback that it jumped in my hand, and I shot one of the sons instead of the father, shot his face instead of the groin, where I'd aimed. I aimed at the father again, fired again, and, in truth, I still didn't want to kill Mr. Valesquez. I only wanted to shoot off his prick. I kept shooting, aiming for his prick, but the shots gouged out his stomach, his chest, his howling face. Blood spurted all over me, all over my hands, and when the cops came, they wouldn't let me clean up properly, though I licked and licked and licked.

⋐§ ⁊⋑

Ah, my hands, scrubbed with Boraxo and a brush, still feel sticky, stink of copper. My lawyer has brought a Catholic priest to the deathwatch cell. No regrets. I am unrepentant.

"Do you have a last request, Felicitas?" the priest says. His eyes pool with tears as I caress my crucifix.

How I adore the moon, the icy light makes eyes sparkle and blood turn black. I recall the window in the antechamber before I entered the deathwatch cell this afternoon.

"Father, is the moon full tonight?"

He nods.

A little window, cut in the stucco for ventilation. Not any sort of security risk.

"May I see the moon one last time? Breathe the air of night?"

"You're on death row, Felicitas. No one ever leaves this cellblock."

"From the window out there. In the antechamber." I smile at him. "That's all." No man can resist my smile.

The priest scurries off with my lawyer to see if the warden can make arrangements. I am certain there is no screen behind the glass, which opens with a latch. The bars must be three, four inches apart. There is probably a ledge, leading down to the first floor. From there, the jump is only eight or nine feet.

It is 11:50 P.M., and I am not prepared to die. I have not fallen in love, I have not conceived a child in the day, and I want this. I want this badly. I don't know if they will understand what they see when they see it, but no matter. I will yowl, I will prowl again, you sons of bitches.

T. Diane Slatton

❧ ❧

JOHNNY CANADA

T. Diane Slatton *writes about a woman who is cursed by the demonic man who enthralled, made love to, and then haunted both her mother and grandmother. She bears a child, and knows that the infant, too, will be possessed . . . unless—*

❧ ❧

Helen Wright smiled at the wave of religious fervor that smelled dangerously like lust. After four years of covering births and deaths, weddings and farm auctions for the *Mid-Town Times*, she had been assigned to write a feature article entitled:

WHO IN HEAVEN IS JOHNNY CANADA?

His arrival was a lie that grew so powerful so fast, it made believers out of three-fifths of the county. A dozen eyewitnesses appeared on local TV news claiming they saw Johnny Canada spat from the mouth of a blood-red dust storm onto the streets of Sweetwater, Kansas.

He reportedly hit the ground wearing nothing on his bronze-gold body except a pair of snakeskin boots. In his hands was a crimson, leather-bound Holy Bible, which he held in front of his genitals like a shy, pagan god.

Posters went up all over town announcing his Saturday night rally at the Sweetwater High School Gym and Auditorium. Johnny Canada billed himself as a "Motivational Speaker Touched By the Wisdom of Ancients". Though tickets to this once-in-a-lifetime event cost three times as much as an evening at the drive-in, they sold out as fast as any of the stadium rock shows that took place up in Kansas City.

"Hallelujah," Helen whispered whenever people at work or on the bus chattered about him. Her tone was only half-mocking, though, for Johnny Canada's arrival promised her salvation too. It was the jump-start her journalism career had been waiting for.

She phoned him to set up a lunchtime interview. But like the spiritual bloodsucker she suspected he was, Johnny Canada said he preferred seeing people after dark. This truth was borne out by his nighttime street ministering. Dressed in a gray sharkskin suit and Western bolo tie, he'd been spotted shaking hands with dirt-collar thugs in the pool hall, paying a whore just to sit on the bank building's stairs and talk with him, addressing train depot drunks as "Sir" even when they cursed him.

Helen had thanked him at least one too many times for taking a night off from being saintly so that she could come and interview him. Now, gunning her old Buick down Route 27, she practiced an excuse for her impending lateness. Then she rehearsed an apology. She shook her head no to both and allowed herself to be tempted by the gloomy stretch of highway that offered a one-way trip out of Sweetwater if she just kept on driving . . . She missed her exit, had to double back.

It was almost 10:30 when she pulled into the parking lot of the Genessee Inn and Resident Hotel. The garish blue two-story building looked forlorn in the middle of flat nowhere on the outskirts of town. The only other sign of civilization was a red-lettered billboard that bragged: SWEETWATER MALL TO BE BUILT ON THIS SITE!

The billboard was eighteen years old.

By the light of the neon 'Vacancy' sign, Helen made her way up an outdoor iron staircase to a row of doors on the second floor. Since every room appeared unoccupied, she wondered why Johnny Canada had chosen the one farthest from the front office and its conveniences of sandwich machine, ice, and the tolerable companionship of Bong-Bob, the hotel's brain-fried hippie owner.

She paused to smooth her hair before firmly pounding at the door. It swung open to reveal brilliant teeth grinning out from a face she'd only heard about in gossipy murmurs. No wonder he didn't like the sun. Hitting his skin, its rays must turn him into a walking slab of polished brass, difficult to behold without sunglasses.

"Ms. Wright," he said with a little bow, "you knock like a Mountie."

Helen stepped back, turned to look down at her car in the otherwise empty lot. The gesture gave her time to catch her breath, and to find a reason for the stark panic that gripped her.

"Ms. Wright?" Johnny Canada called behind her.

She knew him. Helen covered her mouth to stifle a rising scream. She staggered as far as the iron stairs before her trembling legs found the strength to run. He said something else as she descended, but his voice disappeared into the clanking of her shoes and the blood pounding in her ears.

Locked in the relative safety of her Buick once more, it was all she could do to keep the car headed toward the center of town instead of heeding Route 27's call to open-road freedom. But there would be no escape from the memory that ran like a sepia-tinted movie behind her eyes.

She had been five years old, growing up in Sioux City, Iowa. Her kindergarten teacher sent her home one early afternoon to get a note signed. Entering through the kitchen door, she saw her father on his knees drunk and sobbing.

"It was a bet," he whimpered. "I *had* to let him. It was a bet . . ."

Trying to comfort him had only made her feel like crying

herself. She ran to awaken her mother, who usually cherished long afternoon naps. That day, though, the woman was not asleep at all.

Helen's young mind was seared with the image of them on the bed. Her mother's legs were spread wide to accomodate the sweating, muscular, bronze-gold man who slammed into her with passionate brutality. Every thrust made the woman grunt, and caused the bed's headboard to bang the wall like a gunshot.

The little girl did not cry out or run or even blink, for the sight that transfixed her was more fantastic than mere intercourse. It was the man's gleaming skin, which moved in rippling shudders like horseflesh.

She did scream at last, did run at the sight of her mother's hand brandishing a butcher knife poised to plunge into the man's back.

Waves of nausea crashed through Helen at the clarity of her recollection. She eased off the Buick's accelerator, blinked back tears. How *dare* Johnny Canada come up from Hell to open old wounds.

A long-forgotten policeman's soothing, singsong voice flowed into her skull to complete the nightmare memory. He bent low to explain that her Mommy had just killed her Daddy.

"No-no!" five year-old Helen argued. "Mommy killed the *other* man!"

"What other man?" the policeman asked.

"The shiny Indian man!"

There was no one else in the house, she was told. Only her parents—the lunatic one who had stabbed the alcoholic gambler one. The rest of her childhood consisted of growing up with distant relatives who were careful to never mention her father in the ground or her mother in an asylum.

Helen turned off the hissing, overheated car in front of the little Cape Cod she rented from her boss's sisters. She rested her forehead on the steering wheel, only then noticing that rivulets of sweat streamed from her underarms and beneath her breasts.

Once inside the house, unaccountable fever gripped her. She

ran a tub of icy water to cool her flesh and banish an unwel-
come slickness between her thighs.

She slid forward in the bath, drawing knees up to her chest
until the crash of purifying faucet water lapped at the lips of
her vulva. Almost immediately, she shouted fury and surprise at
her bone-rattling orgasm.

No sooner had Helen dressed for bed when exhaustion felled
her like a brick to the skull. Her sightless, soundless, dreamless
rest seemed otherworldly until a ringing phone, followed by an
insistent knocking jolted her awake.

Staggering back, she stared down at her own fist that had
been doing the knocking. Her eyes dropped to her bare feet
below the billowing nightgown, then darted skyward to the
pale-yellow moon. She spun on the cement landing to gaze past
the iron stairs at her Buick sitting lonesome in the Genessee
Inn and Resident Hotel's parking lot. She'd heard of sleep*walking*,
but . . .

The door behind her flew open.

"Ms. Wright," Johnny Canada said in his vaguely disingenuous drawl. "I'm glad you decided to come back. On the phone
you sounded so—"

Helen began to flee, stopped in her tracks at what he said
next.

"You're as beautiful as your mother. Passionate as your grandmother. Spirited and spiritual as your great-grandmother. I
admit I ordered you back here."

Ordered? Hate streaked flame up Helen's back. She spun to
face him, searching for some insult to crush him or at least
destroy the tangle of emotions he stirred up in her.

His eyes were infinitely patient as he waited for calm to
descend. "Wouldn't you like to interview me?" He disappeared
back in the room, leaving the door open for Helen to follow.

She hugged herself and shivered. After a final glance down
at her car, she cursed under her breath, stepped into the room,
closed the door against an unseasonable chill.

"Did you 'order' the weather, too?" she cracked.

"Sure did," he answered, sounding dead serious.

Helen turned to the voice and saw the interview setup. Two chairs were placed opposite one another at a round table beneath a hanging lamp. Johnny Canada's large bronze-gold hands were folded atop his crimson Bible on the table. Beyond a pair of silver *Crucified Jesus* cuff links that held together his crisp, white sleeves, the rest of him sat shrouded in darkness.

Stepping around the disheveled bed, Helen said, "It looks like you're expecting an interrogation."

"Shouldn't I be?" Johnny Canada replied. He motioned toward the empty chair. "I see you didn't bring a notebook. Somehow I suspect you won't forget much, though."

"No, I *won't*, you sanctimonious asshole."

He gave a low whistle and leaned farther back into shadows as she sat down. "I'm mistaken, Ms. Wright. You're not your mother at all. Shall we get started?"

In the silence that followed, Helen avoided looking at his broad-shouldered silhouette by staring at an antique silver hairbrush and neatly arranged shaving kit atop the room's pine bureau.

"I killed a man in Vancouver," he said simply.

Her head jerked his way.

"It's a fact. We got into a feud over land. Just couldn't agree on where his property ended and mine began. It turned out that I was in the wrong, but no sense apologizing to a dead man.

"Montana's my home outside Canada. I moved there to avoid capture after that 'misunderstanding'. Now, this was back in 1916, the year your great-grandmother came into the picture."

It was Helen's turn to lean back into the shadows. "Liar," she whispered, but her traitorous stomach churned to acknowledge his version of truth.

"My neighbor in Montana went away to visit relatives in Tucson one spring. He returned in the summer with a young cousin he'd married. Selena was her name. Knocked me off my feet, that woman. She wasn't pretty in any classical sense but she had . . ." he clenched and unclenched his fists atop the Bible, ". . . *something*. I got real interested. Obsessed, some might say."

Johnny Canada rose from his seat and strolled slowly, heavy-booted, until he stood directly behind her. "Once, I took some undergarments off her wash line and brought them home to sleep with. Do you think that's peculiar, Ms. Wright?"

Heat rushed to Helen's face and she leaned forward again, this time to escape fingers that stroked the nape of her neck.

He gave a low, throaty laugh, then continued walking a slow path around the table. "Selena's husband ran the textile mill about twelve miles away. He asked me to please look in on his wife every day after I took my cows out to pasture. You can understand his worry about her being alone, because she was pregnant with your grandmother at the time."

Helen shook her head, then covered her face with trembling hands. "This is too much," she said.

"Too much," Johnny Canada repeated like a deep, nerve-strumming echo. "After the child was born, Selena complained her husband would no longer touch her. *I* did. Suckled her right breast while the infant nursed at her left. I fucked her in her own marriage bed. And all she ever asked from me was more.

"That's why I've never been able to understand what overcame Selena the night she decided to tell her husband what we'd been up to."

"Conscience?" Helen's hands fell to her lap as he moved behind her once more.

"Yeah, but maybe that conscience of hers would've kept its mouth shut if it knew her husband would kill her with his bare hands, then come over and set fire to my house while I was sleeping."

This time she did not move from his fingers stroking her neck. Eyes closed, she breathed in the heady scent of metal-tinged sweat.

"I escaped," he said, "left town. Thought I'd really come out of that fire okay. But I was different forever. My skin. It's kind of spectacular and awful both now, isn't it?

"Everywhere I went, folks inquired whether I'd been touched by God or Satan. But it was just a jealous husband who knew enough hocus-pocus to make fire curse me instead of kill me. Wish I'd known that before messing with his wife. Not that anything could have stopped me; it just would've been nice to know."

Helen opened her eyes, rolled back her head to see him. "Why don't you age? Or die?"

"I'm very old and worse than dead. Even now I'm carrying out my sentence."

"It seems like a pretty fair prison with you walking free and my great-grandmother murdered."

He touched a finger to her lips. "I'm *never* free. I think you know that. When the baby born to Selena was past its twenty-fifth birthday, desire like the devil's own possession came over me. I had to find her. Seduce her. Then I asked her to kill me."

Memories, brutal in their intensity, swooped down on Helen for the second time that night: His cock slamming into her mother who raised a butcher knife to plunge into his back. Why hadn't she finished it?

A soft rustle of clothes turned her to where he had moved. Johnny Canada removed his jacket, hung it up on the closet rack.

"Destiny," he said, "is sometimes no more than a dog following its nose to dinner. We trust all our senses to steer us toward fulfillment, and sometimes we're steered wrong, Ms. Wright."

Grinning like sunburst, he walked back toward her and deftly unclasped his crucifix cufflinks. He reached past her and opened his crimson Bible to reveal a silver .38 snub-nosed revolver nestled in its cut-out center.

"Once in awhile, destiny gets bigger than most human beings care to face. My destiny is to find you. I've done that. Yours is to free me. Your grandmother wouldn't do it. Your mother couldn't. I am neither god nor man, dear lady. What I am is a promise of misery. Kill me."

Helen stared at the bronze-gold hands that lifted the faux Bible and placed it, still open to display the gun, on the bedside nightstand. When he came close once more she rose to face him, and her hands went up to cup the back of his head.

Blood pounded hot and painful at her temples; every inch of

her body seemed to know him and strain toward him. He removed his shirt, and lamplight seemed to flow into his radiant skin. Standing so close made Helen feel as if his fever were casting reflective glow onto her flesh.

In a single movement he closed the remaining space between them. Breath rushed from Helen's lungs and he sucked it in with his open mouth hard on hers. He lifted her nightgown and slid his fingers into the slickness between her thighs.

His lips tore fire up her jawline to speak urgently at her ear. "You're cursed as much as me. Let me go. *Promise.*" Before she could answer he brought his moistened, pungent fingertips up to touch her mouth. At the flick of her tongue he moaned and kissed her deeper.

Her hands roamed his chest and back as the flesh there began moving of its own accord. A pang of fear shot through her, followed by the ache of need. To her questing fingertips, it felt as if rolling waves of liquid heat were trapped beneath his skin. The effect was a strange alchemy in every aspect of Johnny Canada: metal-cast skin, copper-scent sweat, molten lead kisses with an aftertaste like ash.

He removed her nightgown, pulled her to his rumpled bed. Helen lay back in a pose of brazen seduction, for the first time feeling no shyness about her too-small breasts, and thighs that resisted perfection. He stood motionless above her, his gaze moving over her like caresses she could almost feel.

Then, in seconds compressed to nothing, he knelt naked between her legs. Helen reached down and wrapped her hands around the thick base of his penis, gasped shock at the shaft's serpentine movements on its way to hardness.

"You're not real," she said.

Johnny Canada laughed, removed her hands from him, lifted and impaled her on his erection. He rocked back on his knees until he was sitting on his haunches with her legs wrapped around his back, her arms encircling his neck.

They remained that way, very still except for the tiny earthquake tremors that rumbled through Helen's body and the column of flesh wildly fucking her deep inside. It writhed and throbbed and roiled and lashed until she shouted in a fury of rapture.

"Now!" commanded his voice through the storm. "If you don't kill me now I'll screw *your* child too. Exactly like this someday, I swear it."

Helen felt the skin of his body jump to life like a pond disturbed by a stone. Her arms fell from him and he rocked back, speaking through clenched teeth.

"If you do not give me peace I won't let you have it either. Did your mother die in an insane asylum, Ms. Wright? Did your grandmother hang herself?" The muscles in his face and neck shifted rapidly, changing his impassive countenance into a bubbling, demonic mask.

She snatched the .38 from the open Bible and pulled his head to her breast. The blast and attendant 'kick' from the weapon blew off the entire back of his skull.

He slid out of her, his semen splashing up onto his own chest and chin and into the surprised "O" of his mouth. Helen grabbed her nightgown on the way out. She stopped at the door, glanced down at the gun still in her hand, turned back just in time for the split-second spectacle of Johnny Canada crashing to the floor and bursting into flame. By the time she reached her car in the parking lot, fire had completely engulfed the room.

◄§ §►

THE DEMIGOD SCAM
How A Smart Town Got Suckered By A Smarter Con Man

She had written the story of her life, an expose on the charlatan who had hypnotized the good citizens of Sweetwater, Kansas. Johnny Canada played Savior to stir up religious hunger, then he burned down a hotel and skipped town with the ticket money that so many had paid to hear him speak.

Helen's account of faith betrayed struck a nerve in the national consciousness. Her article was quoted and lauded from Martha's Vineyard to Puget Sound. There were murmurs of a Pulitzer, which never materialized, but the rumor was enough to land her in New York writing ad copy for the *Times*.

In just over two years she had married a paint salesman, gotten promoted, borne a child, and gotten divorced. On an overcast fall day she pushed a stroller down Fifth Avenue. Between window-shopping and maneuvering around dog shit, she went over her battle plan to thwart her ex-husband's custody lawsuit. She paused at Saks to admire some unaffordable piece of haute couture . . .

"As beautiful as your mother," said a vaguely disingenuous drawl beside her.

Helen spun to see a gloved hand slide away from her sleeping infant's cheek. She fell back against the store's picture window and a yodeling cry tore from her throat as a man in a black-hooded jogging suit ran away down the street.

"Liar!" she screamed. "Goddamn bastard liar!"

It was easy at first for pedestrians to ignore a woman flipping out in a city where someone is *always* flipping out. But when she scooped the baby out of its stroller and reached into her purse and put a silver nail file dagger-like to her child's throat, a mass of humanity quickly wrestled her to the ground.

"You have to let me!" she spat at the mob that restrained her. "You don't know. It doesn't make any difference to him—*nothing* does. He'll keep coming back!"

Her struggling melted into limp hopelessness when a policeman pushed his way through. Someone handed him the baby, someone else, the nail file and horrendous story.

No more custody battle, she thought with a bitter smile. Her ex-husband would get their child. And so, eventually, would Johnny Canada.

"Don't kill him," she said flatly, willing the infant to hear her. "No matter how much he begs you to—"

"Shaddap, ya crazy bitch!" barked one of her captors.

"I think killing him gives him permission to keep ruining us. My mother. Grandmother. I think he'll really die if we stop murdering him. Don't do it!"

"Call Bellevue," the policeman said into his walkie-talkie. "This bird'll be flying in that just tried to 'off' her kid with a nail file . . . Yeah, you oughta hear it. Real rubber-room material."

Helen squeezed shut her eyes, concentrated. "It can stop with you. Let Johnny Canada *live.*" She heaved an exhausted breath and nodded, feeling a glimmer of hope at the sound of her infant son's wail.

P. D. Cacek

❧ ❧

MIME GAMES

P.D. (Trish) Cacek *is another one of those writers whose voice is unmistakable. I am willing to bet that after reading this sinister, swift word picture you will never again see a street mime without a shudder.*

❧ ❧

Callie Beaumont was raped on her lunch hour—in broad daylight and in full view of witnesses—and every one of them applauded.

And threw money.

Callie's only thought, when she joined the other working class drones on the noon-hour Exodus, was to put the world temporarily on hold and get lost in urban anonymity.

And the small municipal park across from the office complex in which she was entombed from 7:30 to 4:30 (five days a week, fifty-one weeks out of the year) seemed like the ideal place to accomplish such a task.

Not much more than a greenbelt with benches, the park separated four of the worst lanes of congestion the city had; and offered little in the way of a *challenge* to the League of Corporate Joggers that roamed the city in packs.

The fact that Callie had never seen anyone in running togs do more than traverse the park on their way to indoor tracks (fully equipped with air-conditioning and digital lap counters) only added to its charm as far as she was concerned.

A small herd of nooners crossed with her, complaining about the late summer heat and the price of gas and how that new V.P. in purchasing only got the job because he was the boss's nephew, and continued on . . . still complaining.

Callie leaned against one of the minimally maintained shade trees and watched them go . . . thanking whatever metropolitan god happened to be in the area that they hadn't followed her into the park.

She could feel the tightness across her shoulders begin to ease as she turned. There were maybe a dozen people (if that) taking advantage of the park's smog-drenched seclusion . . . all of whom seemed intent on ignoring each other.

Perfect.

Since most (if not all) of the shadier nooks were already occupied, Callie followed the meandering path to the park's central quad . . . a ten foot by fifteen foot rectangular slab of concrete which hosted a broken drinking fountain and three benches donated by a local chapter of the VFW.

Usually no one sat in the quad but her. Usually.

A middle-aged woman in a summer-weight linen suit was sitting on the first bench, methodically peeling an egg. Dammit.

Veering toward the last bench, Callie glared at the woman and . . .

. . . felt her shoe come down on someone's toe.

"Ohexcuseme I'm . . ." The automatic apology caught in her throat as she turned.

The mime was hopping around in circles in front of her, fanning the "injured" foot with a derby hat as he alternated between mouthing curses and shaking the hat at her. An instant later, he planted the foot and twisted his black leotard body into an old-fashioned fighting stance—derby tipped back, hands curled into knobby fists.

Put up yer dukes. The clown-white lips formed. Put 'em up.

Callie shook her head and sidestepped him . . . or, at least *tried* to. He countered her every move, shifting from pugilist to waltz partner in a manner of seconds. An instant later, he cart-wheeled into a handstand without missing a beat.

"Wonderful."

Callie turned and saw the woman from the front bench stand up and start applauding like a kid at her first circus; her so-carefully peeled egg lay squashed on the cement at her feet.

"Bravo."

Acknowledging the praise, the mime pivoted on his hands and flexed his elbows in an inverted curtsy. When a quarter hit the cement a yard in front of him, he curtsied again.

Seeing her chance for a fast exit, Callie turned toward the trees at the far end of the park just as two more quarters sailed past her face.

"Really something, huh?" A businessman asked, as he and a construction worker bracketed her. "I always love watching these guys. Don't you?"

Callie glanced back at the mime instead of answering. *Just my luck*, she thought, *I have to find the only street-performer aficionados in the whole city.* The mime was still on his hands, lifting himself onto his fingertips as he pirouetted in a silent ballet. When a couple of one-dollar bills floated down to join the change, Callie took the hint and began fumbling with her purse.

Like a dog sensing a forthcoming treat, the mime scurried up to her and began bouncing up and down on his palms.

There was more applause, and more people appeared at the edge of her periphery, but Callie didn't look up. She could feel the blush start at the base of her throat and shoot through her cheeks as someone laughed.

Crumbling a five-dollar bill in her hand, Callie smiled and purposely threw it behind him. The mime darted to the left, faded back and—BOP—caught it between his knees.

Pop fly . . . yer out.

The applause was almost deafening.

The crowd of blue and white collars had somehow sur-rounded her while she wasn't looking, and Callie felt a chill replace the blush left on her skin. When the mime curled forward—feet over head—and flipped into a standing position, then arched his back and shoulders in an Olympic dismount, Callie forced herself to join in the applause ... all the while looking for the quickest way back to her office. Suddenly the idea of sitting behind her desk and listening to all the latest Soap Opera gossip sounded incredibly appealing.

The mime bowed to the crowd and the handfuls of coins that hit the concrete sounded like hailstones. (*Good, it's over.*)

Callie took a deep breath and started pushing her way through the crowd when someone spun her around ... back toward the mime. Again there was the sound of laughter and coins falling to the ground.

The mime was standing directly in front of her, one hand fluttering against his chest—the standard routine—part of every mime's repertoire for showing immediate and undying love.

Standard. Routine. Like walking against the wind ... or being trapped inside a glass box ... (*trapped*)

Callie tried to muscle her way through the crowd, but the same pair of hands held her fast.

"Uh-huh, can't let you go just yet, sweetheart," a deep voice boomed in her ear. "Not after your boyfriend went and got you flowers."

There was nothing she could do but watch the mime pick imaginary flowers (*daisies*) out of the cracks in the sidewalk.

Circling his thumb and fingers to indicate a small bouquet, the mime cocked an imaginary hat into a rakish angle and offered them to her.

She refused.

The crowd supplied the sound effects as the mime visually crumpled. Broken-hearted. Dejected.

"Shit, I wouldn't put up with that from *my* woman."

Callie spun on her heels and glared at the man. He was wearing a sweat-stained *Hard Rock Cafe* tee shirt and biker's glasses .. not the usual type to be seen hanging around the city's financial district during *business* hours.

"Yeah, cold man . . . *arctic.*" This came from a Junior-Executive type in a three-piece suit.

"I don't think we should *judge* her like that." Mrs. Egg-Peeler said. "She's probably just shy. Maybe if he tried again . . ."

"Naw. Lady's as cold as ice. I think he should . . ."

"Maybe candy instead of flowers . . ."

"Maybe a good swift *kick.*"

Callie watched the mime silently entice suggestions from the crowd then act out each in turn. The suggestions, as well as his movements, becoming more violent . . . more suggestive. But only she seemed to notice.

Someone bumped her from behind, muttering "Bitch". Mumbled agreement from the crowd.

(This is getting crazy.)

"Look," she said, forcing a smile at the gyrating mime, *(Jesus, what's he doing now . . . a whip . . . whipping someone? Oh, God.)*

"This has been . . . a lot of fun. Really. B-But I've got to get back to work." To make it as convincing as possible, Callie glanced down at her watch and frowned. "God, I'll be late if I don't . . ."

She turned into the crowd . . . and they turned her back. Again. Toward him.

His face as expressionless as the painted mask it wore.

"Yo mama, you ain't going *nowhere.*" Someone in the crowd answered for him.

"Not until you apologize." A different voice added.

"But I *really* have to go."

"As I've already stated, *you're not going anywhere.*" This voice was different than either of the first two . . . but that didn't matter, Callie suddenly realized, because the faces and voices in the crowd were no longer acting as individuals . . . only parts of a whole.

Snapping open her purse, she withdrew *two* bills and without bothering to notice if they were ones or twenties, threw them at the mime. The money hit his chest and fell, unnoticed, to his feet.

He took a step closer, crushing one of the bills beneath a slippered heel, and cocked his head. Slowly, he lowered himself to one knee and held out a single *(imaginary)* flower *(daisy)*. *(Be nice . . . just take the damn thing and smile. Be nice.)*

Callie tried to clench her jaws to keep the words in but it was already too late.

"Get *away* from me!"

There wasn't so much as a whisper from the crowd as the mime slowly got to his feet. As he backed up he shook his head.

"And I thought you were something *special.*" The teenage girl to Callie's left snarled.

"You people are *crazy!*" She finally screamed at them. "I'm going to find a policeman and . . ."

She gasped and grabbed her chest as the crowd roared with laughter.

The mime was standing a yard . . . *two* yards away, fondling the air in front of him—his long fingers following the contours of her breasts.

(This isn't happening. Can't be happening. I don't believe . .)

He pinched the air and she yelped, her hand automatically covering the throbbing nipple.

"Stop it."

Her whisper was lost in the sudden applause. The mime was undoing an imaginary belt, unzipping an invisible fly . . .

"Yeh, c'mon man, *do* her."

"Teach this woman some *manners.*"

The crowd was back . . . content for the moment just to sit and watch.

Callie screamed as his hands slashed through the air. She felt the skirt of her dress tear apart at the front seam. Dropping her purse she doubled over—tried to hold the pieces together—only to feel his hands on her shoulders . . . pushing her down to the hot cement . . . holding her there.

"Help me . . . please!'

The crowd chuckled.

His fingernails tore grooves down the insides of her thighs

as he worked her panties off. An instant later he was on top of her, prying her legs apart with his knees.

A few men in the crowd whistled their approval.

Callie's back arched an inch off the ground as he tore into her. He lay down on top of her and his weight almost suffocated her. She opened her mouth to scream and found his lips clamped over hers. His tongue tasted like chalk.

Twisting her head to one side, Callie vomited as he came inside her.

The crowd cheered.

Another shower of coins pelted the concrete around her, but this time the sound was cushioned by the layer of bills that preceded them.

Callie pulled her legs into her belly and curled around them. "Help. Me."

Polite applause. Nothing exceptional. The show was over.

"Jesus, look at the time."

Other voices carried the sentiment as individuals drifted back into the real world of summer heat, outrageous gas prices and VPs who were related to their boss.

A man wearing an IZOD shirt and $200.00 jeans grabbed Callie's arm and pulled her to her feet. When she moaned and tried to cover herself with her hands, he chuckled and winked at her.

"Great stuff. You guys ever do lodge meetings? I know a couple of places . . ."

Callie heard his voice rumble on and on like summer thunder as she stared down at herself. The front of her dress was wrinkled and smudged at the hem where she'd rubbed it against the concrete in the struggle, but other than that it was unmarked. Whole. Untouched.

The IZOD man finally got tired of trying to talk to her. Callie watched his shadow shrug then jaywalk against traffic to join the returning Lunch Hour Refugees. When she built up enough courage to look up, the Mime bowed deeply and swept the derby hat low across the scattered donations. A dozen bills tumbled over each other like leaves in the wind.

"You son-of-a-*bitch*. What did you *do* to me?"

Callie took a step forward and doubled over, barely making it to a bench before the second cramp hit. Something gave way deep inside her and she groaned.

A shadow slid up her legs and into her lap.

"Get away from me."

A single daisy fell against her clenched fists as the shadow disappeared.

Callie was still staring at the flower when the evening rush swept through the park and carried her along with it.

☙ ❧

She found him again in February.

Standing with arms outstretched, he was cavorting in front of a late afternoon crowd of business types who normally would have had better sense than to stand out in a misting rain.

Normally.

But there was nothing *normal* about it. If the mime wanted a crowd, there'd be a crowd. If the mime wanted a woman . . .

Callie brushed the damp hair out of her eyes then jammed her hand back into the pocket of her black pea coat. This time he was only going to *get* what he deserved.

Keeping her head down, she slipped into the crowd without anyone noticing. Not that anyone would have noticed. They were all too busy applauding the mime's attempt at capturing the heart of a frightened teenage girl.

"Son of a *bitch*," Callie hissed, but no one heard it over the first faint rumblings.

"Geez, man . . . she's even colder than the weather."

"Hell, no woman of *mine'd* git 'way wid actin' so stuck-up."

"Yeah. Show her who's *boss*."

Not this time, you bastard.

He was on his knees in front of the girl—one hand extended toward her, fingertips touching, the other beating a gentle tatoo against his chest—when Callie shouldered an old man aside and stepped out into the open quad.

For a moment, she was invisible—overpowered by the mime's "performance"—and then someone saw her.

And laughed.

"Whoa there, good buddy . . . mabbe you'd better be checkin' in with the Missus' fore you try brandin' another filly."

The mime turned toward her, pivoting on one knee, and Callie swept the ground in a deep bow. Despite the biting chill, the clown-white greasepaint on her face felt hot and sticky. She had drawn a giant tear-drop under one eye with blue eyeshadow and elongated the downward curve of her mouth in eyeliner.

The crowd loved it.

"Uh, oh," someone snickered, "Mama don't look too happy."

The Mime stood and took a step toward her. As he did, the teenage girl bolted, muscling her way through the crowd.

And only Callie . . . and the mime noticed.

He took anther step and, one black-slippered toe trying to work itself into the damp concrete, offered her the flower. (*a daisy*)

Not this time.

Pulling her hands from the coat, Callie marched up to him and knocked the offering from his hand.

"Oooo," a voice mummered, "you're gonna get it *now*, man."

"Yeah . . . shouldn't be playing around where the old lady can see you."

Callie raised one fist and shook it an inch away from his face. Building on the memories she had of her mother's tantrums, she stamped her feet and tore at her hair. Just for good measure.

The mime backed up a half-dozen steps, circling to the left when the crowd refused to let him pass, and shook his head. Callie followed close behind, ranting in closed mouth silence.

"God, I'd never let *my* boyfriend get away with something like that."

"Men. They think they can get away with *any*thing."

"You *dog*, you."

Callie let him get a dozen steps away, before reaching into her coat pocket and pulling out the gun. The crowd knew it was a gun because she made it out of her fingers—thumb raised, index finger extended and pointing straight at his heart.

"YEAH, do him lady . . . you don't need that shit from him."

"Pretty little thing like you having to put up with a bastard like that."

"Do it."

He knew it was coming and turned to run . . . but it wasn't any use. Callie took careful aim and fired twice, rocking back on her heels each time the silent, pantomimed recoil shuddered through her body.

"All *right*."

"Nailed that sucker good."

"He ain't gonna be messin' around with no other women, that's for sure."

The Mime lay on his belly, arms loose at his side, one leg twisted under the other: The perfect picture of a dead man.

Taking a deep breath, Callie carefully slipped the gun back inside her pocket and bowed.

The crowd was still applauding when she turned and walked away.

Callie was almost out of the park when she heard the first scream. Someone must have turned the mime over—probably wondering why he was still laying there instead of entertaining them—and seen the gaping holes in his chest.

Smiling, Callie lifted her finger to her lips and gently blew over the top of it.

Cynthia Ward

ঌ ৡৢ

THE MIDWIFE

I'm not generally a Gothic fan, but there are exceptions. This is one of them. In **Cindy Ward***'s story, a delusional, naive woman kills her husband's lover, thinking her to be a witch who has enchanted him in order to steal his soul. You decide if, in truth, the husband is willingly monkeying around and the woman is knowingly rationalizing the murder.*

ঌ ৡৢ

Though his estate had fallen upon difficult times, my husband Geoffrey retained the midwife to nurse me through my delirium, for Marguerite Willette had knowledge of the illnesses which come upon a woman who has borne and lost a child. Marguerite little resembled the crude, dull-witted folk who lived in the town, but her humble breeding was evident in the cast of her face, which revealed her French ancestry, and in the swarthy hue of her complexion and raven darkness of her tresses, which betrayed the blood of the savages that once inhabited this land. Her eyes, however, were as green as a wildcat's, and they possessed a gaze of such penetrating quality that, when I opened my eyes and found her looking upon me, I gave a startled cry.

My husband was in my bedchamber, and at once he was at my side. I spoke his name and reached out to him, and he embraced me with all the gentleness one must show an invalid, thanking God I had been restored to him. At length he said, "I cannot express my relief, Emily, that you recognize me! For a month you have lain in delirium. How I feared your mind would not recover! We owe much to Miss Marguerite Willette."

At his words, I recognized the keen-eyed woman as the midwife who had attended me through the long hours of my confinement, and remembered the discomfort I had experienced at the intensity of her gaze. She bowed her head, and I felt an unwarranted relief that she had averted her disconcertingly acute eyes. But she looked frequently to my husband, alert, I thought, for any direction he might give her.

In the candlelight, I saw how thin and wan Geoffrey's countenance had become, marked deeply by grief for his lost son and concern for his wife; I resolved to do all that Marguerite directed, to recover my health, and cease to burden my husband with anxiety for the continuance of his family. Neither must I trouble him with my grief, though it lay on me with an oppressive weight; I would pray for strength. I reached for my cross, which I have worn since childhood, but it was not at my throat.

"Geoffrey!" I cried. "Where is my cross?"

"Emily, your voice shakes as if you think it lost forever. You were restless in your illness, and we feared you might harm yourself, so we removed the necklace from your throat."

"Where is it?" I cried. "I have always worn my cross! I *must* have it, Geoffrey."

"It is here," he said, and opened the drawer of my nighttable. Then my cross depended from his hand, twisting in the candlelight. Astonishment filled me as I saw an expression of distaste pass across Marguerite's face; then I realized my cross must be too plain for a Frenchwoman. The Papists favor a questionable ornamentation, images of Christ upon their crosses.

Geoffrey clasped the gold chain about my throat, and with the cross once more upon my breast, I felt a measure of comfort. I knew our son was safe with God, and God was watching over us, as my husband watched over me.

As Geoffrey slipped his arms about my shoulders, Marguerite

spoke. "I beg pardon for this interruption, Mr. Sylvester," she said in her barbaric French accent, "but you must not keep your wife from her rest. You imperil her recovery."

Geoffrey was stricken at the thought of doing his wife harm, and he apologized to me, and took his leave.

Marguerite cared for me with all the solicitude one expects of a nurse. Her eyes retained their piercing quality, but she maintained a modest and respectful demeanor; I was grateful for her attention, and knew Geoffrey was grateful, as well. Weakened by my delirium and my nine months of bed rest, I could stand only with Marguerite's or Geoffrey's assistance, and, despite this support, I could walk but a few steps.

Geoffrey visited my chamber and assisted me as frequently as his duties permitted. They are considerable, for he is an attorney with a prominent Augusta firm. His business takes him regularly to Portland, and sometimes to Boston, which is where, with God's blessings, we chanced to meet. He is the scion of one of the oldest families of the New World, the Sylvesters, who built their fortune with the tall pines of the land they wrested from the savage Kennebecs. But by the time Geoffrey's father passed on, all the pines had been cut for masts, and most of the land had been sold; so Geoffrey entered a profession that might restore his fortunes.

Geoffrey Sylvester is the last of his line; the son I bore died within the hour of his birth.

I was naught but a burden to this fine man, too frail and sickly to fulfill a wife's duties; yet Geoffrey remained as considerate as the day he asked for my hand in marriage. I prayed to God for a lightening of my husband's burdens, and for the restoration of his fortunes; I prayed for a lessening of my grief, and for the swift return of my health; and I prayed I would learn to bear all my duties cheerfully, as a wife should.

I apologized to Geoffrey for my debility, and told him that if he thought it necessary to put me aside and take a new wife, to assure the continuance of his line, I would understand. At this, his care worn face went white as new-fallen snow, and he said, "I shall *never* put you aside, Emily! Do not trouble yourself with such foolish worries. Your strength improves with every passing day. We will have another son."

My husband was right, of course. My strength improved, and within a month I was walking without assistance. Despite the numerous and exigent obligations of his employ, Geoffrey witnessed my accomplishment, standing ready to give assistance if I should need it; but, with God's help, I did not. Joy transformed Geoffrey's face, almost obscuring his weariness, and when I returned to my bed, he tenderly drew the blankets over me.

That night, Geoffrey returned to my room, whispering my name, and speaking of his happiness that I had recovered. I was startled to find him in my chamber, for I still had much need of rest. He placed his candle on the night-table and embraced me, telling me how much he loved me and missed me, and slipped his hand into my nightclothes, touching me intimately. I knew it was my duty to submit to my husband's desire, but I could not help myself: I tried to push him away. My arms were weak as mist; he never noticed my efforts as he cast back the coverlets and pushed up my nightgown. My anxiety increased at the shock of the cold air and the cold hand on my limbs, and I screamed.

"Mr. Sylvester! Have you no care for your wife's health?"

Geoffrey leaped up from my bed, his face twisting with consternation, and he cried, "Emily, I thought you had recovered—oh, God! Can you ever forgive me?"

Marguerite stepped between Geoffrey and my bed. "She hasn't the strength to be a wife to you now, Mr. Sylvester," she said sternly. "And it will be *months* before she has the strength to carry a child. Go, before you do her more harm!"

My husband's face filled with shame and remorse, and he obeyed my midwife's command; but she hardly noticed, for she had turned to me, to smooth my nightgown and draw up the covers, restoring my modesty. So great was my relief that I barely noticed the discomforting intensity of her regard. Indeed, I fell immediately into a deep and dreamless slumber.

Thenceforth, Marguerite watched Geoffrey with unblinking

eyes whenever he visited me, but she had no reason for concern; he had realized how much strength I had yet to regain, and did nothing which might hinder my recovery. And soon a morning came when I felt stronger at the conclusion of my exercise than I had at the beginning, and, as my husband embraced me with exceeding gentleness, I was emboldened to say, "I am not weary, Geoffrey—might I walk with you to your carriage to wish you Godspeed?"

His tender expression changed to one of concern. "It would not be wise for you to venture outdoors so soon, Emily."

"I have no intention of exhausting myself," I assured him. "I was confined to bed for so many months, I shall not risk a relapse by remaining long outside. I will do no more than see you off on your journey, and say my farewells to our son."

"Emily, you mustn't risk the return of delirium!" Geoffrey said. "You haven't the strength to bear the sensations which visiting the grave will excite. I cannot permit it."

"Geoffrey, I missed the funeral! Almost two months have passed since our child was buried. What sort of mother am I, who does not visit her son's grave?"

Marguerite spoke. "A short walk in the fresh air will do Madame Sylvester good. I shall accompany her, of course."

"If you believe she has the strength, Marguerite," Geoffrey said, "I shall permit it."

At last I would say goodbye to my son.

When we stepped outside, I found that autumn had taken the land. The morning air held a damp chill which penetrated wool and flesh to make the bones ache. The elms which lined the drive stood stark and black against the grey sky, and the spruce forest surrounding the estate formed a dark wall which seemed impenetrable. The lawns of the estate were unmown, and in the dull light filtering through the low, unbroken layer of cloud, the limp grass had an odd, unwholesome aspect, as if it were an old man's hair grown long in the grave. Disquieted by my morbid fancy, I kept my gaze elevated, and my attention upon my husband.

Beside the waiting carriage, Geoffrey embraced me, and we

exchanged farewells. He apologized that he had not the time
to go with me to our son's grave; but he must hurry to Augusta,
as urgent business required that he make the train to Portland.
He climbed reluctantly into the seat beside his stableman, and
the carriage moved away. As my husband disappeared into the
black forest, my grief became heavier with sudden loneliness.

I told Marguerite I must visit my son's grave alone. She studied me with her bold green eyes, to ascertain whether my
strength were faltering, and agreed I might have a few moments
to myself. As she moved away from me, walking silently, her
long hair unbound, and glossy as a raven's wing, it seemed to
me that I looked upon a wild animal, a creature of the night.

I turned away from her, and my gaze fell upon the Sylvester
house, which I had not looked upon in nearly a year. In compar-
ison to the rude shacks of the town, this gabled mansion must
seem a grand palace to Marguerite Willette, for all its neglect.
It had withstood a hundred and more northern winters, which
stripped the paint from the weatherboards and turned the exposed wood grey as cloud. Shutters dangled from broken
hinges, revealing dust-dull panes; the few intact shutters were
closed. Many windows had been boarded up, to cover broken
glass, and keep out the winds of winter. Altogether, the house
presented a sinister aspect which I had not noticed when Geoffrey had brought me here last year through the bright forest of
early autumn; I had seen the neglect, but joy in arrival at my
new home had prevented me from perceiving the extent of
decay. It seemed almost as if some malign force were acting
upon the Sylvester family, and I wondered for a moment if a
pagan spirit were seeking to avenge the dead Kennebecs for
the loss of their land.

The garden had once been orderly and beautiful in the English manner; now the paths were buried beneath dead leaves
that sank wetly underfoot, releasing a foetid odor, and rank
weeds and crawling vines covered the garden like a shroud. No
evidence of the garden remained save a few thorny sticks which
bore dark rosebuds lured forth by the treacherous warmth of
an Indian summer. I bent close to the barbed black stalks,

searching for a bloom, and found the buds had all loosened their petals, but only in frost-stricken death. The lacy tatterings of decay made it seem that worms had gotten into the buds, and, though I searched every corner of the garden, I could not find a rose fit to lay upon my son's grave.

I emerged from the garden near a fence of black iron spears which enclosed a small plot: the Sylvester family cemetery. With effort, I opened the gate, which protested with a hideous screech, as if it had been opened rarely through the years, and I stepped among the gravestones. The more distant were of marble; their chiseled letters were worn, and obscured by leprous patches of lichen. Most, however, were of polished granite, and the letters were as sharp as the day they had been carved. I read the name upon the nearest granite surface, and my legs went soft as melting beeswax; I would have collapsed, had I not seized my son's gravestone.

Grief threatened to steal my senses as well as my strength, but I gripped the gravestone so its sharp edges cut my palms, and the painful sensation revived me. I saw that my husband had placed flowers on the grave, a bouquet of red wildflowers which shone to my tear-bright eyes like splashes of paint. I blinked, and found myself remembering my midwife's aversion to my cross as I saw that the wildflowers were mixed with pine tassels and bound with a knotted cornhusk, in a crude Indian fetich.

Marguerite Willette was neither midwife nor Papist, but a priestess serving the pagan spirits of her ancestors. It had not been lingering illness which had caused me to think a malign force sought the downfall of the Sylvesters; a vengeful Indian demon haunted the estate, and its evil acts were manifest in my ill health, and the deterioration of the estate and decline of the family. Even the death of Geoffrey's heir had not satisfied the demon: it must desecrate the innocent infant's grave!

Marguerite was the most loathsome of mortals, a willing slave of devils. A witch. I thanked God for directing me hence to discover the fetich, and, grasping my cross in one hand, I raised the fetich and cast it out of the hallowed ground.

I realized then that the witch had not confined her evil to her attempt to desecrate the grave. In the guise of midwife, that servant of demons had killed my child!

I rose, intending to flee to my husband's house and lock the witch outside. But I was overwhelmed by the weight of my awful discoveries, and I swooned at the cemetery gate.

When my senses returned, I found myself in my chamber, with Geoffrey sitting beside my bed. The flickering candlelight revealed that the lines in his gaunt face were graven more deeply than they had been when I had revived from delirium.

"In your fragile state, I should *never* have allowed you to visit the grave!" said Geoffrey. "Marguerite says you have been unconscious all day—I feared you might never awaken!"

The witch must be near, lingering to pretend concern for her charge, and to hear whatever words passed between my husband and myself. Therefore, I gestured for Geoffrey to lean close, and whispered softly in his ear. "Geoffrey, an evil spirit is haunting your family! It—"

"Emily, what are you saying?" Geoffrey exclaimed. "There are no evil spirits!"

I realized I should never have told him of my discovery. My words must seem to Geoffrey to indicate only a relapse into delirium. He is an attorney, a servant of law and logic; he sees the world as a place of order and light. He could not see the manifold evidence of the demon's efforts to destroy his family.

"Geoffrey, I apologize for the confusion of my speech. I spoke of an evil dream that came upon me in my swoon."

"God forgive me for allowing you to endanger yourself!" Geoffrey cried. "As I feared, the visit to the grave has revived morbid and dangerous memories. Emily, *promise* me you will venture out-of-doors no more!" He grasped my hands. His felt hot as coals. "I could not bear to lose you!"

I gave Geoffrey my promise, and he gave me a kiss as light and soft upon my cheek as the delicate brush of moth wings. When he leaned back, I saw Marguerite watching us. Her bold gaze no longer made me feel as if I were under the scrutiny of a forest animal, an innocent beast. I had always seen it in her eyes, yet I had not known why her regard caused me such profound unease. But I had discovered Marguerite was a witch; and I knew God's commandment concerning witches.

Marguerite stepped forward, her face a mask of repentance. "I have apologized to Mr. Sylvester, Madame," she said, "and I must ask your pardon as well. I pray you will forgive me for so greatly misjudging the speed of your recovery."

I spoke words of forgiveness, and assured her, "I will do whatever you think best." I could not permit the witch, or the demon she served, to know that I had found them out.

Marguerite said my husband must not remain and weary me further when I had suffered a serious reverse. Geoffrey kissed me, and turned away. I glanced clandestinely at Marguerite, and saw that she was watching Geoffrey with a curiously intent expression; I felt a sickening chill as I recognized her look as one of undisguised ardor. The witch had immoral intentions toward my husband, and did not even scruple to hide her lust from the wife of the man she desired; she was no more troubled by shame than her hot-blooded French forebears, or the black-hearted savages with whom they lay in utter disregard of propriety.

When Geoffrey was gone from the room, Marguerite turned to me, and a look expressive of the deepest hatred passed across her face. It was an expression of inhuman intensity, and my heart quailed as I realized her depraved lust had allowed the demon to enter her soul and take possession of her body; her diabolic master could now wreak direct and grievous harm on Geoffrey!

The loathsome expression immediately vanished from Marguerite's countenance, as if the demon had realized it risked discovery, and Marguerite exclaimed in tones of false concern: "Madame you are so pale! You *must* rest!"

She seated herself by my bed, to wait until I fell asleep. I was weary; despite her terrifying gaze, my lids closed. But sleep was banished by the tumult of emotions in my breast.

My husband had not shared my bed for many months; indeed, I had felt relief that he had not. All men have needs, and the flesh is weak; I had given the demon the means to reach Geoffrey.

Terror for Geoffrey's life and soul wracked me, but I held myself motionless; and at last I heard the scrape of a chair sliding, the scuff of footsteps retreating, and the creak and click of a door closing.

I lay still; I did not want the witch to hear me following. But at last I arose and went forth from my bedchamber. My candle cast a small circle of light, and the corridor seemed limitless; the darkness pressed close on every side, as if the spirit sought to extinguish my light and my soul. I clasped my cross and prayed to God, and He gave me the strength to continue.

I came at last to my husband's room, and found the door closed. But the knob turned quietly beneath my hand, and I found myself looking upon a blazing hearth, and upon my husband's bed.

The sight that greeted my eyes turned me cold again—so cold I felt I had plunged through winter ice into the Kennebec River. My husband lay on his back, unclothed, with the witch upon him. Her face and Geoffrey's were hidden by the straight black fall of her hair, and her bare flesh was dark in the hearthlight; she seemed her own Indian ancestress, restored to corporeality, as she comported herself unlike a woman, taking the man's position upon Geoffrey. Her hands touched Geoffrey's bare flesh, her fingers running down his arm, his chest, his stomach; and she seemed to welcome his touch, pressing her flesh into his cupped hands, her hips against his. I knew the demon possessed her, but still her shameful behavior sent a shock of horror shivering through me, and I fear I betrayed myself with a gasp.

Marguerite raised her head so swiftly that her hair flew back, exposing Geoffrey's face; his countenance was so pale and drawn, it seemed the life was almost gone from his mortal flesh—I realized the demon was drawing the soul from my husband!

The witch turned her terrible eyes upon me. I averted my face and, pulling my cross from about my neck, I ran to the fireside.

She shouted; Geoffrey called my name; but I did not look at them. I dropped my candle to the hearthstone and closed my hands on a sharp-tipped fire iron. There is only one way to treat a witch, but I could not do what was necessary unless she could not resist. A prayer on my lips and the cross against my palm, I raised the iron rod and turned toward the demon.

Geoffrey seemed in the grip of a profound terror, though he had no reason to fear me. Marguerite's dark face showed the most startled expression; it was plain to see the demon had expected never to be discovered.

"Emily, *don't!*" Geoffrey cried, revealing how frightfully strong the demon's influence was upon him.

"In God's name, *begone!*" I cried, and swung the iron.

I was astonished that the skull caved in, with a sound like birds' eggs trodden upon in high grass; I had expected only that the blow would distract the demon long enough for me to thrust my cross into Geoffrey's hand. But the witch's flesh proved vulnerable to iron, or to the alliance of iron and cross, and the witch's body fell at my feet. Blood shone bright red on my hands, and on the black iron, and on Geoffrey's breast and face.

His countenance twisted into an expression of guilt painful to behold, and he slipped off the bed and sank to his knees before me. "Emily, I beg your forgiveness! I never meant to betray our vows—"

I lowered the iron and raised one hand to touch his face. "You must not apologize, Geoffrey," I said. "You did not know what you did! The Indian spirit that possessed Marguerite exerted an irresistible influence upon your fallible flesh." I pressed my cross into his unresisting hands. "You must wear the cross always, for the protection of your immortal soul"

The body lay motionless upon the floor; but death can be feigned, so I struck the skull again. The body never stirred; I had succeeded in driving the demon from its mortal shell.

I dropped the iron, "Marguerite killed our son, Geoffrey." I could hardly speak for the weight of grief upon my heart. "She killed him in service to a vengeful Indian demon which seeks your death and the end of your family! Marguerite was a *witch!* And we must *burn* the witch, as God commands!"

Geoffrey remained silent, but his expression was altered by astonishment and horror as he realized the dreadful fate he had so narrowly avoided. He had always denied the existence of spirits, yet now he had incontrovertible proof that a demon had commanded the death of his son and heir, and very nearly taken his own life.

I seized the witch's arm with both my hands, and attempted to drag the body to the hearth. "Help me, Geoffrey! We must burn the witch, lest the demon reanimate her lifeless flesh!"

Geoffrey raised my cross and stared at it, then bundled me in his arms. "Oh, Emily, Emily." He spoke my name over and over, and he held me tight, as if he thought I would run away from him. I could not help but notice how he trembled at the realization of his narrow escape from death and damnation.

I made him swear in God's name to wear the cross always, for the safety of his soul and his family. Then he said I must return to my room. When I protested, he assured me that he would dispose of the body properly; and I felt so terribly weary that I allowed him to escort me to my chamber, and put me to bed.

Though I reminded Geoffrey that he must not delay burning the witch's body, he stayed with me, sitting by our bed and holding my hand. In my exhaustion, and my knowledge that my husband had the protection of my cross, I fell asleep.

When I awoke, I was alone, and my cross once more lay on my breast. I ran to the door, and found it locked. Terrified, I pounded upon the door, calling to my husband in my loudest voice, warning him that his soul was in grievous danger. He came to the door and assured me that he had taken care of the body, and that he had God's protection even as I did. A doctor was coming from Augusta, he said, to ascertain whether my health had been adversely affected by my exertions of last night. I assured him that I had recovered completely, and expressed how strongly I desired to be with him, but he did not unlock the door.

Though my bedchamber is high above the ground, I ran to the window, desperate to escape the room and confirm that Geoffrey had the protection of a cross. But when I drew back the heavy drapes, I saw that my window had been entirely covered by boards. I shattered the glass as I struck the wood, attempting to loosen a board with blows of my fist; the sharp pain and bright splash of blood immediately recalled me to myself, and brought me to a realization of the foolishness of my actions. Why would Geoffrey tell me he had protection if he were not wearing a cross? He knew his immortal soul was at risk! A loving husband, he feared for my soul, and demonstrated the depth of his concern by returning my cross to me and sealing my room to ensure my safety.

But Geoffrey's love is all the protection I need.

Nancy Holder

❧ ❧

HEAT

Nancy Holder's story taps directly into one of my own fantasies. It deals with an upper-class Japanese custom whispered about in not-so-PC circles. Having had personal experience with the problems this custom creates, I can only say that I did not handle the problem as boldly as the protagonist in Nancy's story.

❧ ❧

It is so easy to blame others, and Genevieve did, but perhaps she had cause. Her husband when he began his affair with her was most attentive, most ardent, and, most importantly, most available. But as soon as their names were on the marriage license, all signs of wooing ceased: no more flowers, no more expensive gifts, and very few passionate hours.

Very few: having tamed the mistress, having made a wife of her, he had lost interest.

She should have anticipated it, perhaps even accepted it as an ironic, although just, punishment. But she was so used to his adoration that it had never occurred to her that anything could happen to change it. In her naiveté she had believed that his offer of marriage was a culmination, a triumph, the prize.

Now, these hot, sultry nights of a Tokyo summer, when the

illuminated Tokyo Tower so resembled the Eiffel Tower that tears sprang to her eyes, she lay alone in bed watching the beautiful soft-core pornography of her native France on laser disc and touched herself, pretending her hands and fingers were his.

As illicit lovers, they had often watched such movies, both aroused by the perfection of the bodies as they writhed and clung together. He had been fascinated to discover that she, too, found pleasure in the beautiful breasts and hips of the women. Most women did, she informed him. They had been trained to from birth—witness the dozens of fashion magazines, the advertisements, the preponderance of closeups in movies and on TV. Their softly lit, airbrushed bodies as men took them in various positions sent her into a dreamlike state of receptivity that drove him wild.

They had coupled in the corporate apartment in Harajuku, in hot spring resorts on Hokkaido, in a charming inn at the southern tip of the Izu Peninsula—the golden tip, the dark pink tip at sunset, dipping into pearldrops of ocean foam as the water eternally tantalized the shore.

He had bought her pearls, and a Mercedes, and fabulous underthings that he would put on her very slowly, and rip off her with his teeth.

Now, he "worked late." Now, he "had to entertain clients."

It occurred to her that he had probably found himself a new mistress. She opened her legs to her lonely fingers and imagined herself confronting him, making a tremendous scene. But his wife—his former wife—had done that, and had it helped her win the battle?

But Hiroyo had lost the moment Kenji had lain eyes on Genevieve. Attached to the French consulate, Genevieve had helped him with some import documents; as thanks, so he said, he had asked her to have dinner. It was the beginning, and it was glorious.

Poor Hiroyo. Now Genevieve recalled their lunch, the defeated general laying down arms before the victor. Genevieve had almost tried to apologize:

"I'm so sorry, Owasawa-san, but he's so perfect. I couldn't refuse him."

Hiroyo had picked daintily at her luncheon omelette, the garnishes of strawberries. "I think living as a wife will go more easily for you, Debeau-san, if you do not think of my husband as perfect." She picked up her coffee cup and held it in both hands. "No man is perfect." She sipped. "They are heartless."

Poor Hiroyo.

Poor Hiroyo, indeed. An earthquake of a divorce settlement, and word was that she had moved in with a man two-thirds her age who was willing to slice open his bowels for her.

Genevieve rolled over on her stomach. Sweat trickled between her breasts. Her silk and lace nightgown twisted around her buttocks; she rotated her hips against the satin pillow positioned there, just so. She let the bodice of the gown pull taut against her nipples as the fabric soaked up the moisture. The thick, wet summer air saturated the flesh of her buttocks. She was hot, and wanting. She wanted him, his thick muscles and his tight chest and his exquisite penis. He knew how to move with her, in her; he knew what to do, and when. He was the finest lover she had ever known, and she had assumed, perhaps foolishly, that it was because he was with her. Skill born of desire, and love.

The door to their penthouse opened.

She caught her breath and listened to the familiar jingle of his keys. He was home. She began to pull her gown over her bottom, but wives did that. Mistresses made sure to put on their highest high heels, to daub a bit of perfume along the Delta of the Nile, awaiting the inundation. She lay as she was, panting a little.

He went into the kitchen and poured himself a drink. She heard the splash of liquor and the tinkle of ice cubes.

She waited.

After a time she began to doze.

When she awakened and heard the TV, a slow anger burned through her. How dare he? The anger built. She moved herself against the pillow. The satin caressed her sex, the shell-pink folds and spirals of pleasure, and she moved against it harder as her mind turned red. Unthinking bastard.

She moved harder.

Pig.

Harder.

Harder.

Harder.

The small of her back rippled and tingled. Eddies swirled in her abdomen, her loins, her thighs. Her nipples were erect.

Arrogant Jap.

The pleasure began to ascend toward ecstasy. Her breath came in gasps, barely came at all. She gripped the headboard. She would slap him if he came in. She would throw something at him.

She saw his face spider-webbed with blood. She saw a bruise on his cheek.

With a tiny shout deep in her throat, she climaxed.

It was not a large orgasm, not her best or deepest, but it was release.

Some minutes later, Kenji came into the room. His suit jacket was slung over his arm, his white shirt unbuttoned three buttons, his tie loosened. His hair was damp from the heat. He was the most incredible man, broad-shouldered and muscular, his hips narrow, his thighs large and well defined. His cheekbones were astonishing. She couldn't believe she had called him a Jap.

"I was awake when you came home," she said.

"Then why didn't you come to me?" he asked. Of course. A Japanese wife would have had dinner and a hot bath waiting. Summer or winter, they loved their hot baths.

Uneasiness washed over her, and though he began to undress slowly, seducing her, she felt absolutely no passion. Nothing stirred within her, and she was astounded: this was Kenji! This was the lover supreme! He smiled his lazy smile and let his pants drop to the floor, followed by his underwear. He was enormous. His balls were full and heavy. The mere sight of his erect penis usually made her very wet. Now she stared and felt nothing. Her lack of interest was not because she had recently played with herself. She could come again and again. When they had first gotten together, Kenji had marveled at her capacity, her appetite. He was thrilled that she was nearly insatiable. Now he approached the bed and stood over her. She made herself smile and open her arms. Like a cat, he began to climb onto the mattress, slinking up and over her. He pulled down her bodice and touched and caressed her breasts, one and then the other, pinched the nipples.

She could only think that she should have made him something to eat.

He kissed her. She opened her mouth and let him slide his tongue in, allowing him to explore before she touched his tongue in return. It was the way he liked it.

She should have made him a bath.

He nudged her legs apart and entered her in a long, sliding motion that filled her.

When he had come home, she should have gotten up and greeted him. He thrust hard; she was still moist from having masturbated. Otherwise, the movement would have hurt her. Bastard, she thought fiercely. Bastard for not making sure she was ready. And since when did her life revolve around someone else's? In Japan it was a man's world, but she was not Japanese. If he'd wanted a simpering slave he should have stayed married to Hiroyo. He was a thoughtless jerk. He was just like—

Heat overtook her. Her nerves overloaded her pleasure centers, and suddenly she was clinging to him, thrusting with his rhythm, crying out. He murmured to her in Japanese, calling her his little fox because there were no words of endearment in his native tongue. She hated it; he knew she did because she had asked him not to ever call her that again. And he had promised, after she told him about the Belgian woman in Paris who had said those same words in German, and Genevieve, not realizing the sexual import of the term, had politely said, "Ja?" and the woman had raped her in an alley with the end of an umbrella.

How could he say that to her? He had held her while she cried. Insensitive boor!

She came, hard, and he followed after. She wanted to scratch out his eyes. Instead, spent, she collapsed into the mattress and lay still as he fell against her.

In the distance, an ambulance bee-booed through the Tokyo dawn. Summer heat, summer fires. Luckily the traffic slackened in the wee hours after the hostess bars and pachinko parlors closed down. She remembered a spring night in Shinjuku when they had gotten their fortunes told. For her, something blasé: Good fortune and conjugal felicity. For him, something odd: Beware a hot wind. How they had laughed at the absurdity. Kenji, her Kenji. He loved her. She snuggled into his embrace and told herself she was imagining things. Everything was all right. Exhausted, she began to drift. She would never be able to move again, speak, open her eyes. She had never felt so wonderfully drained in her life.

"Make me some tea," he said.

"Oh, Kenji," she protested.

"I'm thirsty."

"He waited. She clamped her jaw. He wasn't even asking. He was demanding. Anger surged again.

And with it . . .

. . . desire.

She opened her eyes wide. Allowed the anger to build. Desire built, too.

She looked at him and he nudged her impatiently.

It was all she could do to keep from smacking him.

And sucking him.

Unsteadily she rose from the bed, not because she wanted to obey him but because she needed to think. His seed spilled from her body and she found herself wanting more. Needing more. "First," she said, and put her leg on the bed.

"First, tea." He smiled at her expectantly.

Her anger grew.

She walked from the bedroom into the living room, lay on

the couch, and brought herself to another climax. Then she got up and dutifully made him tea, trembling all the while.

◆§ ℰ◈

He did not have a mistress after all.

So Genevieve invited Arja, a statuesque Finnish girl, to their next dinner party. Arja wore a very revealing black satin dress. Genevieve seated her next to Kenji. He ogled her all night, not bothering to hide it. Genevieve was furious. In the kitchen, on the pretense of preparing espresso, Genevieve brought herself to climax.

Kenji offered to drive Arja home.

Genevieve came three times, and twice more when Kenji finally came home, smelling of the other woman's perfume, of her sex.

It was true, then. She had proven it: her anger at him made her desire for him all the more intense.

Think of the ecstasy if she could come to hate him.

She had lunch with Arja, a complex woman who was obviously wrestling with her conscience and her sense of triumph at the same time. She wore a large ring Genevieve made a point of admiring; Arja colored and murmured something about it being new, from a friend, but the smile couldn't quite stay from her lips. Genevieve was even angrier with Kenji that he would find such a bitch alluring. How dare he? How dare he?

That night she met him naked at the door and pulled off his clothes. She hissed at him, "You're hungry? You want something to eat?" and dragged his head between her legs. He was thrilled. His pleasure made her rage. She came and came; seething, thinking about hurting him in some way, about the knives in the kitchen. About . . .

. . . stabbing, her own form of penetration . . .

She was shocked; she pushed him away and walked to the panorama windows of the penthouse living room, whipping open the drapes and looking down on the vast jewel box of the skyline. Kenji's seed sparkled on her thighs like diamonds; heat rose from the streets, twenty-four stories below.

He came up behind her and cupped her breasts. She clenched her fists as she began to pant. He kissed the side of her neck and whispered, "I have to go away tomorrow. I have to go to Osaka for two days."

With her. Genevieve moved her legs apart so that he could slide his fingers into her. She was sick; she was insane. This had all begun because she missed his companionship and attention, and now she was deliberately courting the absences so that she could get off. She was destroying her love for him for sexual pleasure. But was it not his fault? If he weren't so thoughtless and faithless, would all of this have come about?

"Bastard," she said hotly, but under her breath. Every part of her was hot. Very, very hot.

Would she hate him if she pushed him through the window? If she was left with her remorse and her grief, would she be able to sustain a cold, dark fury?

It seemed that steam sizzled off her body. It would be easy. The windows were actually two horizontal pieces of glass one opened and closed with latches. They were flimsy and she had already asked the manager to replace them.

"I'll need a suitcase for the morning," he went on.

Hate was the opposite of love, they said, but at some point, would it not dissipate? Would she then be left with nothing?

"Kenji," she whispered, turning around, trying at the last to save him. "Kenji, I want a divorce."

He looked startled. Saying nothing, he took a step back from her. She stared at his perfect brown skin, his almond eyes. His sexy, pouting mouth. Would she hate him for leaving her more than she would hate him for dying? He inclined his head and said, "I'll give her up."

She almost smiled. "There will be others."

"No."

"Yes." She opened her arms to him. "There must be others

for you, Mr. Fox." If he lived. And she must hear of them, all of them, and be bitter, and angry, and rich.

For she realized at last that Hiroyo, Kenji's first wife, was correct: no man was perfect. No man.

And there were hundreds of men in Tokyo who could incite her to heights of hot, delirious anger.

Hundreds.

If not thousands.

The sweat rolled off her.

"On occasion," she whispered to him, "we must fuck."

"Nan desuka?" he asked in Japanese, bewildered. What? But maybe not. What had the Shinjuku fortune teller told him? Beware a hot wind. As the old story went: Which shall it be, the lady or the tiger?

"Now open the window, Kenji. It's sweltering in here." He moved. She began to pant. She was so hot.

So very hot.

Carolyn Banks

❧ ❧

SALON SATIN

*I found this story in **Carolyn Banks'** own short story collection and could not resist including it here. It deals with the quintessential sexually rejected wife in a self-discovery story which is bound to speak to many readers.*

❧ ❧

"Oh, my God!" Libby hit the BMW's brakes so hard that both women were jolted against their seat harnesses. "Sorry," she said, laughing apologetically. "But look . . ." She swerved toward the curb so that Joyce could follow the direction in which she was pointing.

"What?" Joyce said. "I don't see a thing."

"There," Lib emphasized, "in that doorway."

"Oh," Joyce put an arch in her voice, "*that* doorway."

It was Salon Satin, the total beauty facility that was touted endlessly on television and in the local press. Salon Satin, which seemed to most of the women of Westlake Hills to be the gaudiest, most outrageous place they'd ever seen.

Consider the Salon Satin logo, made up of seven Gothic windows side by side. And in the worst color combination imaginable: blue, purple, green, orange, white, violet, red. "I mean, really" was all that most of the women could muster to say.

Certainly none of them would ever set foot inside the place, no matter what Salon Satin might promise.

"I see her," Joyce said now, finally catching the point Libby had been trying to make. "I see her!"

It was their friend Shelley, easily the most queen-sized of the group. Or at least she had been.

"She's skinny," Lib almost whispered.

"Maybe it's someone else," Joyce prayed, "not Shelley at all."

But it was Shell, and she came shrieking over to their car. "Are you going to try it?" she asked. "Salon Satin?"

Libby and Joyce exchanged bewildered glances, but they listened to Shelley as she ran through her spiel. She'd dropped twenty pounds. Twenty pounds! And quickly, too. Hadn't they seen her just last month?

"Salon Satin is not for me." Lib was emphatic. She, somewhere between a five and a seven, could afford to be. Joyce, on the other hand, whose jeans had recently become too tight, perked up and really considered it. Why not? She'd tried acupuncture, hypnosis, and a thousand diets. She'd put her aesthetics aside temporarily and give Salon Satin a try. Who knew? Maybe even Emmet, her anerotic husband, would revive.

"If you ask me," Libby said as they drove home, "Shell looks like a hooker."

"Maybe," Joyce said. But really, she was thinking, "Yes, but a thin hooker." Shelley had recently been widowed. Joyce found herself wondering if that was what it took.

Salon Satin was worse inside than she would have imagined, but then, Joyce and Emmet's own quarters were done in an almost industrial gray and muted tweed. Still, it was hard for anyone of reasonable taste to take: the way the rooms spilled into each other, blue into purple into green and so on, complete with stained-glass windows in those hues. Needless to add, there were satin-clad attendants, each dressed up to match the room in which he or she was working. And some of the rooms—the blue, the green, the white, and the violet—had dishes of candies in exactly those colors as well.

Oy, Joyce thought, as she smiled through the tour.

There was one room left. Its door was covered in black satin and it was locked. The girl who led the tour apologized and led Joyce back to Reception: the blue.

"Your reason for coming here?" The girl with the pad wore blue polish on her nails.

"Weight loss."

"And exactly how many pounds?"

Joyce's first instinct was to lie, but then she caught sight of herself in the blue-tinged mirror, caught sight of her midriff and belly merging as she sat. Emmet, Emmet, it had been two years since he'd tried to touch her. "Thirty," she admitted.

"That will take three visits," the girl smiled. "You'll go to the orange room today, then the green, and if you're losing sufficiently . . ." she trailed off, looking at Joyce expectantly. When no questions came, she snapped her pad shut and rang for an orange-clad attendant. "We're required by law to tell you," her voice became mechanical, "that not everyone reaches the weight loss goals she's set."

"How many do?" Joyce asked.

"Oh," the girl with blue nails looked around the room, "one in a blue moon."

◄§ §►

Joyce lay on the orange satin sheet and stared up at the ceiling. She saw a lizard—a chameleon she guessed, since it, too, was orange—above her. It's eyes seemed like colored glass, hard, rigid.

She turned her head to the side and was startled to see three young children, two boys and a girl, dressed in orange harlequin suits. They juggled oranges, tossing them in bold arcs to each.

Joyce laughed. There was a strange sound, part rattle, part swish, as though a beaded curtain had been parted. The children, letting the oranges fall to the floor, backed respectfully from the room. Joyce turned to see what they saw: a tall, slender black man. There was something serpentine about him, though he wasn't in any way repulsive. On the contrary. Joyce felt her insides quiver, turn gooshy and liquid.

He came closer. Joyce's eyes were riveted upon his. It was as though, so long as he stared, she would be unable to turn her own gaze away.

Finally he blinked and Joyce was able not only to look away but to breathe. She closed her eyes now, afraid to lock upon his again. She felt him leaning over her, felt his fingers just inches from her breast. Her eyes flew open. But he wasn't near her, wasn't near at all. He laughed softly, as if he knew what she had been thinking.

That evening, she declined a Scotch and soda. When dinner came,she passed the French bread without taking any. Her husband didn't notice, but Libby, dining with them, did. "Salon Satin?" Lib whispered. Joyce told her, yes.

❧ ❧

Joyce sat in a green satin box. She was naked now, and the box forced her to sit cross-legged, exposing herself, as it were. But she wasn't the performer, she was the audience. Four green-clad ballerinas whirled and vaulted to soft, tender strains. There was something green about the music, too.

When the performance was over, he came again, the black man. He was naked, too. Joyce found herself unable to keep from staring at his groin. His penis, even in repose, was solid and long. Joyce yearned to take it in her hand.

He bent down, almost as if bowing, and reached for her, helped her to her feet. She stood unashamed. Her head tilted back so that she could look at him and with that look say, yes, that she was ready, neither shy nor coy . . .

Again, his knowing laugh. He cupped her chin with his hands and his teeth gleamed in the green streaming light. "Later," he said. "In a week, perhaps. When you are . . ." His fingers left her and his voice grew far away and dim, "thinner."

Joyce looked down at her feet. A young serpent essed across

her toes and away, under the green satin door. Joyce hadn't been afraid, hadn't pulled away. The serpent was beautiful, like a satin ribbon looped and drawn across the floor.

◄§ §►

That night and the next Joyce and Emmet were forced to entertain Emmet's clients, to eat in restaurants. Joyce always looked forward to these occasions, as if the desserts and rich sauces so consumed were calorically innocent. Both nights, however, Joyce was able to look appreciatively but without any hint of yearning at the pastry trays, luxurious creations of puff pastry and whipped cream. "None for me, thanks," she said.

She had lost fourteen pounds. Later, in bed, she turned to Emmet and ran her fingers along the fringes of his hair.

"I'm tired, Joyce," he told her. "Come on, what are we, kids?"

"I have sixteen pounds to lose," Joyce told the girl with blue fingernails. "I'll do anything."

"Anything?"

"Yes."

The girl rang, and six young men in tuxedos—they looked rather like pallbearers, Joyce thought—came out and beckoned to Joyce.

She looked questioningly at the girl with blue nails, but had no hope, she saw, of even getting the girl's attention.

Something made her hesitate, however.

"Tut tut" came a voice. She turned and saw the black man. "You did," he reminded her, "say you'd do anything."

Joyce smiled, nodded, and went willingly now, following the six down the corridors as the light shifted, blue to purple to green to orange to white. In the white room, the six men started to undress, leaning upon one another at first to remove their shoes, their socks, their trousers. Their voices were loud, but the satin on the walls and the floors and the furniture seemed to absorb the shock of the sound.

They made love to each other, their limbs tangled, their mouths continually engaged. Joyce leaned back against the wall—they were totally unaware of her—and watched until they seemed to have sated themselves. One of them finally noticed her. He stood, went to his trousers to retrieve a key, and led her through the violet room to the black satin door.

"You did say *anything*," he reminded her.

"Yes," Joyce said.

With that, he unlocked the door and gave it a push.

It rocked back on its hinges and held itself open. Joyce walked boldly in. It closed behind her, and she heard the unmistakable sound of the key again in the lock.

The pace of her breathing increased. She was sweating, too, though the room was quite cold. She touched her forehead and her fingers came away wet.

The room was blacker than any she had ever been in. Then there was a gonglike sound, and an immediate hiss accompanied by bright red flame. He, the black man, was silhouetted before her.

"Undress," he said.

"I'm cold," she said. Joyce's hand, however, went to the buttons of her blouse. She began to undo them.

He threw something, a fine gold powder of some sort, on the brazier and the flame grew instantly hot. He watched as Joyce stripped.

Joyce smiled. "I am, as you requested, thinner," she said.

He walked about her, inspecting her as if she were a piece of fine statuary. "So you are," he agreed. He took her hand and placed it on his penis. She felt it swell, lifting her hand a foot or more.

Joyce laughed delightedly. Her thumb sought the delicate knob at the end.

"Tell me about your husband," he insisted.

"There is nothing to tell."

This amused him. "I suspected," he said finally. He knelt at her feet. She felt his breath on her thighs, felt his lips on her belly. Emmet had never done that to her, never once.

He pulled back. "You aren't quite thin enough," he said, standing, searching for his clothes.

"No, please," Joyce said. "Please."

"I'm sorry," he said, sliding one leg into his trousers. "It's Salon Satin policy. Unless . . ." he pondered.

"I told you," Joyce fought to keep from sounding shrill, "I'll do . . ."

"Oh, yes," his teeth gleamed at her again, "anything."

❦

He sent her home. She walked through the breezeway with the weapon that he had given her. It was as if it had materialized in his hand.

Sure enough, just as he'd said, there they were: Libby and Emmet, writhing, their bodies glistening with sweat. They didn't even see her, something Joyce regretted. She did as she was told, however, showering them with bullets until neither of them would ever move again.

❦

She went directly to the black satin door, no one barring her way. He was there. He took the weapon from her, lifted her skirt, stroked her bottom.

"No one saw you?" he asked.

"No."

"Good. But before we proceed, do you know who I am?"

"You are Satin," Joyce said, gesturing at the words Salon Satin in vermeil on the black satin wall.

"Very good," he said. "Very good." White teeth gleaming, ebony rock hard and muscled taut. "And do you know—"

"Yes, yes," Joyce interrupted, taking his hand and guiding it under the waistband of her new black satin panties."

"You are thinner," he said, momentarily distracted.

"Thirty pounds so." She had stepped through the bedroom where Libby and Emmet lay, stepped through the bloodspray so that she might reach the bathroom scale.

"Then you do know?"

Joyce was coquettish for the first time in her life, rolling his penis between the palms of her hands and fawning up at him. "About the, uh, typographical error?" She knelt now, about to close her lips upon him. "Yes, Satin. Yes, yes, I know."

"Mmmmm," he answered.

Nina Kiriki Hoffman

❧ ☙

A TOUCH OF
THE OLD
LILITH

Nina Kiriki Hoffman *is one of those enviable people who seems to have no enemies. Not so the protagonist of this story, whose worst enemy is the "self" created out of her grandmother's constant retelling of an old family myth.*

❧ ☙

We inherit much from our families, but sometimes it might be just too much.

❧ ☙

Grandma said there was a touch of the old Lilith in all the Meander women, and she flexed her finger, beckoning, to prove it, saying that under the right circumstances the bones of one's finger became the spine of a snake. "Lilith was the first tempter, who took men one step away from God. She offered them the poison of death. Lilith was a Meander, and you's a Meander woman, little Clea. Don't you forget it."

I didn't understand the connection between Lilith and snakes until later, but I didn't forget anything Grandma told me the summer I turned eleven.

That summer comes back to me whenever I smell aromatic pipe tobacco or violet water. Grandma and I spent a lot of time on the porch together in the evenings while waiting for the air to cool enough for us to sleep. She patted violet water on her throat when the sun beat down, saying violets only grew in shadows, so the scent was cool. She smoked fragrant tobacco in a lady's pipe and blew the smoke at me, saying it would help keep off the mosquitos. She sat in the ladderback rocker like a little old toad, her short white hair boiling around her head, her gray eyes bright as thick summer stars. Her fingersnaps particularly pleased me; my mother had slammed all her fingers in a door before I was born, and her knuckles were scarred, their movements restricted.

Grandma was full of strange tales. Two of them in particular she told me over and over—the touch of Old Lilith one, with no explanations, and the bogey one—and I was a long time getting to sleep each night because of them that summer. She came to live with us just after her house burned down and Grandpa died. Daddy griped about that. Mom was the youngest of seven kids. "She has so many children she doesn't know what to do—why pick on us?" said Daddy. But our house had a guest room, so Grandma came to us first.

I asked Grandma about the fire. She said the police asked questions about why she wasn't home at two in the morning— when a neighbor first smelled smoke and saw flames, but too late to save Grandpa. Grandma was out picking flowers. "Phases of the moon," she said, waving a copy of the *Farmer's Almanac* at the police. She had carried it with her the night of the fire. "Got to harvest in the dark of the moon. Poor old Harvey—if only he didn't have that 'rithmatic in his bones—couldn't take the dew chill, otherwise he might have been out with me and alive today."

The last time I saw Grandpa Harvey had been the family Christmas party when I was still ten. His eyes had white shields over them and he couldn't see, and his hands shook. Grandma whispered to me that the shields saved him from seeing all the wickedness in the world; they were called cataracts, which meant waterfalls which meant cleansing and tears. I never understood that either. Mom said Grandpa had been blind since before she was born.

Investigation proved it to have been an electrical fire, bad wiring in the kitchen walls, nobody's fault. Everybody said I was too young to go to a funeral, so they left me with Lizzy Burns next door when they went off to bury Grandpa. When they got back, Mom's eyes were swollen and the tip of her nose was red, but Grandma looked just as chipper as ever.

That night, when I couldn't sleep, I snuck outside and crept around the side of the house until I was just under Mom's and Daddy's bedroom window. I had had the sense all summer that everybody was protecting me from things without telling me what I was supposed to be afraid of, and I hated not knowing, so I was always seeking out information any way I could. Somehow when I turned eleven in the spring, I figured out the whole world was in cahoots to keep everything quiet, but it was time for me to know. Wasn't I almost a teenager? When I was ten everybody still thought I was a baby, but it was time for that to change now, whether the grownups thought so or not.

Mom and Daddy were talking in the dark. "Poor old Pa," said Mom. "Never hurt a soul."

"Probably a merciful release," said Dad. "I would have done anything to get away from your mother. Maybe even set the fire myself. I might do it yet."

Mom said it was lucky the evidence was so clear, otherwise Grandma made a great suspect, her not shedding a tear over Grandpa or grieving over the loss of the house.

Daddy said, "Will you cry when I'm gone?"

"Peter, you know I will," said Mom, her voice tender.

"Oh, so you're planning to outlive me, are you?"

When I was younger I wished Daddy had a sense of humor like Mom's, but he never did. If he had said that with a smile in his voice, it would have been all right. But he hadn't.

I leaned my chin on my knees and waited for Mom's reply. Around me her carefully tended rose bushes whispered to each other, the flowers spilling a heavy rich scent on the night air. The dark, moist earth chilled me through my thin cotton nightgown and the soles of my feet. After a moment, Mom's voice came again, drifting out the open window of their bedroom.

"We Meander women are long-lived," said Mom in her slow, flat, Scriptures-reading voice.

"You Meander women," Daddy said, his voice sneering. "You sound like your mother. Why do you call yourself Meander? Your maiden name was Stone."

He was off, telling her again how stupid she was.

And when he had finished, run out of voice, she murmured, "Hush." I heard the sheets rustle, and the slide of flesh on flesh, like the sound a snake's belly makes as it crawls across tiles.

I resolved for the fifty-sixth time never, ever, to get married. I wished I hadn't lain awake thinking about the long-fingered bogey that hid under girl's beds and reached up to inject them with zombie juice the instant their breathing slowed in sleep. "When you wake up the next morning, you feel dead," Grandma said. "The bogey whispers the orders for the day and you follow them. You never make another move unless he tells you to. Nobody else notices anything wrong with you, and you can't tell nobody about it." Then she laughed. "I once knew a girl who was bogey-bit and nobody found out till sixteen years later. Nothing to do but kill her, poor thing. They just get too used to being zombies; real life ain't natural to 'em anymore, even if you *could* clean the juice out of their blood. It builds up in the brain."

Between Grandma's stories and Mom's and Dad's fights that summer, I didn't sleep much at all. I was even relieved when I started seventh grade in the fall, though I was at a new school with a lot of older kids at it, when I had gotten used to being in the most senior class. Grandma moved out the week before school started. I thought Daddy must have had something to do with that; he had been nagging Mom about Grandma since the fire. I learned later that Mom wanted Grandma gone just as much as Daddy did. Grandma went to live with my Uncle Kyle, a bachelor who managed an apartment complex—he fixed up a basement for her, and Daddy said that was only appropriate.

With hard work and a lot of reading, I managed to close up my memories over all Grandma's stories, but they still lay under the floor of my mind, like seeds buried deep and forgotten but full of growth potential, with the right sort of care.

◆§ §◆

When Daddy died two years later, and Grandma came to the funeral, I looked at her in her black clothes and little slivers of summer memory struggled free. She kissed my cheek, and her violet scent brought my eleventh summer back in a rush.

That night as I lay in bed, I bit the heels of my hands, trying to cry for my father. True to her word, my mother had cried for him, but I had not been able to; the funeral seemed to be happening on television, with me a distant watcher. So after I crawled in between the cold sheets and turned out the light, I concentrated on the times Daddy took me to the park down the street and taught me how to catch tadpoles with a pet store fishnet. I remembered him buying me a baseball glove when I was twelve, and playing catch in the yard with me. That eased my mind somewhat; nobody at school played with me much, so it was nice to have someone to come home to—when Daddy was in the mood.

Consciously I reached for what had been my favorite memory of Daddy: when I was nine, he came into the room where I was sitting on the floor, watching some show on television. I couldn't remember the show, I just remembered him sitting on the couch behind me, stroking my hair gently. I leaned against his knee and closed my eyes, feeling his hand on my head, a safe caress. I loved him completely in that moment, but it never happened again.

Though I had cherished these memories of him even while he was alive, they refused to stay with me that night. Instead I relived Grandma's summer at our house, her snapping her index finger at me like a striking snake, her old voice murmuring to me like the buzz of a summer fly on a winter window, the words slipping into my mind before I could shut them out. That night I dreamed, not of my father, but of the bogey under the bed, and I woke with a scream in my throat, lodged there like a bone.

A year later, my mother remarried. His name was Patrick, and he was large and loud and friendly, completely different from my small dark father. Grandma came to the wedding. She wore the same clothes she had worn to my father's funeral, and she shook her head no through the whole ceremony. "Eh, Mother, I saw you objecting," Patrick said at the reception after kissing Grandma's cheek.

"I'm an old woman, boy," she said—or I thought she said; she might have said "bogey." "Old women get shaky."

◆§ §◆

I didn't understand why Danny invited me to the senior prom. Nobody had asked me out on a date during my entire high school career, and I was satisfied with that; whenever anyone came near, I felt somewhere within me the lidless, ever-open eyes of snakes looking out at them, waiting to strike. I let those snakes look out through my eyes, and people always backed away.

I thought Danny must have been dared to do it, but facts were hard to come by later, when he was gone. I only know that when he took my hand and led me out on the floor for the first slow dance, I was more terrified than I ever had been before. His arms around me, his hands at the back of my waist, where I couldn't see them. My own hands out of sight behind his neck, where my fingers might have been flexing any moment, without my volition. I felt intensely aware of everything, the fragile orchid touching my wrist, the heat of Danny through his suit, his hands like solid sunlight warming my back, his smell, a mixture of aftershave and an oily human scent I had never been so close to before. The music we walked on, as though it were a staircase. Fear was so strong in me I felt as if the ground had vanished. My hands shook like Grandpa Harvey's had. I felt sweat trickle down my spine.

They said later it was heart attack. His family had a history. But never so young before.

❦

There was a year between high school and college when I ran away. I chased forgetting. When I found it, I came home again.

❦

Being the first one to arrive Monday mornings, I got to wheel the cart away from the library drop chute and check in all the returned books. As I pulled due-date cards out of the pockets and replaced them with check-out cards, I noticed a name: Jeffry Chase. He had checked out a whole stack of books on photography.

I remembered I had encountered a stack like this the week before, books on darkroom techniques, with his name on the check-out cards. This week, I found big picture books about the work of Diane Arbus, Eugene Atget, Richard Avedon, Edmund Weston. I paused, opened the books one at a time, looked at an image in each. Here was a man, wife and large-headed baby, all so much closer to the camera than they would be to a person in the normal course of conversation that their imperfections seemed glaring. Here was a street in Paris at the turn of the century, the road surfaced with wet paving stones, the buildings faced with wrinkled and torn posters and, in the misty distance, a bare-branched tree; here, an ultra-slender woman from the sixties with black kohl heavy around her eyes, her hair cut in a pageboy, her clothes short and stark; here, a bell pepper, photographed in black and white, its smooth curves sensuous and startling.

I closed the books slowly and put them on the filing cart, wondering about Jeffry. I tried to picture him in my mind, though I hadn't checked out any of these books for him. Was he a little old man, taking up a new hobby? Trying to connect with a past he remembered but could not picture clearly? Was he a teenager doing a project for high school? Maybe he had been given a list of books to check out. Maybe he was in college, like I was, doing a photographic internship like my library one.

My supervisor Jenna came in then and got mad at me for forgetting to start the coffee and for sitting over books with my eyes unfocused when there was work to be done.

But later, when a young man came to the desk, his hair curly black and his eyes the color of amethysts, I suspected him of being Jeffry; of course, he also had a stack of large photo books. I thought if I looked as gorgeous as he did, I would probably be interested in photography, too, wanting to preserve my own image in as many ways as possible, and studying which images had survived from the past.

I was the only one at the desk when he came and put down his books and a red backpack. Jenna had taken first lunch, leaving me in charge. I knew that, and still, when he smiled at me, I looked behind me to see if there was someone else who deserved that smile. I went over to the stack of due-date cards and offered him a timid smile in response.

"Hello," he said as I opened his books and took cards out of them. "I'm Jeff Chase, and I've been waiting three weeks for this moment."

"Pardon me?"

"Watching you work, hoping the moment would come when I could speak with you."

I touched my necklace, an amber pendant Grandma had sent me for my sixteenth birthday. I felt an urge to look behind me again, certain this fairy tale prince must be talking to someone else.

"Why?" I said, and would have stepped on my own foot if I had been someone else watching me, to stop me from being so gauche.

"You have a certain beauty—not just in the common run, you know. I was hoping I could talk with you—ask you—I know this must sound like a line—if I could take pictures of you. I'm trying to put together a portfolio."

"Pictures? Of me?" My tone as full of doubt.

He gave me that smile again, his eyes catching light. "So many people say they'll break my camera. It amazes me! Look." He opened the outer pocket on his backpack and took out a snapshot. I looked at a face leaning on a hand, a spill of chestnut hair framing the features. Her pale eyes dreamed, and a smile touched one edge of her wide mouth. She had dark curved brows.

I got an eerie feeling from the picture, the sensation that it was a fossil found locked in a rock, and I wondered why it struck that chord. I turned the picture sideways. No clues.

Suddenly I realized I was looking at myself, a me I never saw in the mirror, where I always focused first on my blemishes, and second on getting the eyeliner on straight. I stared up at the man.

"I took that with my little Pentax three weeks ago. Would you model for me? I can't pay much, but I'll give you proof sheets. Maybe a few prints of the better shots."

I swallowed my first no, and thought a minute. He must have been nuts. Why would anyone look twice at me, especially a man like this? But this picture, maybe there was a me I didn't know how to look for. If we could keep the camera between us, we should be safe. It might be fun. I might see someone I wouldn't recognize who was also a part of me.

"Saturday?" I said.

❧ ❧

He had some clothes he gave me to wear, a black dress with gold embroidery, a little large on me, and a black velvet cloche hat. He had asked me to bring black tights if I had them, and black high heels. I found some tights in a suitcase in the closet, among clothes I had been thinking about getting rid of but couldn't bear giving away. I brought the tights and my church shoes.

We talked about makeup; I never met a man who knew anything about makeup before. He had some rice powder he said Geisha girls used to pale their complexions. I sat in a chair with a towel over the black and gold dress and closed my eyes as he brushed the powder across my face, another strange caress, light as the touch of a butterfly's wing on my cheek. With expert hands he outlined my eyes in black, touched pale pink on my lips.

He handed me a mirror and again I saw someone I didn't know. My sense of myself as fossil returned, ancient and somehow horrible. My eyes looked clear and bottomless, my mouth silent, my expression remote. I could not smile at myself. In some buried corner of my mind, my grandmother's index finger snapped.

Jeffry took me to the graveyard.

He positioned me between the marble pillars of a Greek-style mausoleum. "The contrast between cold stone and warm flesh," he said, smiling at me. I looked at my pale hand against the white marble and thought he was right: my hand looked translucent, but it had its own beauty against the solid rock, a misty, living reality.

As Jeffry told me to turn and lean, to look toward the sky and think of flying, to glance at the ground and think of autumn, I felt disturbed on some other level. What were we really doing here, with me dressed as a corpse in mourning and poising with lambs and little angels on the graves of long-dead children? I leaned my cheek on a lichen-laced rough-hewn stone, smelling centuries locked in rock, and the acid tang of molding oak leaves. I listened to Jeffry's camera click. If he really wanted to contrast life with death, I should have been wearing red, or green. I felt I had wandered into someone else's dream.

The day was overcast. "Pearl light," Jeffry called it. "A diffuse, indirect light that softens edges." The grass and earth stayed wet with yesterday's rain; I shivered, remembering Grandpa Harvey, burned to death because he couldn't take the dew chill. Jeffry asked me to kneel on a grave beside a tombstone that bore a photographic tile depicting a little dead girl. Her face beamed above the date of her death, fifty years earlier. I touched the tile, wondering about parents marooning their child's image in this death camp. My memory jogged. I wondered if this child had died of bogey-bite.

"Can you get her expression on your face?" Jeffry asked.

"No," I said, standing up. "No."

He studied me for a minute, then nodded. "Let's go get some coffee. I bet you're cold."

In the coffeeshop I went to the women's room and splashed water on my face, hoping I could wash away the stranger Jeffry had photographed. I scrubbed my face with the gritty, pink institutional-scented soap. Then I looked at myself in the mirror. The warm water and the soap brought the blood back to my cheeks, and my lips looked dark pink again, but my eyes still frightened me. The day before, I had believed them blue, but this day they looked steel gray. I stared at my self but felt as if someone else were studying me.

When I got back to the table, Jeffry looked at me. "Coffee's not enough," he said. "Can I take you out to dinner tonight?"

The chill began to seep out of me. "All right," I said. "But this time I get to choose my own clothes."

‣§ ß•

He brought some black-and-white prints with him when he came to pick me up that night. I glanced at them, then put them back inside the envelope, not wanting to think about them. I left them on the table by my front door, and we went out to a place with a wine list, and napkins on top of two layers of tablecloths. Jeffry watched me during the meal. He liked how I looked, in my jewel red dress, my hair in a chignon. I could sense his intense appreciation. It felt wonderful. It scared me.

I clung tight to my hard-earned forgetting.

We went to his apartment after supper. When he touched me, it was with reverence, and even in the heat that followed, I had the sense that he worshiped me.

∞ ∞

I went home for Thanksgiving. I wanted Jeffry to come, but his mother wanted him at her house, and it was too soon, he said, to tell his mother about us. "I've never missed a Thanksgiving with Mother," he said. "I don't want her getting suspicious."

Grandma was at Mom's when I got there. "Hello, little Clea," she said to me as she always did, though I was taller than she. She looked exactly the same age as she had when I was eleven, and this time she was wearing colors—a purple and magenta dress, and a straw hat with a large droopy brim and sprays of fake cherries on it.

Patrick greeted me with a big kiss on the cheek and took the pumpkin pie I had bought at Safeway the day before. His bright hair had started to gray, and he was thickening through the middle. He vanished with the pie toward the kitchen. I smelled the rich holiday smell of turkey baking, and wondered why I didn't feel cheerful.

After grace, Patrick carved the turkey and Mom served, silent. I ate a lot of everything, following some instinct I didn't understand—I ate until I felt sick, without really tasting the food. No one talked during the meal, but afterward, when Patrick went in to watch football, Grandma and Mom and I cleared and started cleaning up. I took Jeff's pictures out of my satchel and showed them to Mom and Grandma. "My boyfriend took these," I said. He had tacked prints of me up all over his apartment, so I was getting used to them. "I wanted to bring him, but he couldn't make it."

They were both rock silent as they looked at the black-and-

white photographs of my cool perfection among the tomb-
stones. Mom's eyes seemed to grow shallow. Grandma said,
"Oh, child. Oh, child." She reached out and took Mom's hand
in hers, stroking the scarred knuckles. A tear spilled down her
cheek. "I tried to give you everything, little Clea, but I couldn't.
So the killing starts."

"What killing, Grandma?" I felt disturbed, as if I knew what
she was talking about but didn't want to admit it. An image of
Danny's face surfaced in my mind. I drowned it again, a reflex.
Grandma had never known about Danny's death.

"Killing you into something other than what you are," she
said. "Why can't people leave people alone?"

"Oh, Ma, you know we're put on this earth to be something
to somebody," said my mother, pulling her hand away from
Grandma and shoving both hands into her apron pockets.

"Don't you do what your Mama done, Clea," Grandma said.
"Don't you help him kill you."

"What do you mean?" I asked. My face felt hot now, both
with the meal and the tension. I felt sick.

"I'm going for a nap now," said Grandma. She blinked three
times and walked out of the kitchen.

"Mom—"

"She's an evil woman," said my mother.

"What?" I asked. I had never heard my mother speak with
more conviction.

"She filled my head with tales when I was little. She told us
stories every night. Sometimes she told us Bible stories, but she
talked as if the people were all relatives. She told you stories
that summer, didn't she?"

I remembered. "Yes," I said, feeling again the overpowering
dread that kept me lying sleepless in my bed night after night.

"That's why I begged Kyle to take her away. I didn't want
her filling you up with all those evil thoughts. I didn't want you
to do what I did, and what Jan and Suzle did in their own ways."

I hadn't heard Aunt Suzle's name since I was thirteen. I was
looking at a picture book of Mom's family, laughing because
my aunt and my mother and my four uncles looked so strange

as children. There was another girl in many of the pictures. "That's your Aunt Suzle," Mom had said. "She's dead."

Mom stared at the floor. "Ma told us—oh, Clea, you're too young to hear this. I don't want you to be scared the way I was."

I looked at the pictures spread out on the kitchen table. In one of them, I stared straight into the camera. Behind me, a stone angel prayed with lowered lids. "Mom, if you don't tell me, I'll make up things worse than any reality," I said.

"I don't know if you could," she said. She stood still a moment, staring through the kitchen table. She sighed. "She told us we were powerful women and if we ever married we'd kill our husbands on our wedding nights. She said we had snakes inside us—in our fingers. And she told all the boys to go out and find wives. Then she laughed. We always knew she was scared of the boys, anyway, once they got taller than her. It was like telling them to go and find someone to kill them. She said Lilith was Adam's first wife, but Adam didn't like Lilith because she wanted to be on top. Ma said God was a bully, and Lilith was the only one with integrity. Adam wanted women to serve him, but Lilith walked upright—till he rejected her, then she came back as a snake. She brought death to everyone. And there's a touch of the old Lilith in all Meander women." Her voice came out higher, like a little girl repeating a catechism. Then she began to laugh. "It's so stupid," she gasped, and laughed and laughed. "Hearing it out loud. It's so stupid, Clea!"

I got her a glass of water. She sat on a kitchen chair and laughed her throat raw. After gulping water, she calmed down again. "It was stupid, but it hurt us, because we were children and didn't know any better. Suzle fell in love with a boy when she was sixteen. She was so afraid she'd hurt him, and she loved him so much, she killed herself." Mom stared up at me, her eyes wide, her pupils large and dark. "I found her," she said. "She was lying in the bathtub and she had these wounds on her wrists. She didn't bleed to death, Clea. She poisoned herself. The wounds looked like snakebites."

I sat down, too, feeling sick. "What did Aunt Jan do?"

"Jan became a ballerina. She starves herself, and stays away from men. Her life for art. I wish you'd known her when she was younger, Clea. She as such a funny girl, a little bit plump, but with a wicked tongue and a wild eye. Then when she got to be fifteen or so, she went through this phase where she had a crush on movie stars. She was crazy about James Dean and Steve McQueen. She plastered her walls with pictures out of movie magazines. But she'd been dancing since she was six. One day I came home and all the pictures had come down, the walls were white in her room, and she didn't eat anything anymore except a couple lettuce leaves and a few spoonfuls of cottage cheese. She's saving mankind by staying away from them."

I remembered the one Christmas my Aunt Jan came out. She was pale and thin, with circles under her eyes, and she couldn't seem to look at me without wincing. "You had a girl," I heard her say to Mom. "It just goes on and on."

"What did you do, Mom?" I asked.

"Oh, I was practical! When I fell in love with Peter, I thought through all Mom's stories and figured out that the only real harm I could do him was with my fingers. I used to play piano, you know." She took her hands out of her apron pockets and stared at them. "Snakes' heads. If I could just rid myself of the snakes' heads. I propped open the coal cellar door with a stick, then put my hands on the doorsill and knocked the stick away. I broke all my fingers How I screamed! It hurt for months, but I smiled through it all. Peter married me while my hands were still in bandages. No wedding ring." She smiled down at her crippled hands, her face softened with memories.

After a long moment, she glanced at me. "We're only human, after all, Clea. Ma fed us a pack of lies. I wanted to save you from that, and I did the best I could. I'm so glad you've found a boyfriend."

"But Mom—" I looked down at the pictures. Had Jeff photographed some real piece of me I didn't want to believe in? Who was this haunted woman? I picked up a picture of me next to a small pale angel, my pale eyes looking at her, my hand raised to her. My fingers looked curved in a gradual arc that defied human bones.

"Oh, come on. Do you think models in magazines are anything like their pictures? Your boy seems to have a weird sense of beauty, but you aren't what he makes you look like," she said. She gathered all the pictures together, the top one face down so none of them were visible, and put them in my satchel. "Now, come on. We have dishes to do and food to put away. Do you want some turkey to take home?"

◆§ §◆

Jeffry came to my apartment when we both got back from our Thanksgiving vacations.

Grandma had taken me shopping Friday morning, braving the sale crowds at the Plaza. I found myself a little afraid of her, and I wasn't pleased with her gift to me—a silver apple on a chain. but she insisted. "Don't take away an old woman's happiness," she said, tugging on my hair to get me to bend over far enough so she could fasten the pendant around my neck. "I had seven children, and you're the only granddaughter I got, little Clea. Leave me do things for you."

"Am I the last Meander woman?" I asked her.

"No, no," she said. We stood still in the center of the mall corridor between stores, and chattering people streamed past us on both sides, but I could hear her clearly. "There's no end to Meander women. Maybe every woman is a Meander woman."

We got home around noon, and I had a last family lunch with Mom and Patrick and Grandma. Then I drove the two-and-a-half hours back to my apartment. I remembered applying to colleges all over the state, but when I got accepted at the university and decided it was my college of choice, Mom seconded me. "Close enough to visit, but not close enough for me to look over your shoulder all the time," she had said.

I sat in my yard sale armchair, all the lights in the apartment off, my overnight bag on the living room floor in front of me, as daylight faded beyond the gauze curtains. I held my hand closed around the silver apple. It warmed to my flesh.

Presently I heard Jeffry's key in the lock. I wanted to jump up and turn on some lights, maybe put water on for coffee, but I waited. "Clea? You back yet?" he asked, flicking on the entry light. He carried red roses in rustling cellophane; beads of water shone on his hair. I realized I had been hearing the quiet dance of rain on shingles for some time.

"Yes," I said.

"Why so dark? Are you okay? Did something happen at your mother's?"

"I'm just tired."

He turned on the living room lights and came to me, setting the roses in my lap. Stepping back, he looked at me, and I considered my appearance: my chestnut hair spilling over the wide lapels of my long gray coat; my face, undoubtedly pale; the spray of roses as dark as fall apples, with its accompanying haze of white babies' breath and dark green fern, splashing across my lap; and black tights and black Chinese shoes, under a forest-green velvet dress. If he had brought one of his cameras, Jeffry would be focusing now, trying to decide whether to use a flash, and what to bounce it off.

He smiled at me. "Shall I put water on for coffee?"

"Please."

He walked toward the kitchenette, glancing back at me twice. His smile was almost smug. I felt a flick of anger, like a little bruise inside. Did he think because he liked the way I looked that he had created me?

Hadn't he? Didn't we choose this steel gray coat—"the color of your eyes"—together? Hadn't he bought me this green velvet dress at a second-hand shop, and didn't I drag these tights out of an old suitcase because he asked me to?

I lifted the roses, crackling in their cellophane shroud, and sniffed them, but they proved scentless. As I touched the lip-soft petals, I remembered my childhood resolve never to marry.

"Don't you want to put those in water?" Jeffry asked, coming back and sitting on the couch across from me.

I went to the kitchen and retrieved my yard sale vase, a strange twist of blue-and-clear glass as long as my forearm. As

I ran water into it I glanced back at Jeffry. "Thank you for the flowers," I said. I turned off the water, unwrapped the roses, and inserted them into the vase.

"They reminded me of you. I was glad to have something nice to think about, after that turkey dinner with my mother."

Holding his roses, I stood and studied him. His gaze seemed fixed on the ceiling. "Rough?" I asked.

"It's the same every year," he said, and pressed his face into his hands. After a moment, he ran his hands through his hair, startling raindrops loose, then stared at his wet hands as if they were bloodstained. "She's done so much for me," he told his hands. "I know she loves me. I don't understand why I feel terrible after I see her. She raised me all by herself, you know, and she paid my way through college, and she loves my photography; she supports my choices. I hate her knowing what I do. I don't want her to like it, because then it isn't mine. I don't want her ever to find out about you. Oh, Clea, I know how that sounds, but I just feel—she would steal you from me, too."

"Hush," I said. I set the vase on the counter behind me and walked to him. He stood up. I buried my face in his shoulder, hugging him. He smelled of wet wool, and male animal, and clean wet human hair, but other odors were trapped in his shirt—cigarette smoke and violet water; instantly Grandma was somewhere in the room with us.

He must have felt my arms tighten. "What?" he whispered.

Paralyzed, I tried to sense my fingers on his back. Were they curved, or straight? If I looked in the mirror, would that fossil self show in my face, full of ancient purpose that had nothing to do with me? I wished all the lights were off. Perhaps then my identity would rest totally in my thoughts.

Jeffry knew me as image, though.

I let go of him, putting my hands behind my back. "Let's go to bed." He would take off the shirt and drape it over a chair, leaving his mother and my grandmother out of it. I could lose all these thoughts and live just under the surface of my skin, and we would climb the mountain together—

"You look so strange tonight," he said, and then the teakettle went off. He went into the kitchenette. "Still want coffee?"

"No—unless you do—"

He took the kettle off the heat and came back out to me. We turned off the living room light and retreated to my bedroom together.

✺

I lay awake listening to his deep, even breathing, staring at a narrow slice of street light on the ceiling. Leaf shadows danced across the light, responding to a silent wind. I was blinking, ready to fall asleep, when I saw my own hands rise in the air. Silhouetted against the dim light, I saw my index fingers lash out, fluid movement that looked humanly impossible. I couldn't feel my hands at all; they seemed to belong to someone else.

In that state between dream and waking, I had no feelings about what I witnessed, except a sleepy wonder. Jeffry murmured in his sleep, and my hands, of their own volition, reached toward him.

Waking washed over me like a bucketful of cold water; I was across the room in an instant, the wood floor cold against my bare feet, goosebumps rising along my arms and hackles on the back of my neck.

I went into the bathroom and pulled the chain to turn on the light.

In the blind time before my eyes adjusted, I felt utterly silly and young. I knew I had imagined everything, and it was all Grandma's fault. I closed the toilet lid, put a towel on top, and sat down, studying my hands. They looked very pink and human in the bare-bulb light, and beautiful: I had always loved my slender-fingered hands. It was just a dream; if I had been alone in the house, I would have turned on the radio, gotten out a book, and closeted the fears again, drifting into a quieter sleep.

Like I had been doing so often lately.

I flexed my forefingers. They formed three sides of a bent rectangle. I sighed, and felt tension easing out of my shoulders.

My right forefinger whipped out as though it were as spineless as rope. It struck the side of the sink, leaving a drop of clear, glistening liquid on the white porcelain.

The breath coming from my throat had an edge of voice to it, the shadow of sobs. I thought of Aunt Suzle, entombing herself in bathroom white, mastering her forefingers enough to make them strike her own wrists—was it involuntary, or could one control it? I thought of Grandpa Harvey, whose eyes had been milky and whose mind wandered. Would a touch of venom only half kill? I thought of Grandma whipping her fingers at my four uncles, scaring them all into bachelorhood.

I thought of Jeffry, lying defenseless in my bed. If I went to the living room and finished out the night on the couch, he would surely wonder when he woke alone. And I would not tell him about my strange heritage, though I thought he must know, somehow, considering the contexts he chose to picture me in.

I thought about my favorite bread knife, with its serrated edge. If I just decapitated my fingers—cut off the first knuckle— would that suffice?

I felt cold and sad. I rooted an old cosmetics case out from under the sink, and found two Ace bandages inside, from sprained ankles in my past. I wound the bandages around my fingers, mummywrapping them, leaving only the thumbs free, until I felt constricted and mittened and safe. Then I crept into bed, keeping my back to Jeffry and curling my wrapped hands against my stomach.

"You're cold," he whispered, and he hugged me. His warmth felt comforting. I closed my eyes, and began to drift off to sleep.

Just as the world behind my eyelids began to gyrate in slow, hypnotic loops, I felt the tiny cold prick of a needle. Before my mind stilled, I remembered my grandmother's other favorite story from my eleventh summer.

ఆఖ ఇఓ

We moved to New York two years later, the gallery demands for Jeff's work were so great. New York has graveyards dating back centuries.

Jeff's most famous picture of me depicts me as Ophelia, floating with eyes closed in shallow water, my hair rayed out about my head, and flowers huddled in the folds of my pale gauze gown. Only I know that within the long slender hands folded on my chest I hold my grandmother's apple.

About the Authors

Carolyn Banks coedited two volumes of *A Loving Voice: The Caregiver's Book of Read-Aloud Stories For The Elderly* (Charles Press). She is the author of several suspense novels, including *Mr. Right*, and *Tart Tales: Elegant Erotic Stories* (Carroll & Graf). Her short stories and articles have appeared in numerous magazines, anthologies, and newspapers, including *The New York Times* and *Redbook*. She recently scripted and sold an episode of *Loving*, an ABC daytime serial. Her workshop, "Thickening the Plot," is available on audiotape (Davenport Productions). She lives in Elgin, Texas.

Jan Barette is a pseudonym. The writer's work under that name includes "Eating Cake," (*Erotic Stories: Special All-Women Issue*, British), "Pleasure Cruise," a co-authorship with Dave Smeds (*Flesh Fantastic*, Masquerade, 1995), and a second coauthored story with Smeds for *Club International*, who forgot to include her in the byline.

Janet Berliner (Gluckman) left her native South Africa in 1961 in protest against apartheid. She is coeditor, with David, of *David Copperfield's Tales of the Impossible* and, with Peter, of *Peter S.*

Beagle's Immortal Unicorn, for HarperPrism, both due in the fall of 1995. She recently finished *The Michael Crichton Companion* for Ballantine Books. Her last novel, *Child of the Light,* coauthored with George Guthridge (St. Martin's Press), was part of a trilogy—*The Madagascar Manifesto*—which is being completed for White Wolf Books. Janet's short fiction and non-fiction have appeared in many anthologies, magazines, and newspapers. In her copious free time, she travels (most often to the Caribbean), dances (preferably the lambada), and plays the occasional game of poker.

Poppy Z. Brite has lived all over the South and has worked as a gourmet candy maker, an artist's model, a cook, a mouse caretaker, and an exotic dancer. Her novels include *Lost Souls, Drawing Blood,* and the upcoming *Exquisite Corpse.* (all Dell/Abyss). Foreign rights to her books have sold to Germany, France, Spain, the Netherlands, Great Britain, Italy, and Japan. Her short story collection, *Swamp Foetus,* has been published in limited and trade edition hardcovers by Borderlands Press. Paperback rights were sold to Dell. She edited *Love in Vein,* an anthology of erotic vampire stories. Poppy now lives in New Orleans.

P.D. Cacek was born and raised in California, but she recently had her belly-button surgically removed and replaced with an "I-heart-Colorado" bumper sticker. If the IRS is correct, she has actually been making a living as a freelance writer for the past ten years. Her work has appeared in a number of small press magazines and anthologies including *"Pulphouse", "Deathrealm", "The Urbanite", "Bizarre Bazaar", "Bizarre Sex and Other Crimes of Passion", "100 Wicked Little Witches", "Newer York", "Deathport", "Grails: Visitations of the Night", and "Return to the Twilight Zone."* She is currently editing an anthology of short fiction.

Deidra Cox is well known to readers of many small magazines. She has sold over 100 stories. One of them is included in *Year's Best Horror,* and another is under development for television. In 1991 she received a Harriet Arnow Scholarship. She lives in what she describes as "the wilds of Kentucky" with her two children. The oddest part of all is that she is afraid of the dark.

Dawn Dunn has been writing professionally for three years. She coauthored three novels with her sister and is now working on her own. Her short fiction has appeared in *The Tome, Deathport*, and *Bizarre Sex and Other Crimes of Passion*, Vol. II. She also writes convention articles and takes photos for *Horror* Magazine.

Katherine Dunn is the recipient of the Rockefeller Writing Fellowship, the Music Corporation of America Writing Grant, the Reed Summer Arts Fellowship, and multiple sportswriting and reporting awards. She has been active in radio and readings, nationally and internationally, since 1978. Her novels include: *Attic* and *Truck* (Harper & Row, hardcover; Warner Books, paperback), and the highly acclaimed *Geek Love* (Alfred A. Knopf, hardcover, Warner Books, paperback). Her short story collections include *Why Do Men Have Nipples?*, (Warner Books, 1992.) In 1990, she and sculptor Bill Will were commissioned by the City of Portland for a project called "Streetwise". Quotations, jokes, epigrams, and lone words were chosen by Katherine Dunn and carved into granite paving stones set into the sidewalk of Portland's Yamhill Street. Her novel-in-progress, *Cut-Man*, is under contract to Alfred A. Knopf.

Marina Fitch's short fiction has appeared in *F&SF, Asimov's, Tales from Jabba's Palace, Pulphouse, MZB* and in *Peter S. Beagle's Immortal Unicorn*. She is currently trimming a novel and plotting new ones. She lives with her husband Mark in Watsonville, California, about a mile from the oak tree where the Virgin Mary appeared a few years ago. She currently works as a PIP aide. Of her writing she says, "My experiences and my dreams shape my fiction. Who knows what I might have written had I danced in front of K-Mart in that Kool-Aid suit?"

Esther Friesner, PhD, lives and works in Connecticut. She is a prolific novelist and short story writer. Among her novels are

New York by Knight, Harlot's Ruse, and *Elf Defense,* plus a novel in the "Star Trek" series. As the titles of her books show, she is also well known for her sense of humor. Her most recent short story sale was to HWA's anthology, *Psychos.*

Nina Kiriki Hoffman's first novel, *The Thread That Bones the Bones,* won a Bram Stoker Award. Her short fiction has appeared hither and yon, in magazines and anthologies. Her next novel, *The Silent Strength of Stones,* will be published by Avon in September 1995. She lives and writes in Oregon in the company, she says, of other pulp punks.

Nancy Holder has sold 18 novels and around 60 short stories. Her first erotic horror novel, *Making Love,* written in collaboration with Melanie Tem, has gone into a second printing at Dell Abyss. It was published by Raven in England in January 1995. Her first solo horror novel was *Dead in the Water* (Dell Abyss). She has received two Bram Stoker awards from the Horror Writers Association for Short Story. Her fiction for FTL has been translated into six languages and has been used in Japanese *manga* and TV commercials. Her other fiction has been translated into over 18 languages. She lives in San Diego, California, with her husband, Wayne, and their dogs, Mr. Ron, Maggie, and Dot.

Nancy Kilpatrick normally pens in the horror/dark fantasy/crime fields. Her alter ego Amarantha Knight writes and edits erotic horror. Knight's novels in *The Darker Passions* series include modern erotic versions of *Dracula* and *The Fall of the House of Usher;* her anthologies include *Flesh Fantastic* (Masquerade Books). Knight/ Kilpatrick hail from Philadelphia. Knight is a Citizen of the World; Kilpatrick lives in Canada with her black cat, Shadow, and her poet/husband Mike. Nancy's stories have appeared in many anthologies, among them *Book of the Dead* #4, *By Her Subdued,* and *Noirotica.* Her collection of vampire stories *Sex & the Single Vampire,* and her vampire novel from Pocket Books, *Near Death,* is still at a bookstore near you.

Lisa Mason's acclaimed short fiction has appeared in numerous publications, including *Omni*, *Full Spectrum*, and *Year's Best Fantasy and Horror*. Many have received Nebula nominations, many have been translated into other languages. "Tomorrow's Child" (*Omni*, 1989) was optioned for film to Helpern-Meltzer Productions. She is the author of four novels, including *Arachne* (William Morrow-AvoNova) and *Summer of Love* (Bantam Spectra, 1994). In her new novel, *The Golden Nineties* (Bantam Spectra, 1995), a time traveler returns to San Francisco during the wild and extravagant 1890s. Lisa practiced law in Washington D.C. and San Francisco. Now she lives in the San Francisco Bay area with graphic designer and fine artist, Tom Robinson, and three cats, and writes fiction full time.

Joyce Carol Oates is one of the most distinguished and prolific of American writers. She is the author of 24 novels and collections of stories, poetry, and plays. She won the National Book Award for *Them*; her 1990 novel, *Because It Is Bitter, and Because It Is My Heart* earned an NBA nomination; her novel, *Black Water*, was nominated for a National Book Critics Circle Award and the Pulitzer Prize. In 1990, Oates received the REA Award for Achievement in the Short Story. She lives in Princeton, New Jersey, where she is the Roger S. Berlind Distinguished Professior in the Humanities at Princeton University. Her most recent novel, *What I Lived For*, was published by Dutton in the U.S. and was nominated for a PEN/Faulkner award.

T. Diane Slatton began her writing career in 1990. Prior to that, she served in the U.S. Army (72nd Signal Battalion M–60 machine gun team at Karlsruhe, Germany), and has held such other jobs as security guard, bill collector, electronic maintenance inspector, mail bag thrower (for a photo processing plant and, yes, they *do* laugh at your pictures), teletype repairer, and IRS cashier (fired in one week). Diane has sold stories to *Pulphouse*, *The Ultimate Witch*, *Noctulpa* #8, *Bizarre Bazaar '94*, and *Abortion Stories: Fiction on Fire*. The last earned her an honorable mention in DAW's *Year's Best Fantasy & Horror*.

Martha Soukup has had many stories nominated for the Hugo and Nebula Awards, among them one of those in this volume, "The Arbitrary Placement of Walls." Her short story "Over The Long Haul" was filmed for Showtime. Of her short fiction, she writes: "Short science fiction and fantasy are a wonderful medium to write about emotions. . . .It's an addictive pleasure . . . Love and Obsession are the kind of overpowering emotions which lend themselves very readily to dark fantasy. 'Having Keith' was an early story that took nasty feelings to as dark a place as I could find; 'The Arbitrary Placement of Walls' was a later one. Every so often one of those just happens. I think both readers and writers can take a perverse comfort in stories about people who give in to their weakness, anger, obsession and pain where we soldier on like grownups. You can read about (or make up) people much more dreadful than you are, and then feel better about yourself. The only rub is that on the darkest nights, you might recognize yourself in them, anyway." Martha lives in San Francisco.

Lucy Taylor is a full-time writer whose horror fiction has appeared in *Little Deaths, Hotter Blood 4, Northern Frights, Bizarre Dreams, The Mammoth Book of Erotic Horror*, and other anthologies. Her work has also appeared in such publications as *Pulphouse, Palace Corbie, Cemetery Dance, Bizarre Bazaar '92*, and *Passion*. Her collections include *Close to the Bone* and *Unnatural Acts and Other Stories*. Her novel, *The Safety of Unknown Cities*, has recently been published by Darkside Press. A former resident of Florida, she lives in the hills outside Boulder, Colorado with her five cats.

Melanie Tem has published short fiction in various anthologies and magazines. Her articles have been published in professional journals and popular magazines. Among her novels are *Prodigal* (Dell) which won the Bram Stoker Award for Significant Achievement, First Novel; *Wilding* (Dell); *Making Love* (with Nancy Holder; Dell; Raven Books, London), and the forthcoming *Desmodus* (Dell: Headline). Born and raised in rural Pennsylvania, Melanie Tem lives in Denver with her husband, writer

Steve Rasnic Tem. They have four children and a granddaughter. She was a social worker before retiring in 1992 to write full time.

Lois Tilton has published several dozen short stories ranging in mood from fairy tales to alternate history to horror. Her novels *Vampire Winter* and *Darkness on the Ice* placed vampires in the settings of world war and nuclear holocaust. She has also written books set in the universes of television's *Star Trek: DS9* and *Babylon 5*.

Cynthia Ward lives in Seattle, Washington with her husband. She has lived in Oklahoma, Maine, Spain, Germany, and California. She has stories forthcoming in *The Ultimate Dragon*, *Sword & Sorceress*, *Offworld* magazine, and elsewhere.